Addiction

NEW YORK TIMES BESTSELLING AUTHOR
MARGARET MCHEYZER

Addiction

I CAN STOP ANYTIME I WANT

NEW YORK TIMES BESTSELLING AUTHOR

MARGARET MCHEYZER

For *everyone* who's ever had an *addiction*. Beat it and become a *warrior*.

Foreword

If you're like me, you rarely read forewords. You want to get right to the story. Please make this foreword the exception and read it before you start Hannah's tale.

Methamphetamine (meth) is a powerful stimulant. On the street, it's known by many names. Its use has now become a pandemic, sweeping the world. And we're virtually powerless to stop it.

With so many people seeking an escape from their everyday lives, meth production and distribution has become a criminal industry. Drug dealers outnumber the police, and drugs are available everywhere.

Meth use increases activity in certain areas of the brain and heightens central nervous functions. Heart rate, body temperature, respiration, and blood pressure all increase. Meth also elevates production of dopamine, which causes a "high" and the desire to recreate that feeling makes the drug extremely addictive.

For users, energy, attention, focus, pleasure, and excitement are enhanced. Inhibitions are lowered, which increases risk-taking, possibly suicidal behaviors, and libido. Long-term use can cause damage to the brain cells that produce dopamine and to nerve cells containing serotonin. Serotonin is known as the "happy chemical" because it contributes to feelings of wellbeing and happiness, and low serotonin levels have been linked to depression.

Dopamine is a chemical released by nerve cells to send signals to other nerve cells. Dopamine pathways play a major role in the motivational component of reward-motivated behavior, like the use of meth. Over time, the damage to dopamine-producing cells dampens the reward—*the high*—experienced by a meth user, and the user requires more and more of the drug to achieve the same high.

Over the long term, users can develop cognitive and emotional issues such as:

- Aggressive behaviors;
- Violent outbursts;
- Anxiety;
- Depression;
- Paranoia;
- Confusion;
- Visual and auditory hallucinations; and
- Delusions.

Physical effects include:

- Skin sores and infections from compulsive picking;
- Tooth decay and gum disease, also known as "meth mouth";
- Weight loss;
- Increased risk for infection or sexually transmitted disease; and
- Respiratory damage (if smoked or snorted).

The statistics are startling. The National Institute on Drug Abuse reports that in 2015, six percent of Americans aged 12 or older had tried meth at least once. In 2011, meth accounted for 103,000 emergency department visits, and was the fourth most-mentioned illicit drug by patients.

Thirty percent of law enforcement agencies see meth as their greatest drug threat, and the threat that requires the most resources. In Portland, Oregon, more than one in five burglars and nearly forty percent of car thieves were also charged with meth crimes.

In 2017, the United States Department of Justice issued a National Drug Threat Assessment stating that 897,000 people aged 12 or older currently use meth. Deaths from meth overdose rose 225% between 2005 and 2015. In 2015, 5716 people died of stimulant overdose.

So you see, Hannah's story isn't isolated. Drugs aren't something only supplied to those with low socio-economic backgrounds. Unfortunately, drugs are easily available everywhere.

Hannah goes through so many changes, physically and mentally, once she's hooked. She, like most who are addicted to drugs, have altered brain functions. The drug clouds an addict's perception. There are a lot of times in *Addiction* where Hannah believes something other than reality, because she's affected by her meth high.

Addiction will do to you what it does to a family of a drug addict.

It will frustrate and anger you. Especially when we catch Hannah in lies about what occurred, replaced by how she interpreted the same events. The inconsistencies in *Addiction* are deliberate, so we can fully understand how Hannah sees things from within her drug fog.

After the first experience taking drugs, a lot of people will say "no" and stay away. But some think "once won't hurt." Unfortunately, the first time is the ultimate high, and if they choose to continue, they will chase it over and over again. Meth is manufactured in "labs" where there is no quality control, no code of conduct. There are no safe practices. There are no government regulations. But once a person becomes addicted, the drug alters their level of comprehension and their only goal is to achieve the ultimate high they got from the first time using.

It's hard to break the cycle of addiction.

It's harder to integrate back into society as a productive member.

It's even more difficult to look a family member you've wronged in the eye and apologize.

Please, while reading *Addiction,* remember Hannah is still a human being. You'll be angry and frustrated, and you'll want to shake her. You may even want to save her. Her journey is not uncommon. Hannah needed to hit rock bottom before she could break the chains of her addiction.

She needed to crash before she could save herself and become a warrior.

Addiction

is a hard book to read.
It isn't a young adult book, a sweet romance, or even a light read.
It's a dark story about a young lady who's lured into a world where everything hinges around her next hit from the meth pipe.
One bad decision starts her down a path that nearly leads to her death.

Prologue

"Is she dead?"

Groaning, I try to roll over so I can see where the voice is coming from.

"She's moving. We have to help her," someone else says. Their voice is breathy, sounding panicked.

My limbs are heavy, my head is fuzzy, and I swear I can hear my mother's voice.

"Hannah, are you high?" She aggressively holds my chin and stares into my eyes.

"No, Mom," I respond, and giggle.

"Your eyes are bloodshot, and you're barely looking at me."

"I'm just tired," I say and giggle again.

"What's so funny?" she asks as she lets go of my chin and steps backward.

Shrugging, I look around the room.

"We need to call an ambulance," someone says, reminding me that my mother isn't here with me.

My vision is blurry. I can't focus on anything at all. Turning my head, I look straight into the eyes of a girl. She's probably around my age, but I bet she hasn't seen half the stuff I have. She kneels beside me, and behind her are another two girls and three guys. One of them looks bored; he's scrolling on his phone.

"What do you want?" I bark toward her, but my voice comes out broken, and slurry.

"Jasmine, she's a junkie. Look at her. Just leave her. She's not our problem," the bored guy says.

"We can't just leave her," she snarls back at him.

Suddenly, my stomach starts contracting, and my breathing becomes challenged. Gasping for air, my body tightens with spasms, trying to get oxygen into my lungs.

"Shit, she must be overdosing. We gotta get out of here before anyone finds us," bored guy says.

"I'm not leaving her. She's just a kid."

"She ain't my problem. I'm outta here," the bored guy says and takes off, the others going with him.

The girl stays with me, and as I try to focus on her, all I can see is the pretty chain around her neck. It looks like it's worth a lot, I'm sure I could give it to Edgar for some crystals. Man, maybe a few days' worth. I need money big time.

"I'm going to call an ambulance," the girl says as she takes her phone out of her pocket and dials it. "What have you taken?" she asks.

Everything is fuzzy. Her voice sounds disjointed and almost robotic.

Reaching for my pipe, I scream in pain. But she doesn't seem alarmed by my screams, maybe I'm actually not moving. Everything hurts.

"I need an ambulance…" her voice is frantic as she tells the operator where she is.

My eyes keep drifting shut, and she screams at me to open them again.

"She's frothing at the mouth, and she's barely moving."

I try to turn over, but whatever those fuckers gave me was strong. It's weighing me down. I can barely move.

"Her breathing is shallow…"

If I can just get up, I'll find my way back to Edgar's. He'll look after me. He always does. Sometimes he asks me to do stuff for him. "I'm alright," I mumble.

"She's trying to say something," the girl says into the phone. "Okay, I won't touch her." Her eyes are filled with pity and sadness. I stare up at her, and can see how concerned she is. I can see her. Can she see me?

"There's a syringe beside her. I think she might have injected something. There's a pipe, too. Maybe she smoked crack or meth?"

Yeah, baby. Crystal meth. Meth. Crystal. Ice. Tina. Glass. I love it. I love getting iced. It's the best feeling in the world. Being invincible, even when there are a million people in the room. Being free. Floating. That floating is what I love best. Anything can be happening around you, and when you smoke a bit of ice, you're floating above everyone. Free and happy and high.

"I'm here!" The girl jumps up and waves her arms frantically.

"Thank you for calling, we'll take it from here," another woman says to the girl.

The girl steps back and continues to stare at me. I'm being rolled over, and talked at by someone in a uniform. "What's your name?"

"Hannah," I respond.

"She's unresponsive," the woman says as she looks up to someone. She presses into my chest plate with her knuckle, and a shooting pain rips through me. "She's barely coherent. Heart rate is down, pulse is weak. She's overdosing."

"Get me back to Edgar's," I say.

"She's crashing. Administering Narcan."

There's a tightness in my chest. Pain soars through me, every part of me is like someone is stabbing multiple sharp knives into my body.

A darkness overtakes me.

A blanket of warmth is thrown over my entire body. My last breath escapes past my chapped lips.

Suddenly, I feel weightless. This must be what heaven feels like. It's so peaceful.

"We're losing her!" I hear someone yell.

Who's losing who? What's happening?

"ETA sixty seconds," someone else says in a calm voice.

I'm not sure what's happening, all I know is I like the quiet.

"Breathe, damn it, breathe!"

"Great, another dead junkie," someone snickers.

"I haven't lost her yet."

"She's just a junkie, Sally. Who cares if she dies? It's another one off the streets."

"Hey, she's someone's daughter. You want to be the one to knock on her parent's door?"

I hear a grumble from behind me. More like a pained sigh.

Who's talking?

What the hell is happening?

As it turns out, this is far from the end of my story.

Chapter 1

"MOM, THERE'S A PARTY ON SATURDAY NIGHT AT KRISTEN'S HOUSE. Can I go?"

"Will her parents be there?" Mom asks as I help with dinner.

"I have no idea. I can ask her if you want."

Mom looks up from preparing the meat and tilts her head to the side. "I'd be more comfortable knowing her parents are there. If they are, then yes, you can go. Make sure you've done your homework first though. You've got that English paper due on Monday, so that has to be done."

"Thanks, Mom," I say as I give her a hug and a kiss on the cheek.

Heading into my bedroom, I take my phone out of my back pocket and send Kristen a message. **Mom wants to know if your parents are gonna be home.**

Firing up my laptop, I open the document for my English paper. Reading over it, I begin making notes about what I need to do so I can get an A for this paper.

My phone vibrates, and I lift to see Kristen has responded.

Yeah, olds will be home.

Smiling, I push up from the bed. "Mom," I call as I leave my room.

"Yeah," she responds from the kitchen.

"Kristen's parent's will be home. Can I go?" I smile at her, looking forward to Kristen's party.

"As long as her parents are home. I'll give them a call to make sure."

"Okay," I happily say.

Walking back to my room, I send Kristen another message. **Mom said I can come.**

Almost instantly she replies. *Baby, need mommy's approval for everything?*

I let out a laugh, Kristen always teases me about the close relationship I have with my parents. She's always rolling her eyes at me and telling me I'm a mommy's girl. Hell, yeah I am. And damn proud of it.

Yep, totally do. ;)

I grab my laptop, take it to my desk and placing my phone down beside me. I'm reading over my English assignment, plotting it out, when Kristen replies. *Baby.*

Yep.

Must be nice being an only child. Always getting whatever you want.

I send her the middle finger emoji. But I'm really laughing. Kristen has eight brothers and sisters, and they all have to compete for everything. Her parents are super nice, but in a house with eleven people, her parents need to make a lot of things stretch. Like rooms. Kristen shares a room with her twin sister, Sasha. She likes coming over here because everything is so much quieter. There aren't a thousand voices yelling while you're trying to do your homework.

What's this party for? She's told me, but I've already forgotten.

25-year anniversary. They've been married forever.

Wow. That's a long time. So, they'll def be home. LOL

My parents have been married for sixteen years. They got married after I was born. They told me they were happy living in sin, but decided they should get married once I came along. Not that I care whether they're married or not. I don't think society really worries about that anymore. But they did, so they got married.

Yeah. Can I crash at yours the night before? It'll be crazy here, and I need to get this stupid English paper done.

Picking my phone up, I head back out to Mom. "Mom, can Kristen stay on Friday night? The party is for her parents wedding anniversary, and she said it's going to be busy there. Can she stay and we'll go together to the party?"

"That's fine, as long as she tells her parents," Mom says.

"Thanks, Mom."

Walking back to my room, I text Kristen. **Mom said yes, you can stay.**

I turn my phone off and chuck it on my bed. I need to get this paper started, or I'll end up getting a B or C on it. Moving the mouse, the screen lights up and I start researching.

"Dinner," Mom calls. I look at the time and haven't even realized I've been working on my paper for over two hours with no break. My shoulders are tense, and there's a pain in my neck from the way I've been sitting at my desk. Standing, I roll my shoulders and try to release the stiffness.

"Hey, sweetheart. How was your day?" Dad asks as I start setting the table for dinner.

"Hi, Dad." He stands and gives me a hug and a kiss on the cheek. "My day's been okay. Like any other. Went to school, came home, and now I'm doing homework."

"You work too hard. You need a break every now and then."

I help Mom bring dinner over and sit beside Dad. "I won't get to be a teacher if I don't study."

"Yeah, but you're only seventeen. You need to learn to relax." I chuckle and roll my eyes. "What's funny?" Dad asks as he places some of the fried rice on his plate.

"Most parents would be worried their kids are into partying, alcohol, sex, and drugs, and you're worried that I study too much. Kinda funny, don't you think?"

"Well..." Dad looks at Mom, who's smirking. "Don't do drugs," Dad adds and quickly looks down to his food.

"And don't drink, and try not to have sex until you're ready," Mom continues.

"You're never allowed to have sex," Dad grumbles. "Not until your sixty-five. *Maybe*."

"So, by your standards, I can't have sex, do drugs or drink alcohol. But I can smoke and go to crazy insane parties as long as I don't do those three things. Check. Got it. I'll keep that in mind for the party I'm going to at Kristen's."

"No smoking!" both my parents shout at me in unison.

"Man, you two are no fun," I chuckle at them.

"We're heaps of fun." Dad draws his brows together and scowls at me with a 'serious' look. But I know he's kidding. "Just no to *you* having fun."

"Seriously," I say with a wide smile. "How was work, Dad?"

"It was alright." He shrugs. "Being a loan officer at the bank isn't really exciting. Granted some loans, and declined some others." Dad loosens his tie and takes it off. He rubs his temple and I can tell he's frustrated with himself.

"Why don't you do something you love?" I say.

He snorts. "Because there's no money in tap dancing," he says and chuckles.

"Come on, Dad. What makes you happy?"

He puffs his chest out, his gaze going between me and Mom.

"You and your mother make me happy. You two will always star in my proudest memories. Nothing can compare to the both of you."

"Aww," I say and look at Mom, who's got the biggest smile ever on her face. "You're almost nauseating," I tease Dad. "Lucky I love you too."

Mom bursts into uncontrollable laughter. The rice she's eating sprays out and some lands on Dad. "Note to self, don't say anything sappy in front of teenage daughter again. If I do, I'll remember to wear a raincoat."

My family is small but so tight. Nothing could come between us. The bad and the ugly couldn't destroy the love we have for each other. It just couldn't.

Chapter 2

"YOU'RE GOING TO WEAR JEANS?" KRISTEN ASKS AS SHE SPRAWLS across my bed.

"Yeah, why?"

"It's my parents' anniversary. Wear something nicer."

Opening my wardrobe, I grab a flowery dress and hold up against myself. "Like this?" I ask.

Kristen scrunches her nose at me. Her long blonde hair falls over her face, and she blows it out of the way before tucking it behind her ear. "You've gotta have something cuter than that. It looks like a beach dress."

"I don't want to wear anything too dressy. It's just at your parents' house. What are you wearing?" I ask.

Kristen is slim, like really slim. She's on the cheer squad at school, so you can imagine how gorgeous she is. "I'm wearing this," she says as she jumps off the bed, goes to her bag and produces something ultra-small.

"What? That's a headband." I point to the black scrap of material she's holding.

"Look." And of course, Kristen with no modesty at all, strips down to her bra and panties and slides the black material over her vivacious curves.

"Oh, it's a dress. Well part of a dress." I make her spin to see exactly how tight it is. "You have the best body in the world. And you can pull that off, but don't you think it's maybe just a bit too short? My Mom would freak and say, 'you can't wear that,' so what's your mom gonna say?"

"Mom bought it for me. And hey, it's covering everything." She tugs it down over the top of her thighs.

"Please tell me you're not wearing hooker heels with it."

"Nah. Don't be dumb." She pulls out a pair of black flats that are super cute. "These won't hurt my feet."

The dress really isn't that bad, but I hate showing any part of my body. I'm not a prude or anything, but showing too much just isn't for me. I don't feel comfortable doing it, but hey, power to whoever does.

"You'll look super-hot," I say.

"Yeah, I know." She wiggles her brows at me and gives me a sexy smirk. "Guess who I invited tonight?"

"Don't tell me you invited Brad?" Brad's her long-time crush. Kristen can barely talk around him. She becomes a blubbering mess whenever he says anything to her. It's really kinda cute because he's totally into her, but she's an idiot who loses all her social skills around him.

"Maybe."

"How did that conversation go? You can barely string a sentence together when you see him, so how did you get the invite out without stumbling over your words?"

"Well…here's the thing. I technically didn't invite him. I made Sasha do it."

I start laughing. "I can see this is going to go really well for you," I add sarcastically. "What happened?"

"Sasha said we're having a party and does he want to come?

He said yes."

"Why don't you just talk to him?" Instantly, Kristen's face burns with a wild red glow. "Oh yeah, that's why." I point to her face.

She lifts her hands so I can't see how red her cheeks are turning, but she's giggling like a little school girl. "Help me, Hannah. What am I going to do? I can barely think of him without breaking out in hives. I like him *sooooooo* much." She flops on the bed, face still buried behind her hands.

"Just talk to him. How about I start talking to him, and you can come over and join in the conversation?"

"You'd do that for me?" She peeks at me from behind her hands. Her eyes are wide with excitement.

"Duh, of course. You're my best friend."

"Thank you." She leaps off the bed and throws herself into my arms. "I love you."

"Yeah, yeah, I know. I love you too." I exhale a big breath and turn to look at my closet. "What about this?" I take out another dress. It's knee length, red in color and kind of fitted with a small split on the side.

"Oh, yeah. This'll make your eyes pop. Oh, my God! Can I do your hair and your make-up? Please?" She places her palms together like she's praying. "Pretty please?"

"Jeez. Okay, you can do my hair and make-up. I was just going to put my hair up in a bun."

"Ugh," Kristen grunts and sits on the side of my bed. "You always have your hair in a bun. You look like a nerdy librarian."

"Librarians are not nerds. They're cool. And they love to read."

"Nerd," she mumbles with a smile.

"You know what?"

"What?"

"You hurt my head."

She laughs out loud. "You hurt mine, nerd."

"Fine, do my hair and my make-up. But no making me look cheap."

"Pffft." She waves her hand at me. "You're way too classy to look cheap. Unless you got fake lips."

"Fake lips don't make people look cheap."

"They do when they overfill them."

"Who'd overfill their lips?"

"They say 'go big or go home.'"

I place the red dress over the back of my chair and kneel so I can see what shoes I have to wear with its. "I have no idea what you're talking about. We were discussing one thing, and now we're talking about plastic surgery."

"I think I want a boob job," she says as she squishes her boobs together to make them bigger.

"You're seventeen. You don't need a boob job. Your boobs are big enough as they are."

"But don't you think they'd look good like this?" She squeezes them together.

"Yes, wear them under your chin. Totally normal. You need to worry about the English paper we have due, not your boobs."

"You should get a boob job too."

Slowly I turn to look at her. She's lying on her back now, and she's playing with the ends of her hair. "My boobs are fine. I don't need or want any extra attention. Thank you very much. What I do want is to get an A on this English paper."

"Have you ever gotten anything but an A?" I pick up my slipper and throw it at her head. "Hey!" she protests. "What was that for?"

"'Cause I felt like throwing it at you. And you'd get A's too if you studied like I do."

"Nerd," she mumbles again.

I stick my middle finger up at her. Although she's pretending she can't see me, I know she can. The smile is a dead give-away. "Hey, what about these shoes?" I hold up a pair of black pumps.

"Yeah, they're nice. Bit high for a nerd, don't you think?" she teases with a slight head wobble and big grin.

"I swear, Kristen, the next thing I throw at you won't be a soft slipper." She laughs at me and buries her face beneath my pillow. "I'm going for a shower, I'll be out in a few."

"I'll make you look like the prettiest nerd known to man," she says from under my pillow.

It's no use trying to rein her in. She's just so... so... so... Kristen.

"You look beautiful," Dad says to both Kristen and me when he drops us off at Kristen's house.

"Thank you," I say, leaning over to give him a kiss.

"Thank you, Mr. Mendes," Kristen says as she closes the car door. "I think Mom or Dad can bring Hannah home tomorrow. If not, Eva should be able to." Eva is Kristen's oldest sister. She's twenty-four and a total brainiac. She's going to college and studying to be an honest-to-God rocket scientist. She's already got a job at NASA lined up, and she's by far the smartest person I know. But just like the rest of the family, she has blonde hair and a slim body. Everyone in that family looks like they belong on the cover of *Vogue* or *GQ* magazine. They were all graced with amazing genetics.

"Call if you need anything," Dad says.

"Thanks, Dad. Bye."

Kristen and I head up to the house. Their house is cute. It's a gray colonial-style home, with white shutters on the windows and a darker gray roof. It's a stark contrast to ours, which is more a traditional style. Hers is cute and cozy, mine is more refined and expansive.

"Mom and Dad have hired a band for tonight."

"Wow, that's impressive," I say as I adjust my dress. "You sure this isn't too much? I brought jeans and a t-shirt, I can always change in them."

"No, it's a party. You look hot. Anyway, there's no time to change, people have already started arriving." She points to the few cars parked along the street.

"I feel like I'm overdressed." Then I look at her dress, and smile. "I suppose if I stand beside you all night, I won't look overdressed at all."

She cheekily smiles as we walk into her house. "Mom...Dad, we're here," she calls. "I look hot, you can say it." She wiggles her hips at me.

"Yeah, you do." The dress could almost be spray painted on her. But man, she carries it so well.

"Hi, Krissy," her mom says when we walk out to the back deck. "Hannah, wow. You look so beautiful. And so grown up." Her mom comes around to give me a kiss on the cheek, and hugs and kisses Kristen. "You both look gorgeous."

I look around and see how they've transformed the back deck into a wonderland. The band is set up and playing soft music, the singer, a younger woman, is singing in the background. There are lanterns and fairy lights, and big vases with brightly colored flowers springing out of them. It's beautiful. There's a chill in the air with fall closing in quickly, but it's definitely not cold yet. The temperature just reminds us what's around the corner.

"This all looks amazing," I say as my eyes draw onto every detail.

"Thank you," Kristen's mom proudly says. "Not every day you celebrate twenty-five years of marriage."

"Congratulations," I say smiling.

"We've gotta put our stuff in my room. Where's Sasha?" Kristen asks her mom.

"I'm not sure, she should be around here somewhere." Her

mom looks around for Sasha. "I have to go; more guests are arriving."

"Come on," Kristen says as she grabs hold of my hand and we head toward her bedroom. When we get in there, she shuts the door and plonks her bag down, before sitting at her desk to start touching up her make-up. "Do I look alright?" she asks. There's a trace of worry to her voice. "I mean, do you think Brad will think I look okay?"

"I think if Brad doesn't go weak at the knees for you, then there's something wrong with him. You look so hot. I wish I looked half as hot as you do."

"Girl, you're gorgeous. A nerd…but gorgeous."

Standing behind Kristen, I try to look at myself in the mirror, but she's a hog and has taken it over. "You sure I'm okay?" I run my hands over my stomach, trying to suck in while I straighten my back. "I think I look terrible. This dress isn't me."

"Stop it. You look really beautiful. That lipstick is killer on you."

"It's red. Red doesn't suit me."

"Your dress is red, and your lipstick is red, and you definitely look hot in the color red. If you didn't, I'd tell you."

This is true. She's definitely honest, even when I don't want her to be. But that's one of Kristen's best qualities, I know she'll never lie to me. "Fine," I say as I pace back and forth in her and Sasha's room. It's a large room, with two double beds, and two desks and two night lights. It's spacious enough so when I stay over, I can either sleep on a fold-out, or sleep with Kristen on her bed. I'm still nervous about what I'm wearing, I feel like I'm dressed up like a doll.

"Hey, losers," Sasha says as she bounces into the room.

Kristen is up on her feet in a heartbeat. "Is Brad here yet?" Kristen asks.

"Not yet, but he messaged me and asked if you were gonna be here. The boy is missing a brain cell or two, right? How can *you* not be here when it's our parents' wedding anniversary?"

I chuckle at Sasha, but Kristen is already in panic mode. "He asked if I'm going to be here?" she says in a dreamy, excited voice.

"I think that's all she heard," I say to Sasha, who laughs. Sasha is Kristen's identical twin, but anyone can tell the difference between them. Sasha's hair is cut in a short pixie style, whereas Kristen's is long, half-way down her back.

"Anyway, I'm going. I just wanted to tell you he's on his way over. See you losers outside." And with that, she's gone again.

Kristen runs over to me, grabbing hold of my hands. She starts jumping up and down. "Oh my God, oh my God, oh my God!"

"Calm down."

She lets go of her death grip on me, and steps back, taking several deep breaths. "Okay, I can do this. Just don't let me make a fool out of myself."

"I promise I won't," I say to her.

She turns to look at herself in the mirror again, fixing her micro dress and fluffing her hair. "I got this." The confidence in her has increased in a matter of seconds. "I got this," she says with more sass.

"You've got this," I agree, nodding.

Kristen has been crushing over Brad for ages. I hope he treats her well. Kristen pulls her shoulders back and lifts her chin with confidence. "Yeah, I do."

We both head outside, where more people have arrived.

People are stopping Kristen to talk to her, but I can see she's looking for Brad. I say hello to a few of their extended family and friends I've met over the years, but quietly make my way over to get a drink.

There's a bartender serving, and when he sees me he smiles. "What would you like?" he asks when he finishes serving someone.

"Just a soda, thank you."

"Coming right up." He opens a can of soda and pours it into a glass. "Here you go," he says with a huge smile before turning to serve the next person.

I place a straw in it, and turn to watch the room. I can't believe how many people are here. The music is louder, the deck is spilling over with people, all sharply dressed. There are some little kids running around and playing with the balloons. It's very family-oriented. I like this about the Watsons. They have a large family, but everything they do always includes all of the family. And they always make me feel at home whenever I come here. It's just the type of people they are.

Mr. and Mrs. Watson are wrapped in each other's arms talking to people. There's lots of laughter and love here tonight, and that makes me happy.

"Hi," I hear from behind me.

Turning, I come face to face with one of the most beautiful men I've ever seen in my life. He's half a head taller than me, with ruffled, dark brown hair, and eyes so blue they instantly remind me of a clear sky.

"Hi." I manage to keep my composure and not act like a giddy school girl.

"What are you drinking?" he asks as he eyes my soda.

"Just a soda. You?" I look to the bar and notice he's got nothing yet.

"I'll be getting a bourbon." I can feel my face starting to burn so I offer him a quick smile before I turn away from him. "I haven't seen you at the Watson's house before," he says which forces me to turn around to answer him.

"Funny that, because I was just thinking the same thing about you," I say.

A smile tugs the ends of his lips. "I'm Zac and I'm Uncle Jason's nephew." He points to Mr. Watson. "And I know for sure I've never seen you at one of these things before, because I would've noticed."

"Well...Zac," I say his name slowly, commanding his attention. "I've been to almost all their parties over the past ten years. I'm Kristen's best friend."

Zac takes a deep breath in. He lets his eyes roam down my body then back up again. "Then I'm a damn fool. Because I never noticed you, until now...and phew, I *definitely* noticed you tonight." He lifts his brows, as if he's approving my choice of clothing.

"Well, nice meeting you, Zac, but I should go find Kristen." Leaving my drink on the bar, I leave.

I barely make it a few steps before I'm tapped on the shoulder, Zac's holding my drink out to me. "You forgot this." He thrusts it forward so I can take it.

"I wasn't born yesterday, Zac. I'm no longer thirsty." I wink at him as I turn and walk away. Sashaying my hips a little more than usual. I doubt he's spiked my drink, but my mamma didn't raise no fools either. Better to be safe than sorry. Kristen stands out in her tight dress, and immaculate, long blonde hair. "Hey," I say to her.

"Brad's here," she half squeals. "I saw him and smiled."

"Have you spoken to him yet?"

"Yeah, I said 'hi.'" Her cheeks pink.

"That's it? You said hi? Nothing else?"

"Oh my God." She ducks her head down so her hair flings over her face, covering it. "He's walking toward us."

Turning, I see Brad. "Hey Brad," I say. "How are you?"

He quickly glances at Kristen, whose face now is a lovely shade of candy apple red, then looks back to me. "I'm really good." He shuffles on the spot, looking awkward.

Brad's not really my type of guy, I've never had a type I've drooled after. Until Zac. Now, he's mighty fine. Brad can't stop looking over to Kristen, and Kristen can't even make eye contact with Brad. "So, Brad, what are you doing over summer?" I ask, trying to fill the uncomfortable silence between him, Kristen, and myself.

"I've got a job at Target. Nothing really special. I restock the shelves, and whatever else they tell me to do."

"Which Target?" Kristen asks. Her face brightens as she stares dreamily toward him.

"The new one in town," Brad answers. He turns his body toward her, and she mimics his pose, essentially cutting me out. I'm okay with this, because it means she doesn't need me here to help her along. I look over to the bar and see Zac still standing there, his eyes glued on me.

Smiling, I give him a wink, to which he lifts his glass and gives me a nod. *Cheeky.*

Slowly, I make my way over to the bar, purposely standing on the opposite side. I look around the room as I wait for the bartender, but I can see Zac out of my peripheral vision, still watching me. I'm stubborn, I'm not going to him. He can come to me if he's interested.

The same bartender comes over to me, already holding a soda. "Here you go," he says as he places it on the bar.

"I didn't order a soda," I say while I discreetly watch Zac.

"Gentleman down the end of the bar, said you'd want it."

"Did he now?" I pick the drink up and turn to Zac, giving him a small nod of thanks. "I'll have a water please," I say to the bartender.

The bartender eyes the soda, then turns to pour me a water. Zac smiles, and slowly walks over to me. "You're a hard person to impress," he says.

"You think buying me a drink when the drinks are free would impress me?" I ask.

He lets out a deep chuckle. "Touché, Miss…?" He waits for my name.

"Hannah."

"Finally, I get a name to put with the beautiful face."

"Nope." I shake my head at him. "Nope," I say again. "That's super cheesy, and I don't fall for cheesy lines."

"Well, how about this?" He turns his body and leans both elbows on the bar. "I want to take you out to dinner. Next Saturday night. Dinner and a movie."

"Better than the cheesy lines." I crinkle my nose. "But I'm busy." I'm so not, but playing hard to get is totally fun.

"You're not busy. You just want me to beg," he says, catching me out, damn it. "See, there you go." He points to my face. "Your eyes give it away. And so does your smile."

Double damn it. "Fine, I'm not busy," I admit.

"Good, what time should I pick you up?"

This is so much fun. "You don't know where I live. And, I prefer it that way."

"Then you can pick me up," he counters.

"I don't drive yet."

"How old are you?" His brows draw in together while his tone drops.

"I should be asking you the same question. I don't go out with old men."

"Old?" he quips. "I'm twenty-one."

"Ewww." I scrunch my nose at him and pretend to gag. "You're almost ancient."

He steps closer to me, and suddenly my cheekiness is overtaken by this strong, incredibly beautiful man in my personal space. I don't try to move away, because truthfully, I like it. "Am I too old for you, Hannah?" he says in a low voice.

His aftershave takes over the sane part of my brain. His mere presence does something to me. My stomach flips, then flops, then flips again. The aroma from his aftershave is something familiar, yet sexy as sin. It's like a woody smell with an overtone of sweet spice.

Closing my eyes, I inhale deeply. His scent is deeply attractive, so recognizable that I'll never forget it. "You smell so nice," I say aloud. My eyes spring open, and I'm momentarily shocked at what I said out loud. "Tell me you didn't hear what I said?" I beg.

"I heard it, and I loved it."

A burn rises inside me, slowly making its way up to my face. Although I can't see myself, I know my face is turning a lovely shade of crimson. *I'm such an idiot.* "You didn't hear anything," I say as I step away from him trying to gain control over my dumb brain.

"I did. Would you like me to repeat it, just to make sure?" Now he's teasing me. I should be angry, but I can't be. Self-inflicted stupidity. "It went something like this…'You smell so nice.' Does that sound familiar?"

As quick as anything I retort with, "Well if you have to ask, then my point is proven. You're way too old. Which means your hearing is on its way out. So, you actually heard nothing. Phew." I wipe my hand across my forehead and pretending to the wipe sweat away. "Geriatric," I mumble under my breath.

Zac lets out a laugh, and in one smooth movement grabs my hand, and leading me out to the part of the deck where some people are dancing to the song the band is playing.

"What are you doing?" I ask.

He brings me in close to his body, his right hand on my lower back, his left hand holding mine close to his chest. "I want to dance."

"Maybe I don't." We sway together among the other couples. I take a moment to study his face, and notice a scar running about an inch across his chin. It's faint, but it's definitely there.

Mr. and Mrs. Watson are dancing nearby and they both see us. They move toward us, and smile. "Zac, I see you and Hannah are getting along."

"She's definitely something else," Zac replies.

"She's part of this family," Mr. Watson says to Zac in a warning tone.

"I have no doubt."

"Good."

Mr. and Mrs. Watson keep dancing but this piques a question in my mind. "Why would he warn you like that?" I say to Zac.

"When I was younger I got myself into some shit. I'm on the straight and narrow now. But it's something the whole family holds on to, keeps reminding me about it."

"I've never heard them talk about you, so it can't be that bad. What did you get involved with?" I ask. Curiosity is getting the better of me, but my walls are rising too. I don't want to get involved with someone who's trouble. That's definitely not what I'm about. I want to be a teacher, and I can't be if I fall in with the wrong crowd.

"I was running with a bad group of people. Small crap. It could've potentially become much worse, but thanks to my parents and the rest of my family, I was pulled out of it before it got worse."

"Like what?" I push.

Zac's jaw tightens, and I can see by the faraway look in his eyes, he doesn't want to talk about it. But at the same time, he's chasing me, wanting me to go out with him. I need to know what kind of guy he is. "Just shit," he says as he slows his dancing.

"Right." I pull away from him and watch as his features harden. "Thank you for the dance." Turning, I walk over to Kristen, who's hooked on everything Brad is saying. "Hey," I say as I glance at Zac. He's left the dance floor, and heading out through the house.

"Zac's into you, huh?" Kristen asks. She wiggles her brows, and bumps hips with me.

"I'll grab us a drink, what would you like?" Brad says to Kristen.

"A Coke please."

"Hannah?" he asks.

"Nothing thanks."

Brad smiles at Kristen. Her face brightens like it's the first time she's ever seen the sun. "Oh my God. We've been talking about everything. He's so cute. And perfect for me. Hannah!" She grabs hold of my hands and squeezes them with excitement.

"I'm happy for you. Finally. Now you can stop fantasizing about him."

"Tell me...you and Zac huh?"

"I don't think so," I say, not entirely convincing to her or me. "Your dad warned him that I'm a part of your family. When I asked him about it, he said he'd gotten involved in some stuff but wouldn't tell me what the stuff was. He asked me out, but I'm not sure if I want to go." I mean, I do, but not at the risk of my life path taking a turn for the worse.

"He got himself involved with some people who were into petty theft and drugs. He was stealing stuff, but never got involved with the drug part. I think if his parents didn't get involved, it would've been just a matter of time before he did get caught up with drugs."

"Does he still see them? The people he was hanging out with?"

"Nah, he turned his life around. Studied hard to get into college, and now he's working and going to college to become something like an accountant. How boring." She rolls her eyes. "He was destined to become a statistic, but as it turned out, he really pulled it together."

"He asked me out."

"Go! He's really nice. Girls go crazy for him for some reason. But since he straightened himself out, he doesn't do anything. He just stays at home and studies. Go out with him. You're both kinda the same. You know, nerds."

"Here's your drink," Brad says, handing Kristen a soda.

I poke my tongue out at her for calling me a nerd. "I'll go talk to him," I say feeling bad for judging him before I knew the story.

"Yeah, go find my nerdy cousin. Tell him I said he's a dork," Kristen shouts after me.

I'd like to give her the one finger salute, but I doubt her parents would appreciate it.

Heading in the same direction I saw Zac disappear, I make my way out to the front porch and notice how many cars are now here. I can see Zac sitting on the hood of a car. As I walk over to him, he sees me and puts his phone away before jumping off the car.

"Sorry, were you busy?" I ask indicating his phone.

"Candy Crush," he says.

"About what happened back there." I hook my thumb over my shoulder gesturing to the party. "Kristen told me about what you went through. But, I judged you. And I shouldn't have. For that, I'm sorry."

"It's probably something that's going to stick with me for the rest of my life. The low-life screw-up who was stealing shit."

I lean up against the car beside Zac and fold my arms over my chest. "We all deserve a second chance. Maybe some people want you to work for your second chance."

"Do you want me to work for it?" he asks.

"I don't know what I want," I truthfully admit. "I'm studying hard because I want to be a teacher, and I can't afford to screw anything up. Otherwise, all my hard work will be for nothing, so I have to be careful."

Hurt flashes across his face. "I get it." He's trying to hide his disappointment, but I can see it. "I get it," he says again, this time straightening his shoulders. "Thank you for the dance, Hannah. You truly are the highlight of my night."

Something draws him to me. He has this alluring quality about him that's raw and honest. "You can pick me up at six.

And if you're late, you can forget about another date."

"I won't be late. Matter-of-fact, I'll be early."

"Give me your phone," I say to him holding out my hand.

"You know, a please wouldn't go unnoticed."

He's not letting me get away with anything. "Please," I say and rapidly blink my eyes at him.

Zac clears his throat and looks away from me. "Yep, okay," he says with a gravelly voice. Obviously, I'm affecting him. I like how I have this power over him. It gives me confidence and makes me feel alive on the inside.

I type in my address, and when I finish, I give myself a call too. "You now have my address, and my phone number. But I won't be calling you first. You have to make the effort."

"You're a tiger, and I'm loving it," he says as he reaches for his phone. He grabs hold of my hand, and his thumb strokes my skin, leaving a blazing trail of heat.

I like this.

I like *him*.

Walking away from him, I'm smiling to myself. I'm not going to look all eager and like I'm a giant marshmallow. He has to work for it.

My phone rings in my hand, and I automatically know it's Zac. The giddy feeling in my stomach tells me he's watching me as I'm walking away.

"Hello," I answer without even looking at who it is. *I just know it's him.*

"Watching you walk away is definitely a sight for sore eyes," he says.

My smile grows wider. "Then put your sunglasses on," I respond and hang up on him.

Hannah — one.

Zac — zero.

Chapter 3

"ZAC CALLED ME YESTERDAY AND WANTED TO KNOW MORE ABOUT you," Kristen says to me when she sees me at school.

"Did he?" I smile as I shove my bag in my locker, take out my laptop and close the door.

"So, tell me. What happened?" Kristen leans against my locker, and stares at me as she eagerly waits for the gossip.

"Nothing to tell." I shrug.

"You already told me on Saturday how you two are going out. What else happened?"

I turn to stare at her. "If you stopped talking about how wonderful Brad is, then you would've heard what I said."

Kristen's face reddens. "Yeah, I know, all I did was talk about him. Sorry. But now I want to know about you and Zac."

"There's nothing to know. He asked me out. I said yes. We're going out this weekend."

"What about your parents? What are they going to say?"

"I haven't told them everything yet, but I told them a little bit last night. They said they're willing to meet him and give him a chance."

"Your daddy will be standing at the door with a shotgun," Kristen says with a laugh. "Actually, nah it won't be him, it'll be your mom. She's hardcore protective of you."

I shrug again because truthfully, I don't mind. Sometimes it gets in the way and becomes a bit much, but most times I don't mind. I know that what she says and does isn't to make my life miserable, but to keep me safe. "I have no idea where this is going to go. If I go out on the date with him, he might turn out to be a huge jerk." I place my hand on Kristen's arm and stop her walking. Suddenly, it hits me hard. "If it doesn't work out between Zac and myself, does that mean you and I…" I point to her, then me, unable to continue with the sentence.

"No way, girl. You and I are best friends for life. You're stuck with me, through thick and thin. Ten years ain't getting thrown away 'cause it didn't work out with my cousin."

"It won't put you in a bad position? He *is* family."

"Yeah, he's family, but so are you. Besides, I only see him like three or four times are year, you I see all the time. Oh my God!" she shrieks in the highest pitch.

"What?" My pulse quickens.

"If you marry him, you and I will be best friends *and* cousins." She grabs hold of my arm and starts bouncing up and down. "Marry him!" she nearly shouts in my face.

A few of the other kids walking in the hallway turn around and stare at us. "Great, now there'll be rumors about me getting married. Thanks, Kristen," I say, adding an eye roll.

"Sorry," she mumbles. "It just came to me, and I got super excited about it."

"Next time, don't shout it. One…" I hold my finger up to her and continue saying, "I'm way too young to get married, and two…" I hold a second finger up to her, "We may not even work out."

"I know, but…"

"No, 'buts,' no marriage talk. Let me date him first and see where it leads."

"You're no fun." She playfully pokes her tongue out at me and we resume our walk to class.

"If you're so into marriage, you should be marrying Brad."

"Trust me, in my mind we already *are* married. He just doesn't know it yet. He will, one day. And we'll have the perfect life. Two-point-three kids, white picket fence, a dog named Rex."

"A chauffeur named Charles and a house in the Hamptons. Right?" I purposely walk into her, throwing her off balance. "It's okay, Dylan O'Brien is my husband too, he just doesn't know it," I say.

"You're a nerd," she says.

"I'm not the one with two-point-three kids. You are."

Kristen lets out a laugh just as the bell rings, telling us it's time to get to our first class.

Chapter 4

TODAY WAS LONG. AND BY LONG, I MEAN TEDIOUS AND BORING. But I had thoughts of Zac to keep me company. Thankfully the end-of-day bell has sounded, and I'm walking toward my locker to get my bag so I can go home.

There's a history essay due at the end of the week, and I need to finish it. Crap, there's also math homework and I still have that English essay to finish, too. Lost in my own thoughts of everything I have to do when I get home, I don't even realize someone is standing in front of me until I collide with them. "Sorry," I say as I look up to see Brad standing in front of me.

"Hey, Hannah. It's okay. You alright?" he asks.

"Got a lot on my mind. What are you doing?" I ask as we slowly both walk down the corridor.

"Waiting for Kristen."

"Oh, cool," I say. A smile dances on his lips as the tops of his ears begin to turn pink. "I'm not sure where she is. I think she had gym, so she's probably getting changed."

"Yeah, okay."

Noticing how the sun is blinding me, he turns his body, so we're both side-on to it. "I came to see you."

"Don't you have class?"

"Early lessons today. So, I have the rest of the day off."

"Cool," I say. There's an awkwardness between us, like neither of us knows what to say. "I gotta get home. I've got homework to do."

"Want a ride? We can stop off and grab a coffee on the way." I'm torn on what to do. I want to say yes, but I have so much homework. Zac misinterprets my silence for uneasiness because he backs away from me and straightens his back. "It's okay, I'll be seeing you Saturday, anyway."

"It's not that," I say trying to defend my silence. "I just have so much homework to do."

"Yeah, cool." He drops his shoulders slightly forward, he's not as tense. "I'll um…" He steps further away from me.

"Let me send Mom a text to let her know I'll be a little late. It'll be okay as long as we're not out for too long. I really do have a lot of homework," I say again.

His face lights up with a huge smile. "I promise, we won't be."

I quickly send Mom a text telling her I'll be home later than normal because I'm going for coffee with Kristen's cousin.

He opens the door for me, and I get into the passenger side before he joins me in the car. "Nice car," I say as he merges into the smooth flowing row of cars.

"You like Mercedes-Benzes?"

I shrug my shoulders. "I'm not interested in brands. I like how it's shiny, but I couldn't care less what type of car this is."

He lets out a laugh as we drive toward the town center. He finds a parking space in front of a small café. He parks and jumps out of the car, running around to my side. But I'm already out before he reaches me. "I wanted to the open the door for you."

"I've got two legs, two arms and a heartbeat. I can do it for myself." My phone vibrates in my hand, and I know it's a message from Mom. I stop walking as I open the message from her. *'Whose Kristen's cousin?'* it reads.

His name is Zac, and I met him at her parents' party. Remember, I'm going out with him on Saturday? I reply.

"Everything okay?" Zac asks as he looks at my phone then to me.

'You and I need to talk about this when I get home tonight.'

Okay. X. I reply. "Yeah, all good."

We enter the café and find an unoccupied seat at the front window. It overlooks the sidewalk and the street. We both sit, and I look outside, watching as people walk by. It's not too busy, more like a trickle of people.

"I was thinking about you yesterday," Zac casually says as he picks up a thin menu and peruses it.

"Were you? Were you thinking how fantastic I am and of course you couldn't wait to see me, so you decided to surprise me today?" I cheekily reply.

"You could say that." He returns with his own brazen smile. "I was thinking how I wanted to call you but I didn't want to make myself look like a desperate stalker guy."

"Yes, this is a much better approach. Show up at my school. Nothing screams stalker about this scenario. How long were you waiting for me?"

He lifts his hand to rub at his temple, and adds a chuckle. "I might've asked Kristen what time you finish, and I might have said I wanted to see you today."

"Might have?" I question.

"I'm not confirming that's what I did. But, would it be weird if I did?"

"No, not weird at all. But would you like my phone so you can put a tracking device on it? You know...not weird or anything."

"If you're not against doing something like that…then…" he drags out the word 'then' as if he's seriously considering it. I lean over and smack him on the shoulder. It's a playful smack, not a real one. "Hey, bruiser. You could hurt someone with that right hook of yours."

Laughing, I look over the menu too. Although, I'm not hungry, more like thirsty. "Well, I think it's sweet how you were waiting for me. Thank you."

He gives me a small smirk, and my heart beats quicker when I notice his cute crooked smile. "What would you like?" he asks.

"I think I'll just have a mocha, thanks."

"That's not a real coffee. That's chocolate and coffee, no one will take you seriously if you have mochas," he teases.

"What do I care what other people think of me? I like it, so that's what I want."

Zac stands and moves toward the counter to order our coffees. "You're headstrong, I like that."

I like how he appreciates me the way I am. It means he's not one of those guys who's going to try and change anything about me. I think that's cool.

He comes back and sits opposite me, placing a table number down so when the coffees are done they know where to bring them to. The café is quaint and cozy. There's a bookshelf on the back wall with a bunch of novels, newspapers, and magazines. The café itself isn't overly busy, but it shows remnants of the end of a hectic few hours. Some tables still have coffee cups sitting on them, and the bookshelf is a mess where people have searched through to get reading material. There are only two people working, and they both look flustered.

"Mom and I have been here," I say to Zac. "Mom likes the wraps, and the coffee. I'm partial to their key lime pies and of course, their mochas."

"I come here too. I like the breakfast menu they offer."

"I've never seen you here before."

He shrugs. "I don't come often, but when I do…you know."

"You go to college?" I ask, trying to get to know him better. He nods his head. "Accounting?"

"Yeah, I like numbers. They make sense when I look at them." I scrunch my nose in disgust. "You don't like math? I can tutor you," he offers eagerly.

"I hate math. Can't stand it, but I'm good at it too. Like really good. I could probably tutor *you*," I counter.

He sits back in his seat and crosses his arms over his chest. "Oh, it's a math off, is it?"

"Are you throwing the gauntlet down?" He nods his head, giving me a cheeky look. "Name the time and the place." I counter his moves.

"Is this a wager?"

"I will outnumber you any time, any place you set. I'll take you down," I say in a sassy voice and add a snap of my fingers.

He smiles even wider, leans in and whispers, "I hope you'll take me down."

I can feel the redness creeping up to my face. My eyes widen, and my mouth falls open with shock—more at myself than at him. "Oh, my God, I can't believe I walked straight into that one." Shaking my head, I try to laugh it off. But judging by the heat rising in my body, I know it's going to take some time for my embarrassment to ease.

"You're even cuter when you get flustered. Sexy when you're head strong, and sweet when you're red."

I rub my hand over my eyebrows, trying to conceal my blushing cheeks. "Thanks," I say.

"Mocha?" the server asks.

"That would be me, thank you," I say as I move my hand to pick up my coffee mug.

"And your black coffee." She slides Zac's over to him and promptly leaves us.

"Saved by the coffee," I say. My face isn't as hot as it was, which means the redness is dying down. Thank God. How embarrassing. "So, you want to be an accountant."

"I do. And you? You want to be a teacher? High school?"

"No, I want to be an elementary school teacher. I'd like to be able to mold them when they're young. And besides, little kids listen more than high school kids."

"You're a high school kid," he points out. "Don't you listen?"

A mischievous smile stretches my face. "I'm the exception; I'm the awesome one."

He laughs so hard he nearly spits his coffee out. "Warn me before you say something like that in the future."

"You don't think I'm awesome?" I joke.

"I think you're better than awesome," he says in a serious voice.

The mood around us changes instantly from light and playful to serious. He looks over his coffee to me, intensity rolling off him is sudden.

I take a sip of my mocha and try to avoid his hungry eyes. I'm jolted out of the intensity when there's a knock on the glass beside me. One of three guys who are walking past has knocked on the glass. Both Zac and I turn to see who it is. I don't recognize any of them, but when I look over to Zac I can tell he does. A different expression flashes across his face, almost like he's in pain.

The three guys walk into the cafe, and over to us.

"Zac," the tallest one says as he holds his fist out to Zac.

"Hey," Zac's reply comes out rigid and rough. He's changed again. His shoulders are tight, and his jaw is clenched, the muscles jumping. Zac slowly lifts his arm to bump knuckles with the guy.

I remain quiet, but I watch the three guys who've intruded on our impromptu date. The one who's most vocal is tall and clean-shaven, and judging by his tailored suit, steely dark eyes, and immaculate haircut, he's the leader of this trio. The other two are wearing jeans and t-shirts and look more like hangers-on than actual friends. The main guy has a thick gold chain around his neck and a pinky ring that looks way too gaudy. The other two are standing behind him, almost like they're flanking him and on the lookout for any potential dangers that might lurk in this quiet little café.

One of the two peers over at me. My skin crawls at the way he's looking at me. I avoid his greedy stare, and look back to Zac, who is completely uncomfortable.

"Who's this?" the main guy asks as he changes his focus to me.

"A friend," Zac replies quickly and coldly.

I have a sick feeling in my stomach. I'm guessing that these guys all have something to do with Zac's shady past. "You must have a name, pretty girl," the main guy says to me, ignoring Zac. He holds his hand out to me, and the gold of the ring he's wearing glistens as a ray of the afternoon sun catches it.

I don't want to take his hand. There's something really wrong with this. Zac flinches as the main guy extends his arm to me. But I pull my shoulders back and refuse to let them see how intimidated I am by them.

"I'm Hannah," I say as I reach for his hand to shake.

When my fingers touch his, his hand is icy cold. Like he's dead. I remember when my grandfather died, and we went to see him before he was cremated, I leaned down and gave him a kiss on the cheek and he was so cold. Colder than stone, colder than ice. And that's how this guy feels too.

"It's a pleasure to meet you, Hannah. I'm Edgar," he says as if I should know who he is.

I smile at him, though the smile is fake. I don't care who he is. His posse is making me feel uncomfortable.

"How can I help you, Edgar?" Zac says, dragging Edgar's eyes away from me.

I look behind him, and catch the creepiest one still staring at me. He blows me a small kiss and winks at me then licks his lips slowly.

Bile rises to the back of my throat. He's creeping me out big time. I try to swallow back the lump in my throat, but it's lodged there and won't move.

"I haven't seen you for a while, and I noticed your shiny Benz outside. I thought I'd see how you're doing." Edgar looks out the window toward Zac's car.

"I'm fine," Zac replies in a tight voice.

"Did he tell you how he bought that car?" Edgar turns and asks me.

He's baiting me and trying to make Zac look bad. Shrugging my shoulders, I reply, "Not my business what or how he paid for it."

Edgar throws his head back and laughs. This makes me angry, but I hold it together. His taunting is incredibly annoying. He's teasing me, and I hate how he's gotten under my skin in a matter of minutes. Usually, no one really bothers me, but Edgar is condescending and frustrating.

"You didn't tell her?" Edgar asks Zac but keeps his intense gaze on me.

"No, it hasn't come up yet."

The two guys behind Edgar giggle like school girls at Zac's response. The double-entendre is not lost on me. Edgar shoots them a glance and both quiet down, lowering their eyes to the floor.

Out of the corner of my eyes, I notice one of them scratching his arm, but the up and down movement doesn't stop after a few seconds, instead it intensifies, like he's trying to get under his skin. The other guy slaps him on the arm, and both look up at me.

"Did you know our boy Zac was a drug dealer?" Edgar asks me but turns to look at Zac.

My gaze catches Zac's. His face is filled with pain and embarrassment. "Was?" I ask picking up on a word I'm sure Edgar didn't realize he said.

Edgar turns with a smirk on his face. "Yes, was," he replies slowly.

"Then I'm not interested in how he got that car, unless he's still a drug dealer."

Edgar laughs again. He's getting more annoying by the minute. I want him gone. "I like this one," he says to Zac.

"So do I," Zac replies in a smaller voice.

I smile at him because I like that he likes me. What I'm not liking is this part of his past. It's not for me and I'm not sure if it's something I can forget about. Especially if spontaneous visits from this Edgar guy happen. I'm not an idiot. I can pretty much tell Edgar is probably a high-level drug dealer, and Zac worked for him.

"And he worked for you, right?" I challenge Edgar.

"He did. One of my best. Such a shame he got himself clean. He brought in big bucks, which is how he's putting himself through college, and bought that beautiful car," he shamelessly replies.

The more he talks, the more I dislike him.

"How about you?" he asks me.

"How about me what?" The moment I ask the question, I instantly regret it. I know what he's asking, and I hate myself for falling for it.

"Do you like to party?" He leans on the table, blocking my view of Zac. But I'm a tough girl, and I can give as good as I get.

"I love to party," I say in a swoony voice. "And by party, I mean I love to stay away from low-life drug dealers who make a living screwing up people's lives."

A glint passes through his eyes. A cross between anger, and humor. He leans in closer, his face only a few inches from mine. My heart beats crazily with anxiety. Something passes though me too, a little thrill. I kinda like this dangerous encounter, but I'm also smart enough to know he's not the type of guy I want to be associated with.

What's wrong with me? Why am I attracted to this guy? But it's not attraction, it's something else. And I can't quite put my finger on exactly what that is, either.

"I'd like to screw you," he says in a low voice. "I'd like to screw you real good."

Spit pools in my mouth, and a switch is flipped inside me. He's playing me, and I'm being the naive school girl who's falling for it. "Sorry, I don't screw walking STDs."

"You *are* a cute one." He leans down to grab my chin, and gently plays his thumb over it. Stroking my skin. I turn my face, unsure at how I'm feeling at this unwelcomed touch. But in my head, it's not unwelcomed. I kinda like it. *Stop it, Hannah. He's a drug dealer.*

"Please leave," I say finding my voice.

He stands straighter, and smiles at me. "I'll see you around, *Hannah*," he says with a devilish look in his eye.

"I hope not," I reply.

He and his two goons leave, and I sit back staring at Zac. He's made me angry. At no point did he jump in and tell Edgar not to touch me or to leave me alone. "You okay?" he asks when the three are gone.

I arch an eyebrow at him, and purse my lips together tightly. I want to tell him off. "I can't believe you just sat there and said nothing to him."

"You don't get it," he instantly responds.

"Then tell me."

"Edgar is…" He looks off to the side, avoiding my intense gaze. "…dangerous," he whispers.

"And you're gutless for not standing up to him. Gives me very little hope that if I'm ever in a bad situation around you that you'll help me. It makes me think you'll run and leave me to fend for myself."

"It's not like that. Edgar, he's not a nice guy. What he wants he stops at nothing to get."

Zac isn't who I thought he was. I have more balls than he does. I can't see a future for us, not after he sat there and did nothing while his former drug-supplier boss basically hit on me in front of him. "Still, you could've said something."

"I'm sorry," he says.

Picking my mocha up, I've found it's tepid and not pleasant to drink when it's lost its heat, or when I'm around company who doesn't defend me. The silence between us is uncomfortable. I don't want to be here anymore. Zac really isn't who I thought he was. I place my cup down, and smile at Zac. "I've got a ton of homework to do, so I think I'll get going. Can I get my bag out of your car?" I ask.

"I'll take you home," he insists.

I look at the time on my phone and shake my head. "It's okay, the bus will be here soon. I'll catch the bus home."

"It's no trouble," he says trying to weasel his way back into my good graces.

We walk to his car, and when he unlocks it, I grab my bag and back away from him. "It's okay. Really. The bus drops me off right in front of home. Thank you for the coffee." I smile and step further back.

"What time should I pick you up on Saturday?" he eagerly asks.

Crap, we've still got our date. But after today, I don't think I'm interested in going anywhere with him. "I'll call you," I say with no intentions on calling him.

"You sure you don't want me to take you home?"

I start toward the bus stop shaking my head. "No, it's all good. Thank you." I turn and walk away, not waiting for his response.

Walking to the bus stop, I replay the whole scenario in my

head, from the moment Edgar and his "bodyguards" walked into the café, until right now. Zac disappointed me. I can't get over how he sat there and didn't say anything to Edgar. Nothing. Zip. Nada.

Clutching my school bag closer to my chest, I internalize what happened and try to make sense of it. Edgar is, at best, a drug dealer. At worst, who knows what else?

Zac sat there, not talking or even sticking up for me. I had to do it all for myself.

When I reach the bus stop, I take my phone out of my pocket to see what time it is. There's a message from Zac, it simply says, 'Sorry.' Rolling my eyes, and without responding, I put my phone away and decide to take some time so I can think about this all.

Looking down the road, I notice a parked black car idling. It's not Zac's and something tells me, it's Edgar's.

I know he's not a good guy, and it's not a smart thing to entertain thoughts of him. However, in our short interaction he's gotten under my skin. The two guys he was with creeped me out. They looked sketchy. But Edgar…

Ignoring the sleek, black car, I turn away from it.

The bus arrives, and I get on, but keep an eye on the black car. I hope he doesn't follow me home. That would be super creepy, even more than those Instagram and Facebook weirdos who message you to proclaim their love without ever talking to you.

I notice the black car pulling over behind the bus as it makes its stops on the route. It's making me feel even more uneasy now. Edgar will know where I live. Nervousness takes over, and my leg bounces as we approach my home. The stop before home is quite isolated, so I don't want to get off there, and the stop after home is isolated too. So, I decide to make a round trip, and hopefully Edgar will get bored with following the bus and just leave. It's the safest thing to do. That way he won't know where I live, and I don't have to tell my parents about the freak who's followed me home.

This situation is best left secret. My parents don't need to know. They would worry about me.

The bus stops at my stop, and of course the black car does too. But I stay on the bus, and when I get back into town, I get off at the mall and head inside. Some of the stores are still open, but the smaller ones have started to close. I take my phone out of my pocket and call Mom.

"You're not home yet," she says before anything else.

"Can you come pick me up please?" my voice is slightly higher than normal, and even to my ear, I sound panicked.

"Where are you? Are you okay? What's happened?" the rapid-fire questions are an indicator of Mom's stress level.

"Yeah, I'm great. I um…" I don't want to lie, but at the same time I don't want to tell her about Edgar. I duck into Target, and hide toward the back. I keep looking over the displays, hopeful I don't see Edgar and his goons. Thankfully, no one seems to have chased me in here.

"What is it?" she sounds terrified.

"Nothing, I missed the bus. That's all. I was walking fast because I wanted to get into Target before they closed. I'm looking for…" I turn to see the closest thing to me. "…for a notebook." I grab the first one I see.

"A notebook? And you're stressed because you wanted to find a book? What happened with Zac and coffee?" Mom's suspicious. I would be too.

"I don't know about him. Anyway, can you pick me up please?"

"I'm already on my way. Wait for me outside."

My stomach churns with anxiousness. I don't want to in case Edgar is there. "Yeah, sure. I just have to try to find a notebook. So, if I'm not there, I won't be long."

"I'm only a few minutes away."

"Okay, thank you."

"Bye, darling."

I absolutely despise lying to my parents. But in this case, I know how much she'll freak out if I told her what happened. I have to tell her how coffee with Zac went, but there's no chance in hell, I'm going to tell her about Edgar. No way. I'll have to leave that part out.

Chapter 5

MOM HASN'T SAID MUCH TO ME SINCE WE'VE GOTTEN HOME. BUT I know she's waiting for Dad to arrive from work before she broaches the subject of Zac.

I'm in my room working on my paper, dreading the interrogation to come at the dinner table. I know she's going to ask me about Zac, and why I sounded panicked. I have to put on the performance of a lifetime to convince them. *God, I hate this.*

It doesn't take long for Dad to come home. Looking at my phone, I notice the time and think it's weird how he's home early. Within moments, there's a knock at my door. "Come in," I say.

"Darling, you've got flowers," Mom says. Her features are filled with questions and doubt.

"Flowers?" I ask as I push up off my chair and head out to the family room. On the dining table, sitting in the middle is a huge vase filled with red roses. I've never seen an arrangement so large. "Did a card come with it?" I look around the giant bouquet trying to find the card.

"No card." Mom places her hands to her hips and takes a step back. "They're pretty," she says.

"Yeah, they are." I look at them and take a deep breath.

"You don't seem too impressed with them. Who are they from?"

"I don't know. There's no card." I point toward the flowers. "Probably from Zac."

"Probably?" Mom's voice squeaks.

Or Edgar, but I don't want to even mention his name. "I can't see how they'd be from anyone else." Dad's not home yet. It was the flower delivery I heard.

"What aren't you telling me, Hannah?" Mom asks as I stare at the enormous bouquet of roses.

There's a sinking feeling in the pit of my stomach. These aren't from Zac. "Nothing!" I reply with too much enthusiasm.

"Tell me about this Zac guy." Mom pulls out a chair and sits on it. She's not going to let this one go. She is intent on knowing what's happening.

I start to formulate the answer in my head, careful not to mention anything about his past or Edgar or anything that's going to freak Mom out. "Zac is Kristen's cousin. He asked me out on a date, I liked him and so I said yes. He asked Kristen what time school finishes, and he was waiting for me today. That's it. Nothing else."

"Um, no, that's not it. How old is he?"

"He's twenty-one and goes to college. But truthfully, I'm not all that into him. I thought I was, but after today, I know I'm not."

"What happened today to change your mind?"

Edgar happened. "He was talking about himself and I don't think he's really interested in me, more like parts of me." It's the only excuse I can give that I know Mom will be proud of me for deciding not to pursue him.

"What's that supposed to mean?" Mom asks.

"Sex, Mom. I think he just wants sex from me." These lies are getting out of hand now. I can't keep them up.

I should tell her the truth, but I can't. She'll lose it if I tell her about his past, and Edgar, and how I think I'm attracted to Edgar but I know I shouldn't be. I feel like screaming and pulling my hair out. He's a bad guy, and I'm drawn to him. What is wrong with me? I shouldn't be feeling like this. I should be strong. I know he'll screw my life up if I get involved with him.

"Then I'm glad you've decided he's not for you." Mom stands and pushes in her chair. "Is that all, or is there something else you want to tell me?" She's staring as if she's testing me.

Swallowing back the lie, I smile at her and shake my head. "No, Mom. That's it."

"What do you want to do with these flowers?" Mom asks as she looks at them.

"I don't know." I shrug. "But I do know I have homework to finish. Do you need help with dinner?"

"No, go finish your homework. I'll call you when dinner's ready."

"Thanks, Mom." I move around her, but stop, and turn to give her a kiss on the cheek. "Thank you."

She smiles at me, gives me a quick hug, and goes to the kitchen to continue making dinner.

As I take myself back to my room, I'm mentally kicking myself for feeling anything but disgust toward Edgar. I know he's way older than me. I know he's a drug dealer. I know intellectually I shouldn't be thinking about him. But I can't help it. He's in my head, and under my skin.

Flopping on my bed, I think about today and how it's panned out. I don't *want* to think about it, but everything is so fresh in my mind, that I can't really concentrate on anything else. And now I've received flowers. Even that gesture has crawled under my skin and is messing with my head.

My phone vibrates and I get a sinking feeling in my pit of my gut. I know it's not Kristen or Zac. Somehow, I know it's Edgar.

A smile tugs at my lips. *And I hate myself for it.*

Dragging myself up from my bed, I lean over and grab my phone from where it's been sitting on my desk.

Hope you like the flowers — the text reads from an unknown number.

My smile widens, and I feel sick to my core. I shouldn't be smiling. I shouldn't even be thinking about responding to him. But my fingers are already in place to send a message back. I don't know what.

My hair falls over my face, and I tuck some in place before collapsing on the bed again. Lying on my back, I bring the phone up so I'm looking at it. A weird feeling takes over my body. A few years ago, Kristen and I sneaked a cigarette from a relative of hers. We waited 'til Monday and before school and went out the back behind the bleachers to have it. Neither of us knew what we were doing, and both of us choked like we had something stuck in our throats. But after we smoked the cigarette (more like choked 'til we were red in the face) we went to class feeling invincible.

We knew we'd done something wrong, but we walked in with our heads held high and our shoulders back because we had a secret no one else knew about.

Still, to this day, no one knows we tried (and hated) the taste of a cigarette.

Oh, that feeling… It was exciting and dangerous. But so much fun, because we both knew a secret no one else knew.

And that's how I'm feeling right now. Responding to Edgar means I'm stepping into a world of danger. Different danger than smoking a cigarette out back behind the bleachers.

A shudder of mixed emotions flutters over my body.

I shouldn't reply.

I really shouldn't. I should ignore it and ignore him. He'll get the message that I'm not interested and move on to the next girl. But that idea pains me. I don't want him to want someone else. I don't want him looking at anyone else the way he focused his powerful stare at me.

Standing from the bed, I leave my phone, choosing to walk away from it. "What are you doing?" I say to my reflection in my floor-length mirror.

I stare at myself, conflicted by what's happening in my head. Clashing tornadoes colliding with one another. Darkness and danger entwined.

"Nope, I can't do this." I take in a deep breath and decide not to respond to Edgar. I mean come on, what kind of name is Edgar? He *sounds* like a drug dealer. And I'm way too smart to get involved with someone who sounds like—and is—a drug dealer. I have too much at stake to succumb to the temptation of a person with the potential to ruin my life.

I stare at myself, satisfied to have made that decision. I turn, grab my phone, and delete the text without responding. Instantly, I feel like a huge burden has been lifted from me. This was just a momentary lapse of judgement. Something I don't have to tell anyone about. And something I *won't* tell anyone about. I'll take this to my grave. My brush with the wild side.

Smiling at myself, I feel good about the decision I've made.

Real good.

Chapter 6

SCHOOL TODAY WAS A BLUR.

I haven't really been able to concentrate on anything. Each class has blended into the next. Even lunch was *meh*. Brad spent lunch with us today, and Kristen is so into him. I don't mind how into him she is; I think it's totally cool. But Edgar has been on my mind all day.

I can't shake the thought of him. In a way, I hope he messages me again. In another I hope he doesn't. I made the decision last night to not respond to his text about the flowers, and I felt good for deleting it. Later, though, as I was lying in bed I couldn't help but replay how he talked to me at the café. It disgusted me, but it turned me on like crazy. Heat slowly crept through me, making me want to hear from him again. I realized I was hanging on his words, wanting him to say something to me.

But even now, thinking about him, I slightly shake my head, hoping to dislodge the thought of Edgar that's etched itself in the center of my mind.

I'm in the last class of the day, and I feel like a robot who's drifted from one lesson to the next, not really knowing what I'm supposed to be learning.

It's been a haze.

And I hate myself for giving him any more of my time.

The bell sounds at the end of the last period, and I go to my locker, grab my bag and laptop, and head out the main gates. Checking my phone, I have a text from Mom saying she's going to be late home tonight. And a text from Dad saying he'll pick dinner up on the way home from work.

Heading over to the buses, I wait in line absentmindedly looking out over the cars. Truthfully though, I'm disappointed Edgar didn't try to reach out to me again. I'm also relieved. That takes the pressure off me. *What is wrong with me?*

"Didn't you like the flowers?" a husky voice whispers in my ear.

Instantly my skin pebbles with excitement and my heart leaps in my chest. Closing my eyes, I savor the sound of the deep voice.

His fingers find my hip and dig in possessively. My brain fights with itself. *Stop it, Hannah. You can't like this. It's not primal, it's dangerous.*

I grab his hand and yank it away from me. Turning, I'm immediately assaulted by his dark eyes. "Don't touch me," I say with venom in my tone.

His lips quirk into a mocking smile. His eyes follow suit with hints of danger and amusement. His brow lifts arrogantly, and a lump forms in my throat. My body defies what my brain is telling me to do. I want to kiss him.

Stop it, Hannah! Stop it right now!

Shaking my head, I attempt to dislodge the sick thoughts assaulting me. Not sick because I'm attracted to him, that's part of life. But sick because he's deadly dangerous, and I'm crazily attracted to him and everything represents.

"The words you're saying don't match your body's

reactions," he whispers as he reaches out to gently take my upper arm. This is a direct contradiction of everything he is. He's not a nice guy, a gentle guy. I know this. But the softness of his touch is causing all the signals to go fuzzy

I have to stay strong. I can't and won't throw away my life on a guy who's bad for me. "I said don't touch me." Turning, I step on the bus. I can't do this. I can't let him get under my skin like this. *But he already has.*

"Get off the bus, Hannah," he says as he crosses his arms in front of his chest. Two different guys flank him today. They look much more menacing and deadly than the guys from the café. He notices my reaction to them. "I didn't like the way they were looking at you, so I got rid of them," he says as if he can read my thoughts.

I stare at him, swallowing the even bigger lump in my throat, but continue to get on the bus. I sit toward the back and try to not look at him. But I can't help it. Turning, I see him standing outside, he's shaking his head at me but looks amused. For a second, I feel happy because I think he's going to leave me alone. But then realization hits, and I know this is nothing more than a game for him. He's going to follow me home.

The bus leaves and I exhale deeply, glad I was able to fight my libido on this one. Why must I feel like this?

As the bus travels and makes several stops before reaching home, I keep looking behind me hoping to *not* see his car. But, all my hopes are squashed when at every stop his car is there. When it gets to my stop, he's already waiting. He's outside his car, smoking a cigarette. The two guys he has with him are out of the car too. Both wearing black shades, both dressed in identical suits, both standing like they're protecting our President.

Lowering my head, I don't make eye contact with him as I make the trek up the hill, and around the corner to my house.

"You can't ignore me forever, Hannah." He catches up to me in a few long strides. I ignore him. "I'm not going anywhere."

Anger begins to bubble inside me. I want to tell him to leave me alone, but I know if I engage in conversation, it'll mean I'm opening the channel of communication. I don't want to do that. Not with *him*.

"If you don't talk to me, then I'll make sure I'm here when you're leaving for school in the morning too."

"No!" I shout as I turn to face him. Damn it. I spoke. "Just leave me alone, Edgar. I'm not interested in you." I clutch my bag to my chest and keep walking.

He grabs hold of my arm, stopping me from walking away. I quickly gaze at the two men in suits, who look around them as if they're making sure no one is near to bother us. "I can't leave you alone. You're mine," he says.

"What? I'm not yours, I'm not anyone's. I'm my own person." He lets out a belly laugh and throws his head back. This makes me so angry. Any attraction I was feeling for him is now long gone. "You're an asshole. Leave me alone." I break the hold he has on my arm and try to walk away…*again.*

This time he grabs me by the hips, and pulls me back into his body. "What you don't get, Hannah, is if I see something I want, I get it. I'm not a man who takes 'no' for an answer. I'm a man who gets what he wants. And right now, I want you." He loosens the hard grip he has on my hips, and I step away from him.

"You saw me for all of ten minutes at the café, and you decided you want me. Even though I'm clearly not interested in you," I say defiantly.

His eyes narrow and his lips curl up. He steps closer, and I turn my head away. I don't want him this close to me; it's messing with my head. I can't do it and keep my sanity.

"Problem is, my little kitty. I want you, and I know you want me too. It's all over you. When you take a breath, it hitches. Your eyes dilate with excitement, and your nipples… hmmm your nipples."

Horrified, yet turned on, I look down to my breasts. Damn him. "Go to hell," I say and step away from him. "I'm not your *kitty*, I'm not your anything. Stay away from me, or I'll get the police involved."

As I'm walking away, he laughs at me again.

Lowering my head, I walk as fast as I can to get home. When I'm there, I lock the front door, and check all the others are locked to make sure he can't get in. But I know that's useless. I suspect a man like him could find a way to get in if he wants.

My heart rate is crazy high, and I'm shaking like a leaf at just the thought of him setting his sights on me. I have to break this stupid effect he has on me. In just the few interactions I've had with him, I know he's dangerous. And he *will* hurt me. One way or another, he'll wreck me.

I look out the window, and see his black car sitting across the road. He's sending me a message. A very loud one. He wants me, and he's not going to stop 'til he gets me.

But I don't think going out with him will make him cut this possessive crap out. I think that would intensify it.

I decide to not look out the front window anymore. I head to my room and try to start on my homework. But every sound, every movement freaks me out because I think it's him. Everything is intensified, and I can't concentrate on anything.

My phone vibrates beside me, and I leap in response to it. A message from Kristen comes through. *Hey girl, what's happening?*

NMU — I respond.

Nothing. Just talking to Brad. There's a heap of love hearts next to his name.

Awesome — I reply, still nervous and jittery about the guy sitting outside my house. I'm really not in the mood to talk. And I'm not going to tell anyone that a drug dealer has taken a liking to me and wants me. And I'm *definitely* not going to tell *anyone* how attracted I am to him, but I don't want to be.

U OK?

Yep. Just doing homework.

God, I hate lying. Hate it with a passion. But I'd rather lie then tell the truth in this case. It's not something anyone else could understand.

K – talk 18r.

Curiosity gets the better of me, and I go out to the front window again to see if he's still there. Thankfully his car is gone. But in place of his car is one of the two men. Standing across the road, looking at my house. *What?*

I check up and down the road. Edgar's car is gone. I decide to go and see why he left behind one of his men in black.

I have a gut feeling I know what he's going to say, but I have to hear it for myself. Unlocking the front door, I peek outside, making sure this isn't an ambush. I know in my heart it's not, but still I have to be careful. Crossing the street, I stand in front of the guy. "What are you doing here?" I ask.

"I'm the first shift," his voice is deadpan.

Staring at him, I don't quite understand what he's saying. "What?"

"I take the first shift guarding you. You'll have a replacement when you get to school."

"What?" This is now insane. "I don't need a… " I wave my hand over him, not sure what to call him.

"A bodyguard, Miss Mendes."

"A what?" I shriek even louder. "A bodyguard? Why the hell do I need a bodyguard?"

"Mr. Zaro has appointed me to be your personal bodyguard, ma'am."

Edgar's last name is Zaro? Seriously? Edgar Zaro? Even his name sounds like he's dangerous. Next, I'll be finding out he's known as Edgar *'Big Daddy'* Zaro. I chuckle to myself. What a stupid name. "You can call *Mr. Zaro* and tell him I'm refusing you and I don't need you because the only person I need protection from is him."

This earns me a smirk. "He said you'd say that. And he told me if I leave you alone for one moment, he'd kill me. Sorry, ma'am, I value my life too much."

"He told you he'd kill you if you leave me alone?"

"Yes, ma'am."

"Can't you see how insane this is?"

"I get paid well to protect you."

"That doesn't answer the question. *Can't you see how insane this is?*" I ask again, stressing the actual question.

"My job is to protect you, and that's what I'm going to do."

This is beyond a damn joke. "Call him," I say firmly.

This guy is tall, maybe two heads taller than me. I'm over five foot eight, and he'd have to be six foot three easily. He looks down at me with a puzzled stare. "You want me to call him?" Suddenly, fear is clearly present.

"Yes."

"I've been told not to interrupt him unless it's an emergency with you."

"Call him. Now." I don't give in.

Hesitantly, he takes his phone out of his pocket, and calls Edgar. I snatch the phone out of his hand. He's much bigger than me and could easily overpower me, but I already have it to my ear when Edgar answers. "She better not be hurt," he says into the phone.

"This is not normal. Get rid of him," I say to Edgar.

"What a pleasant surprise. It's my kitty."

"Stop calling me that. I'm not your anything. Get rid of this guy. I don't want him here."

"No can do. He's there to stay. Get used to him."

"Edgar, this is crazy. You're forcing yourself on me, and I don't want you."

"You and I both know that isn't true. You want me, but you

don't like the idea of me being a drug dealer. You think I'm going to be bad for you. Admit it, tell me you want me the way I want you."

"I don't want you," I say too quickly and in a crackly voice. He's playing with my head. And I hate myself *and* him for it.

"Then having a bodyguard shouldn't bother you."

"Of course, it bothers me. Because THIS IS INSANE," I yell. He's so frustrating. "Leave me alone. I won't do this with you." I hang up abruptly and throw the phone to the ground, adding a few stomps to it too. The bodyguard looks at me and shakes his head. "Leave," I yell at him with annoyance.

He stands taller, and crosses his arms in front of his chest.

I walk away from him. Angry and frustrated, I head back into the house and lock the door. The bodyguard stands outside, positioned like a military armored guard.

Protecting.

But who is there to protect me from but the man who hired him?

Chapter 7

THANKFULLY, MOM AND DAD DIDN'T SAY ANYTHING ABOUT THE guy standing outside our house because he'd left by the time they got home. *Finally.*

"I have to leave in the next half hour, if you get ready I can take you to school," Dad says as he sticks his head inside my bedroom the next morning.

"I won't be ready. I'll catch the bus, it's okay."

"Sure? I can wait for a few extra minutes." He looks at his watch, and I can tell by the stressed look on his face that he really can't wait.

"Dad, it's all good. I'll catch the bus."

Dad sighs, and purses his lips together. With a concerned scowl, he sighs again. "I can wait."

"Go to work, I'll be fine."

"Okay, love you," he says as he comes in, gives me a kiss on the forehead and turns to leave. "Do you need money for school?"

"Nah, I'm good."

"See you tonight, sweetheart."

"Love you," I call while he's closing my bedroom door.

I hear the front door shut a few moments later, and I make sure it's locked. I don't know anything about Edgar, but what I do know is he obviously has the means to do whatever he wants. Exhibit A — the flowers. Exhibit B — the bodyguard yesterday.

As I approach the door to check if it's locked, I notice his black car on the opposite side of the road. Something stirs inside me. It's a combination of frustration, anger, and excitement. None of which I shouldn't be feeling. The worst thing is I've been expecting it.

I decide to confront him — face to face.

I head outside, no shoes on my feet, and not even ready for school yet.

I get to his car, and rap on the back window. I know he's not the type to drive himself around. The door opens, and he steps out.

"You're looking very adorable this morning, Hannah," he says as he leans in to give me a kiss.

I step back to avoid him. "What part of 'leave me alone' is hard for you to understand?" Angrily, I place my hands on my hips and fan them out to make me look more imposing then I actually am.

"What part of, 'you're mine' do *you* find hard to interpret?" he smarmily replies.

"And how do you think this is going to work? I'm seventeen, you're how old?" I ask pointing to him.

"Twenty-eight."

My face scrunches up on its own. "Ewww. That's disgusting. I'm not interested in someone as old as you. Nor am I interested in dating a drug dealer. And I can tell you right now, my parents won't like you. You're wasting your time with me. Find someone else to harass and stalk."

Turning away, I've said what I need to say. But he wraps his fingers around my wrist and yanks me back to him. "You don't fucking walk away from me, Hannah. I gave you the benefit of the doubt yesterday, but this childish, bullshit behavior stops right now."

"You think *you* demanding I go out with you will work?" I step away again. "It won't. And you're insane. I'm not yours and I never will be."

He steps closer to me, and I automatically flinch. He lowers his head as if he's embarrassed, but looks up to me with a fire burning in his eyes. "I'll put it to you this way, so your pretty little head can understand." He steps further into my personal space, and I step back. "You're mine and no one on this planet is going to stop me from taking you. No one, Hannah, including you."

I stand staring at him for a second, before I feel the tears stinging my eyes. I will not cry in front of him and give him the satisfaction. "I don't want you," I say with conviction. "I will not be yours. Leave." I back away from him, not daring to turn my back on him.

"When will you be ready for school?" he calls after me.

I ignore him as I break into a run back to my house, and lock the front door when I'm inside. I lean against the door, and bury my face in my hands, crying. He's insane. My phone rings from inside my room, and I run to get it. Wiping the water from my cheeks, I take several deep breaths so I can compose myself before I answer the call. I swipe to answer, "Hello?"

"I'm sorry for my behavior, kitty. I didn't mean to scare you. I just… " I hang up on him, before he can finish talking. My phone rings again. I ignore it, knowing it's him.

He's relentless. As soon as I hang up, he calls again. Then I hear someone thumping on the front door. I know it's him or one of the men he's employed.

Sitting on my bed, I take several deep breaths, trying to make sense of what's happened. He's dangerous. There's not one iota of doubt in my mind about that.

But… God, how I hate the 'but.' He's overtaken all my thoughts, and the danger borders on thrilling. *What is wrong with me?*

I keep making the decision to walk away, but then a part of me screams how this is exciting, illicit. Almost taboo.

For now, I have to push him to the back of my mind, and get ready for school. Changing into jeans and a tank top, I slip my feet into my shoes and get my school bag ready. Checking the time, I know I'm already running late thanks to Edgar and his primal outburst.

I open the door, to find his car still across the street, and him leaning up against it, smoking. I scrunch my nose when I see the cigarette between his fingers. He sees me, immediately stamps out the cigarette and jogs across the road to where I've already started walking toward the bus stop. "Go away," I bark toward him. In a swift move, he grabs my bag, and begins walking back to his car. "Hey!" I yell.

"You want it, you have to come with me."

"No! I'm not coming with you, Edgar. Leave me alone."

He turns and shows me a smile. "I like the way you say my name. The only thing sexier would be for you to call me Mr. Zaro when we have sex."

I arch a brow at him, disgusted at how sure he is we're going to have sex. Ugh. "Well, imagine it as much as you want. You and I are *not* going to have sex. Ever. Now, give me my bag back. I'm already running late thanks to you." I point at him, but hold my hand out for my bag.

"I tell you what. Say Mr. Zaro, and I'll give you your bag back."

"What?" I ask, perplexed.

"Say my name, and I'll give you your bag back."

"You'll walk over to me, and give me my bag. I'm not going anywhere near your car. You're a stalker and a weirdo who'll most likely push me into the car and kidnap me."

"I'd do no such thing," he enunciates clearly. "But they would." He chuckles as he points to the two bodyguards.

If I say his stupid name, then he'll give me my bag back, and hopefully I'll make it to school on time. Taking a breath, I stare at Edgar. "Mr. Zaro," I say then hold my hand out for my bag.

"See, that wasn't so hard, was it?" He continues walking toward his car.

"Hey, give me my bag back."

"I have every intention of giving your *bag* back to you." He opens the passenger door to his car, pulls the zip of my backpack down and empties everything on the seat. He walks over with my bag and hands it to me. "There you go," he says with amusement. His eyes are smiling as much as his lips. "Your bag."

"Edgar!" I shriek when he hands it to me. "I need my things for school. I don't have time for this crap. I need my stuff."

"Then you better get in my car. And I'll give you everything back when I take you to school."

"This is insane, just like you are."

"But it's the only way you're going to get your things back. If you want them, then you better hurry up and get in the car." He looks at his shiny, gold watch. "We're going to have to speed to get you there in time. And I'm a law-abiding citizen. I wouldn't want to be stopped by the police." He sarcastically chuckles. *Yes, a law-abiding drug dealer.*

Defeated, I walk toward his car. I need my things for school, but it doesn't mean I'm going to talk to him on the way there. He holds the back door open for me, and I slide into the plush, leather back bench seat.

"Nice of you to join me," he says. He's laughing at me. But I'm not replying. He slides in beside me, but on the opposite side. I look out the window, as one of his men packs my bag, and holds it in his lap on route to school. "You're an interesting woman, Hannah," he says.

Rolling my eyes, I keep looking outside as the car travels, slowly, toward school.

"Your parents are interesting too."

The hair on my arms stand as my skin pebbles. I swallow. What does he mean? But I still remain quiet.

"Did you know your father hasn't been promoted for three years?" I want to ask him how he knows, but that means I'll be talking to him. "And your mother earns more than your father? Did you know that's causing your father to gamble?"

What? Dad is a gambler?

More questions burn with the need for answers.

"Your mother has been seeing a man for two years now. Would you like to read the emails she's shared with him?" My head turns so fast, I'm almost dizzy.

"No, she hasn't. And my Dad's not a gambler." My life is perfect. Everything is perfect, except for Edgar, who's forced himself into my life. "Why are you lying to me."

"Lying?" He taps one of the men on the shoulder, and he hands Edgar a thick manila envelope. "Here you go." He hands me the same envelope.

Hesitantly, I take it and slide out the contents. My heart is going crazy, and I'm shaking like mad. I don't want to see what's in here. The first thing my eyes land on is a printout of an email. It's from my mom's email address at work to someone other than Dad. The first line makes me gasp.

This email is intimate, and personal, and says things I don't want to know. It's also vulgar and disgusting. What they want to do to each other. What they've already done with each other. Fantasies, pleasures, everything.

My stomach is hit with waves of nausea as the bile quickly makes its way up to the back of my throat. "This can't be true." My whole world, everything I know, has been a lie.

"And if you flip to the next page, you'll see how much your

father has gambled away." He turns the page, and I see the bank account details. How dismal it is, for how much my parents work. It doesn't add up.

"Why are you showing me this?" I ask, tears brimming in my eyes and my stomach churning with worry.

"Because your perfect world, the parents who you're insisting won't like me, aren't saints. We're all sinners, Hannah. I refuse to hide my sins from the world. I embrace them."

"You're a monster, Edgar. You're not a good person." I throw the papers at him, and turn to keep looking out the window, silently crying as we near school.

We reach school, and I try to open the door, but I can't. It's locked. *Of course.*

"I'll be here this afternoon to pick you up." He hands me my bag, and suddenly my door opens. Standing outside, holding my door open, is the guy from outside my house yesterday. He smiles at me, trying to make me feel safe, but right now, I feel like my world is about to implode, all because Edgar showed me my parents' secrets. Mom is a cheater, and Dad's a gambler.

"Don't bother, I won't be here," I say to Edgar unsure of what I mean by my own words. But I don't want to see him.

Walking away, I hear Edgar give instructions. "Follow her, and make sure she's okay," he says to the one who's supposed to be replaced by another bodyguard.

This is all too much.

I break into a run, trying to get away from everyone. I can't deal with this, not now. Not after what I've seen. I run through the hallway at school, and see Kristen and Brad standing near her locker. In tears, I fly past her. She sees my destressed look, and gives chase. She's on my tail, only a few steps away. "Hannah!" she calls.

But I go faster. Leaving through the back door, out into the field, past the bleachers as far as I can go.

Looking behind me, I can see Kristen still running after me, but she's lagging further and further behind. I have to get away, to be alone. I can't do this. Not with anyone.

I need to be alone, and away from everyone. How can I trust my parents after what Edgar showed me? They're supposed to be the people I can depend on most in my life, and I saw proof that they're anything but dependable.

There's only one place I can go, a place I know is isolated enough not to be bothered by anyone. It's a place Kristen and I have been to several times. It's the place where she brought a bottle of tequila out, and we both tried it. I had only one swig from the bottle. It burnt my throat and I didn't like the taste.

It's also the place where she told me she let Jason Masters feel her boobs in seventh grade.

I haven't been there in a while, but it's quiet and calm. It's the park on the other side of town. No one likes going there, because there's a cemetery behind it that's overgrown and unkempt. It looks scary, although it really isn't. It's peaceful. Maybe that's why I like it so much.

I run toward the park, making sure to keep an eye out for Edgar's black, shiny car, or the guy he's set up as my bodyguard.

Not today.

When I get to the park, I slow to a jog as I look around and notice how isolated it actually is. There's no one here. Not a single person. Good, because I couldn't deal with anyone. Not after those two huge bombshells Edgar dropped on me.

Toward the middle of the park is a swing set and a slide. No one uses them, and the slide has so much graffiti on it, that you can't see the original color of it. There are three swings. One is completely broken; the other two are old and worn. This park is clearly neglected, but at least it's still here. I reckon in the next few years, it'll be demolished and probably developed for housing or something else.

Placing my bag on the bottom of the slide, I walk the couple of steps to the swings, and sit on one of them. My phone vibrates in my pocket, but I don't bother even looking at it. I know it's either Kristen or Edgar. And I don't want to talk to either of them. Edgar has unleashed a world of pain on me. I suspect it's intentional, and my head is so foggy I can't see why he'd do it. Kristen, well, she just cares about me. She saw me running while I was crying and wants to know what's upset me so much.

She's a beautiful person. And I don't want to bring her into any of this.

Pushing myself on the swing, I look out the back at the overgrown cemetery. Tears fall from my eyes as flashes of what I read keep replaying in my head.

Oh baby, I can't wait to see you tomorrow. My mother wrote. And it makes me sick to my stomach.

Withdrawal of thirty-five hundred dollars at the casino. My father's gambling addiction.

This hurts so much. How can they lie to me? How can they do this to each other?

I bury my face into my hands and cry. My soul is hurting. My entire world is nothing but a lie. It's crumbling beneath me, and I can't stop it. How… why? *Why?*

My phone continues to ring, and I opt to turn it off. I don't want to hear it anymore. I don't want to be bothered by anyone. I just want to be alone.

Standing, I take my phone out of my pocket and notice the insane amount of calls I've missed. Kristen's name keeps popping up on the screen. Followed by a number I haven't saved, but I know whose it is. *Edgar's.*

Kristen calls again, and I answer it on the first ring. I can't have her worrying. "Hey," I say through a heavy sob.

"Where are you and what's happening?" she asks.

"I'm not at school. I can't be there, not today. Cover for me?" I ask even though I have no right to ask her for a favor.

"Tell me what's happening."

"I… " Taking a deep breath, I rub at my temple with my free

hand. "I can't. Not today."

"Are you in trouble, Hannah? I talked to Zac and he said you might be in trouble."

"What? Why would you talk to him?"

"You've been kinda quiet for a few days, and I called him to see if everything is going okay with you two."

"I can't believe you. Why would you do that, Kristen?" I snap at her.

"Because something's going on and you're not talking to me."

"Maybe because you think it's a good idea to go and ask everyone. You're a gossip queen, Kristen!" I yell at her before hanging up.

Jesus, what have I done? I know Kristen didn't ask Zac about what happened because she wants to snoop. She genuinely cares about me, and I just made it ten times worse by snapping at her out of anger and saying horrible things.

I can't deal with this today. I just can't. Everything is getting worse by the minute. Turning my phone off, I slide it back into my pocket and sit on the swing. Pushing myself, I'm left alone with my thoughts, and the pain of knowing how my parents are just pretending to be loving and happy. Why would they do that? If they're not happy, they should divorce and be done with it.

Dad was in a rush to leave this morning, did he really have a meeting, or was he going somewhere to gamble what's left of their savings in hope he can win back everything he's lost?

Is Mom really at work, or is she in some hotel room somewhere, doing something with someone other than my father?

I burst into tears again, face in my hands.

"Kitty." Edgar pulls me into his arms and hugs me tight to his body, stroking my hair. I cry into his chest. I hate how he found me, but I also knew he would. Although, I thought it would take him longer.

Wiping at my eyes, I step back and sit on the swing again. "How did you find me? I lost... " I point backward indicating the bodyguard who's nowhere to be seen. "... him back at the school."

"I have my ways," he says gently.

"I hate how I feel about you," I blurt.

"How do you feel?"

"I know you're not a good person, and you're certainly not a good person *for me*, but... " I'm about to tell him, and I know I shouldn't, but in my moment of vulnerability, I say what I've been thinking. "... I'm attracted to you despite the fact I know you're not a good person."

"Just because I deal drugs, doesn't mean I'm not good for you."

I stare at him blankly. "That's an oxymoron if ever I heard one." He laughs easily, seeing the humor in this. But truthfully speaking, there isn't a funny side. This is deadly serious. "I might be attracted to you, but I can't be with you. Being involved in that world isn't where I see myself heading, and it would ruin the future I want for myself. I'm anti-drugs. Even when I saw you were smoking, it turned my stomach."

"You really don't have much of an option, Hannah." Anger sneaks in to settle with all the other emotions I'm experiencing. "You're mine."

"Do you know how cheesy that sounds? You're not a caveman. You're a drug dealer."

"Who gets what he wants."

"I'm sorry, Edgar, I'm not something you can acquire. I'm not a possession, and I'm not a *thing*. I'm a person."

His mouth draws up into a smile, and I notice how perfectly symmetrical his strong, square jawline is. And how incredibly nice looking he is. Beneath the scruff of the stubble and his sinister, dark eyes, he's an attractive man. I'm sure he can have anyone he wants. "You're my possession, Hannah."

"What's drawn you to me? Because, really, no matter how you look at this situation, it isn't normal."

He shrugs his shoulders. "Normal is subjective. What's normal for you, may not be normal for me."

"That doesn't answer my question."

"Your feistiness makes me hot and bothered. *And hard.*"

I balk at his admission. But my nerve endings spark alive. Knowing the effect I have on him is turning me on. And I hate myself so much for feeling anything but pure disgust.

"So, you're saying if I was more giggly and stopped fighting you, you'd lose interest?"

"I'm saying, I prefer you this way because it means I'm the one who's going to break you in."

"Now I'm a wild horse?"

"I hope you buck like one."

Ugh. How disrespectful. "You know, for a second I was considering giving you the time of day. But now, after that remark, I know I'll mean even less to you then whatever hooker you're going to pick up tonight. I'm not interested, Edgar."

"Your words don't match your actions. I know you want me, and that's sexy as sin. What's better is how much I want you, too. So, there's an easy solution. You come out with me on Friday night. I take you to dinner, then back to my house and we have sex. My itch will be scratched, and you'll be addicted to me. It'll be a win-win."

I'm staring at him, speechless. The words spinning around in my head can't make their way to my mouth. He's staring at me, like he's expecting me to say "yes," and fall at his feet. He has another thing coming if he thinks I'm going out with him, especially after that last sentence. "I'm not interested." I stand from the swing, grab my bag, and start making my way back toward home. But I stop when I hear his heavy footsteps crunching on the dry grass behind me. "How did you find me?"

"I'm a resourceful man, I can find you wherever you are.

Here." He holds out a cell phone to me. "This way I can contact you," he adds as he thrusts it toward me.

I turn my nose up in disgust. "Seriously? Have you got a learning disability? I don't want anything to do with you. Leave me alone, Edgar, or I'll have to go to the police."

He laughs at me. "I have them on speed dial, want to call them now?" He takes his phone out of his pocket and gives it to me. He's basically saying he knows them all, and they're in his pocket. Great. Not just a drug dealer, but one who owns the police.

I shake my head at him, looking down at both phones in his hands. "My world is crashing down, and you're hitting on me. Thanks… but no thanks." Turning, I leave him and his dumb offer.

"I can take care of you," he calls after me.

"I don't need taking care of, Edgar," I shout without turning around.

The guy he had stationed outside my house is only a few feet away. When I pass him, I can hear him following me. It's no use in telling him to leave. He doesn't listen to me, he listens to Edgar. He's merely the pawn in the big picture, nothing else.

I head back to school, already knowing I'm going to get a slip for being late. It's not like this happens often, if ever. I make my way toward the office and find the school principal standing just outside in the hall, talking with another student. She sees me, and gestures for me to stop.

I hang back and wait. Great, now I'm going to have to come up with some excuse as to why I'm late. *I hate lying.*

The student, a girl from a younger year, leaves and Mrs. Lewis approaches me with a wary glint in her eyes. "Are you okay, Hannah? You look worried," she says. Man, she's so observant.

Plastering a fake smile on my face, I nod my head. "Yeah, sorry. I forgot my laptop at home, and had to go back to get it."

That came out way too easily.

Her brow crinkles together, and for a split second I'm fearful she doesn't believe me and will be calling my parents. Uncertainty thumps through my veins. I'm petrified she's going to call me on my lie.

"Get a slip and head straight to class," she says. Breathing a sigh of relief, I head to Mrs. Jones at the office, and get a slip. She heard what Mrs. Lewis said, so she doesn't ask me anything. She simply writes the slip out, hands it to me and offers me a stern glare. Mrs. Jones isn't very nice. She snaps at you if you ask her a question, gives you the stink eye if you're waiting for her. And she's old. By old, I think she has to be pushing seventy. But she says she loves what she does, which is why she's here and not retired. I think she's horrible.

Taking myself to class, I hand in my slip and sit beside Kristen. She's staring at me, anger rolling off her. Her eyes are large and her mouth is pursed into a tight line. I try avoiding looking at her, but I can't help it. She's my best friend, and I snapped at her.

"I'm sorry," I whisper as I lower my eyes in shame.

"So you should be," she snaps back. I deserve that. She's right.

"I'm really sorry," I whisper again.

The enormity of everything over takes my emotions. I start crying, holding in the sobs so the teacher doesn't hear them. I try to wipe the tears away, but my attempt is futile. They keep falling.

Thankfully, I'm only in class for no more than ten minutes before the bell sounds. Standing, I walk as fast as I can to the bathroom and lock myself in the stall.

Kristen is right there, knocking on the door. "Hannah, what's going on?"

Through the sobs, I say, "So much. I... I can't tell you right now though." *Mom... Dad... Edgar.*

Everything feels like it's sitting on my chest, a strain so heavy it can never be lifted.

"Come outside, talk to me." I shake my head. Inane, because she can't see me. "Hannah?" she says in a softer voice. "Open the door."

I open the door to the bathroom stall and embrace her. "I'm so sorry, I have so much going on and I snapped at you. I just want to go home, crawl under the covers and go to sleep. I want today to be over already."

"What's going on?"

Hmmm, where to start. Let's see. The guy I'm attracted to is a drug dealer, who's dangerous and possessive. I found out my Mom is cheating on my Dad. And my Dad is no better, gambling away whatever my parents have saved. I can't tell her any of that. "Stuff... everything." It's the best I can do at the time.

"Tell me," she pushes, trying to get me to open up to her.

But I can't. It's impossible. Wiping at my eyes, I step back and go to splash water on my face. It's the only thing I can do for now. "I think everything seems worse cause I'm getting my period."

She smiles weakly at me. "Oh, so you're in the emotional stage," she says sympathetically. "Lucky, only forty or so more years to go before that ends," she jokes.

"Yeah," I respond, happy she's not pressing me about what's happening in my life. "Let's get to class. I don't want either of us getting in trouble."

"I'll choose detention any day of the week over having my best friend so upset." She gives me a hug. "If you want to talk, you know I'm here for you."

After how poorly I've treated her, I don't deserve her understanding. "Thank you," I say and return her hug.

I spend the rest of the day under a cloud. So many things are dancing around in my head, making it virtually impossible for me to concentrate on anything. I drag myself through the motions, smiling blankly at people, nodding when conversation is happening and sitting next to Kristen at lunch, pretending to be listening to things our group is talking about.

When school finishes for the day the shiny, black car is waiting for me. I ignore it as I catch the bus home.

It doesn't stop him from following me home.

I want a redo of today.

Chapter 8

LAST NIGHT AT DINNER, I OBSERVED MY PARENTS. BOTH SEEMED totally normal, but this instigated more questions I have no answers to.

Are they both so used to faking everything that they have no idea how to be real with me? I had no appetite for dinner, so I sat there watching them and how they interacted.

Our family is built on a fault-line. The cracks are below the surface and unless you're looking for them, you don't see them. I looked, and I looked hard. I didn't see the cracks, which makes me believe we're in a more delicate state then I originally thought.

Mom talked about a new guy starting at her work, and my ears immediately pricked up. Is he the one she's having an affair with? Or is it someone else? Is it someone I know? Is it someone Dad knows?

Then Dad told us he'll have to start work early for the rest of the week, and finish late next week. Does this mean he's spending time with his own mistress? The slot machines? Or is he a poker kind of guy? Maybe he bets on the horses. Who knows? Something inside of me aches with hurt sitting at the table having the dinner Mom had taken time to prepare. It was homemade pizzas. Mom had made the dough herself. My mind ticked over frantically. Is she taking the time to give us beautiful meals because she feels guilty for letting another man near her?

Is this the first time she's cheated on her family?

How long has Dad been gambling?

Too much was going around in my head. And when dinner was over, I had a quick shower and collapsed on my bed, crying. I fell asleep with tears in my eyes, and I woke this morning with a heavy heart.

I reach over and grab my phone from beside my bed.

There are several text messages, most of them from Edgar. I read the first one. *Call me.*

I roll my eyes and delete it, along with all the others before I even read them. I don't need to read them to know he'll be demanding in whatever he wants from me.

There's a message from Kristen too. It's simply a love heart. This one makes me smile, a lot.

I reply by sending her a love heart.

The sadness returns, and I stand from my bed and make my way out to the kitchen. There's a note on the kitchen counter from Mom.

Dad and I had to leave early. We'll see you tonight at dinner. Pick somewhere you want to go. Anywhere you want. Love you, Mom X

There's a knock on the front door. I know who it is, so I ignore it. I make myself a coffee and some cereal as the knocking becomes more insistent.

By the time I sip my coffee, I walk over to the door an open it. The bodyguard is standing there, dressed impeccably, waiting for me. "What?" I ask with a clipped tone.

"The car will be ready to take you to school," he replies.

"I'm catching the bus."

"Mr. Zaro would prefer I get you to school," he says disregarding what I've said.

"I don't give a rat's ass what Mr. Giant-Pain-in-my-Neck wants. I'll be catching the bus." I slam the door on him, but I know this is far from the end of the conversation.

Slowly, I finish my breakfast, and head into my room to get ready for school.

I grab my jeans and a tank top and change into them. The top is a bit tight, highlighting my curves, and usually I wouldn't wear something so revealing. But I don't have enough energy to care about what I'm wearing.

Once finished, I brush through my hair, and throw it up in a high ponytail. Grabbing my school bag, I head out the front, where Edgar is waiting for me. He's leaning against the car, smoking. I hate how good he looks in his super expensive black suit, his gold watch around his wrist, cigarette hanging out of his mouth. I could honestly snap a photo of him like this, and sell it to an author for a cover of a mafia book. He's so nice to look at.

"I don't like what you're wearing. Go change," he demands of me as I walk past him.

I keep walking, opting not to obey.

"I don't want anybody looking at your tits except for me, and with this, everyone can see everything."

I snarl toward him, "Go away."

He grabs me by the hips, stopping me from walking. His body is so close to mine, I can feel the warmth rolling off him, and onto me. His grip is nearly painful, possessive, and such a huge turn-on. Why am I so attracted to him when he's a Neanderthal?

It screws with my mind.

"I don't like you dressed like this. I want you to wear

something less revealing," he whispers in my ear.

My breath catches in my throat, as I lean my head back onto his shoulder, loving this crazy-ass behavior. I know I shouldn't, but I do.

"I'll wear what I like," I respond, though take a small step back melding my body into his.

His arousal is evident. I love how I'm sending him crazy. But nothing good can come from this. *Nothing.*

Of course, my body and my brain don't want to communicate. They're not friends at the moment. He greedily splays his hand on my hip, and draws me back further. My skin pebbles with excitement. My blood pulses as the thought that this bad man, a drug dealer, wants me for himself. My heart jumps with anticipation at what he's going to say and do next.

A part of me wants him so badly. But another part of me, the *sensible* part, wants to tell him to leave me alone. Right now, I'm not sure which part is winning.

He's making my body sing, sparking alive as a hazardous fire rips through me, risking my sanity and safety.

There's a devil whispering in my ear, telling me to give him a chance. And there's a saint in my other ear, screaming how he'll ruin me. No, not ruin, utterly annihilate me.

But I'm strong. I can fight this effect he has on me.

Can you? The devil whispers.

"One date. If you want to leave after that, I'll take you home myself. And, if you don't want another date, I promise to never bother you again. One date, kitty. One little date." His voice is filled with sin, sex, and a promise I'm not sure I can believe.

My mouth answers before I have a moment to stop myself. "One date." I swing around in his arms, and look into his dangerously wicked, dark eyes. His mouth is close to mine, his eyes are locked on mine. His body, damn, his hard body is pressed against mine.

My throat dries, as I internally scold myself for agreeing to this.

"I'll pick you up tonight at six," he says, not giving me an option to say no.

"Tonight? It's a school night. And I'm going out."

"Where are you going?" He steps back, but leaves his hands on my hips. His fingers tighten and dig into me.

"Out." I walk away, furious at myself for giving him this opportunity.

"Where's 'out,' Hannah?" he asks again, but this time his tone is tight, as if he's talking through a clenched jaw.

"Out with my parents." I continue walking toward the bus stop. He sweeps me up, and carries me back to his car. "This confirms it. You're insane. Put me down, Edgar."

With a stupid smirk on his face he keeps walking, ignoring my plea. He gets to his car, where his bodyguard opens the back door and he slides me in. "I'm taking you to school, and I'll pick you up."

His possessiveness is frustrating. But I can't lie. It's a bit sexy, too. *What is wrong with me?*

The driver has already got the car in motion, before Edgar hands me the phone he was offering me yesterday. "I'm not taking this," I say as I turn to look away from him.

"I need to be able to get in contact with you at any time. So, you *are* taking it."

"No!" I shake my head and crinkle my forehead. "I don't want it. And besides, this is one date. Nothing more."

"Yes, you didn't tell me where you're going tonight with your parents," he scoffs in disgust when he says 'parents.'

"What's that supposed to mean?" I ask defensively.

"One can't keep his hands off the family savings, and the other can't keep her mouth off… "

"Hey!" I voice loudly before he says anything vulgar about my mother. "They're still my parents. They may not be perfect, but they still love me."

"Is that what you call love? Your father gambling away your college fund, and your mom sleeping around with whoever she can?"

"Stop it. Or else this is the last time you and I will have any kind of conversation."

He snorts, as if he's the one who's disgusted. Seriously. He's a damned drug dealer. I'm sure his past isn't all rainbows and unicorns.

If I can change the conversation, hopefully the tension in the car will ease a bit. "Why do you sell drugs?" I flatly ask. No use in beating around the bush. He's not that kind of guy. He's very forthcoming, so I may as well be, too.

"Because I wanted to be a millionaire by the time I hit twenty-one." His answer is candid, which makes me believe him.

"Did you make it?"

"I made my first million before I was twenty-one," he answers smugly. "Then my second million soon after my twenty-first."

I stare at him blankly. "Hmmm," I grumble. "So, you're a millionaire?"

"Multi-millionaire," he corrects.

"All from drugs? Are you proud?" I notice his smug smile drops slightly. "Are your parents proud?" He flinches when I mention his parents.

"They're dead," he says in an expressionless voice. But for some reason, I don't think they're actually dead. More like, dead to him.

"Do you think they'd be proud of you obtaining your wealth this way?"

"I'm not talking about my parents, Hannah. They aren't a topic of conversation you should bring up again." His tone has changed, it's more somber and clipped. There's clearly a story there, but I doubt it's one he'll ever tell me.

"But you can demand to know where I'm going? Right, so this is one-sided. Not a two-way street."

He furrows his brows together, then his lips draw up into a sneaky smirk. "It's whatever I want it to be, and right now, I want you." He lays his hand on my thigh and squeezes it tightly.

We arrive at school, and my bodyguard opens the door for me. "Does he need to be here?" I ask, almost resigned to the fact he's here to stay.

"Yes." He gives me no other option.

"Can he stay outside. It'll be hard for me to explain him to... well... everyone."

Edgar stares at me, considering my request. It takes him a few minutes before he answers. "If you try to leave without him, I'll know, and I won't be happy." It's not a direct threat, but it's definitely his way of telling me not to try to ditch the bodyguard.

His deadly, grim stare sends a shiver down my body. I know he's serious. "I won't," I say trying not to make him angry.

His demeanor immediately lightens as he smiles at me. "Then he can wait for you outside the school," he says loudly enough for the bodyguard to hear him. "I'll pick you up when school finishes."

"Okay," I respond as I slide out of the car.

"Do I get a kiss?" he asks.

"Um, no."

He smiles again. Much more relaxed. "I'll see you this afternoon." The bodyguard shuts the door, and the black car drives away.

We're both left behind. "Do I get to know your name?" I ask.

"No." He steps back onto the grass, and resumes "bodyguard" position.

"Right." I look at him, feeling awkwardly out of place. "I'll just go to school then." He slides his sunglasses over his eyes, and stares ahead. *Okay then.*

"Hey, girl. What's happening?" Kristen calls as she does a double-take, looking between me and the bodyguard. "Who's the guy?" she whispers as we walk into school.

I'm not sure how to explain him, so I don't. "I'm not sure." I shrug my shoulders to add conviction to my lie.

"Huh, well he's cute for an older guy. And kinda scary. I wonder what he's doing here. He looks like he's a cross between a secret service agent and an assassin."

My brows fly up, mocking her. "An assassin?"

"Yeah, he has that deadly 'don't screw with me' demeanor." She glances over her shoulder as we enter school, giving my secret bodyguard another look. "Definitely. He's probably packing a gun."

I shudder at the thought. "Anyway, what's happening with you and Brad? I haven't really talked to you much lately. I've had a few things going on, you know?" The moment I said Brad's name, her eyes light up, as if she can see little love hearts dancing in front of her.

"Oh my God!" she nearly shouts as she grabs onto my upper arm and squeezes. She's walking on air, I can tell how happy he makes her, and I love this so much. "He's such a nice guy. We're going on our first proper date on Saturday. He's taking me to the movies. He even came home and asked my Dad for permission to take me to the movies. How old-fashioned." She giggles like a little school girl. "He's been walking me home every day, and he waits for me so we can walk to school together. Except today, he said he had to help his mom with something." Her dreamy gaze is infectious, because I start thinking about Edgar. I'm a more than a little jealous of how tightly Kristen and Brad fit together and what they have with each other. "Tell me what happened with Zac," she says, hurtling me back to reality.

"He came to the school and offered to take me for coffee. We went, but… " I screw my nose up. I don't want to tell her about Edgar, because I know what she's going to say. She'll tell me he's not a good guy, and I shouldn't be involved with someone like him.

"But?" she pushes. I look away. We reach Kristen's locker first, and she opens it. She's waiting to hear what I have to say, but I'm not sure what to say without telling another lie. "But?" she asks again once her locker door is flung open. "Come on? What happened? Did he try to hit on you? Feel your breast? Stick his tongue down your mouth? What?"

"No, nothing like that. He's just not the type of guy I'm interested in. I thought I was, but as it works out, I'm not." *No, I prefer the broody, dangerous ones.*

"But you were both so into each other."

"I'm not interested in him, Kristen. I thought I was. It's hard to explain. There wasn't any chemistry." *Edgar on the other hand. Hmmm.*

"What a shame, I thought you two would be cute together."

"It's okay. It's not meant to be. If it was, I'd get those stomach flutters and a huge smile every time I'd think of him. And he doesn't give me anything like that. Nothing. He's a nice guy, just not *my* nice guy." *Nothing like the shivers I get when I look at Edgar.*

"Well, who knows? Maybe you'll meet someone else who will give you those things."

She doesn't know it, but I already have.

I remain tight-lipped; I don't want to say anything about Edgar. I simply can't.

The bell rings and we head off to class. Kristen is still in a dream-like state, talking about how wonderful Brad is; I'm thinking about Edgar. Even though I know I shouldn't be.

The day goes by fairly quickly, and before I know it, the last bell rings. Packing up my things, I head toward my locker, where the bodyguard is standing. "I asked you to stay outside," I say as I approach, open my locker, and get my things out.

There are lots of kids trying to get out of here as quickly as possible. I'm trying to covertly talk to him, so no one sees or asks any questions. Looking around, I'm trying to avoid Kristen, or even Brad. Especially after his 'friendly' chat last week.

"I do what Mr. Zaro wants me to do," he says. His tone is stern, and could be interpreted as offensive.

"Can you please go outside and wait for me?" I beg in a small voice.

He straightens his shoulders, and looks ahead. I guess he's giving me a definitive answer. *No.*

I try to kill some time, hoping the hallways will empty before I leave. I don't want the questions. Man, how many people go to this school? It's a never-ending stream of people.

If I don't go now, someone will see, and questions will be asked. I slam my locker shut, lower my head, and clutch my bag. I make a bee-line for the front door, not looking up so I don't have to make eye contact with anyone.

I see the black car waiting for me.

I know he's in there, waiting. I head straight for it. the bodyguard beats me to it, opens the back door and I slide in. I slide down and tilt my head. Not that it matters. These windows are so dark, anything could happen in the back and no one would see a thing.

"Kitty, how was school?" His voice drips with sex. It's liquid gold. His tone is deep and sultry, with a hint of a rich baritone. God, it's sexy.

"Good," I reply as I keep an eye out to make sure no one saw me.

"Who are you hiding from? Is there a problem?" his voice changes again. It becomes darker and deeper. More protective.

"I'm not hiding from anyone. It's just… " my voice trails off to nothing.

"You're embarrassed?" he asks, angry.

"Yes. You're not exactly someone I want to be seen with. How do I explain you? How do I explain this?" I point to him, then me. "I can't. It's easier to not say anything. And let me tell you, not saying anything is difficult when you have him standing beside my locker." I gesture to the bodyguard. "Can you not send him in to do that, please?"

He rubs his hand over his chin, considering my request. "He can stay out." The bodyguard from the front laughs, as if he knows something I don't.

"Thank you," I say.

The bodyguard laughs again. Now, I'm definitely worried. He looks back and gives Edgar a wink. They're sharing a secret I'm not invited to be part of.

I turn to stare out the window. I feel like an outsider, and not welcome in here.

This is confusing everything inside me. I started coming around to Edgar, accepting him more, but now, they're sharing a secret and I feel awkward and out-of-place.

The moment the car gets to my house, I open the door and I'm out before the bodyguard has a chance to do it. "Thanks for the ride," I say as I make my way to the front door. Neither of my parents' cars are in the driveway, which means I'm on my own.

What a weird ride home. Edgar seems to have changed a bit. He's colder toward me.

I unlock the front door, and turn to see Edgar and his posse are already gone. What's going on? Why is he acting like this? Did I do something wrong? I look down at my clothes, and notice I'm still wearing the top he doesn't like. Maybe that's it. Tomorrow I'll wear something more appropriate. Ugh, this is frustrating. What have I done?

I take my phone out of my pocket, and press the button to wake up my screen. There's so many messages. Mostly from Edgar. I didn't even realize he'd messaged. There's one from

Mom saying her and Dad will be home by five so be ready for dinner.

I open one of Edgar's messages.

Hope you're having a great day. It reads.

I text back to him. **Is everything okay?**

He reads the message immediately. The three little circles down the bottom indicates he's replying. Then... nothing. The three circles disappear, and I get no reply.

I sit on the sofa, waiting. Maybe he erased what he was going to say, and is typing something else.

No reply.

Minutes pass.

Still nothing.

Worry overtakes me. What if something's happened to him? I dismiss it nearly immediately, knowing he can take care of himself. Why isn't he replying? What have I done?

Stress replaces the worry, and I become anxious at his silence. He's usually quite vocal, annoyingly so. Now he's quiet and isn't responding. I don't like this.

I wait a few more minutes. But it feels like hours. Time seems to drag on. And with every second he doesn't respond, the more my gut churns with tension. "Wait until four-thirty, and if he doesn't respond, then send him another message," I say to myself.

Looking at the time, I make a mental note to message him in about an hour. Taking myself to my bedroom, I sit at my desk, pull out my laptop and text books, and start on my homework.

But I can't seem to concentrate. Instead, I stare at my phone. It's sitting beside me, and the screen hasn't lit once. I'm completely distracted by him. He's gotten into my head and won't leave.

Ugh.

I should feel thankful he's left me alone. Wait, is my

bodyguard still on duty? I jump up out of my chair, and run to the front window to see if he's outside. He isn't.

My heart falls.

Dragging myself back into my room, I sink to my bed as tears sting my eyes. I feel so rejected, like I've done something wrong. Picking my phone up, I contemplate sending him another message.

"Don't do it, he's not interested anymore," I say to myself aloud. I should be happy, but I'm not.

I stare at my phone and the time on it. I open his message thread for what feels like the hundredth time, hoping he's responded. But I get nothing. With every passing moment he doesn't reply, more cracks appear in my already damaged heart.

After what seems like hours, but has only been minutes, I look at the time and know my parents will be home soon to pick me up for dinner. I have to get ready.

Standing, I force myself to stop thinking about Edgar and his radio silence. I don't know what's going on with him, or why he's treating me so coldly. I'll never know, I guess. I just have to push on, and pretend it doesn't bother me.

Maybe, it's for the best. He *is* a drug dealer, and nothing good could come from a relationship with him.

I head to my closet and find something nice to wear. I want to dress up a bit, to feel better about myself. How dumb. A man breaks my heart, and I need to feel better about myself. *What is wrong with me?*

I look through everything, and find a cute black mini-skirt. Pairing it with a red off-the-shoulder top, I wear some heels to show off my legs. I'm not much into dressing up like this. Actually, I prefer jeans and a t-shirt, but tonight I want to wear something sexy. Make boys look at me. I want to feel good about myself.

The front door opens, and I hear Mom call out to me. "In my room," I call as I fluff up my hair to try to make it look like it has more volume than it does.

"Hey, are you ready?" she asks as she opens the door to my room. "Wow, look at you." Her eyes travel up and down my body, taking in what I'm wearing. "Whose skirt is that?"

"Mine." I look down and smooth it with my hands. "I think. I found it in my closet. Yeah, you bought it for me, last year. Remember? We went to the mall, I saw it and you liked it."

"I thought it was longer."

I laugh and shake my head. "Apparently not."

"You look incredible," she says. "But, I swear, I thought that skirt was longer."

I shrug and smile. "Maybe I've had a growth spurt."

"You look so much older like this."

I walk over to hug her. I get a whiff of a new perfume she's wearing and inhale it deeply. It's different than what she usually wears, more woodsy than her normal citrus scent. "Did you get a new perfume?" I ask as I inhale again.

"I was at the department store, and tried it on. Not sure if I like it. I don't think it suits me." She sniffs at her wrist.

"I like it," I say.

"Well, your father is having a quick shower, so he won't be long. And I'll go get changed. Do you know where you want to go for dinner?" she asks.

"Wherever."

"Considering how beautifully you're dressed, I think we might go a little bit upscale. No use in going to iHop when you're all tricked out." She leaves to go get ready, and I spend a few minutes applying some simple make-up. I'm not a make-up person. Mascara and lipstick is pretty much the extent of my expertise.

Once finished, I wait for my parents in the family room, and look at my phone.

I had pushed Edgar to the back of my mind, but looking at

my phone and lack of messages, has propelled him front and center. Ugh, I can't have a good time tonight if all I'm doing is staring at my phone. I walk back into my room, turn it off, and leave it on my desk. I'm spending tonight with my parents, and not worrying about him. I'm going to pretend I don't know about my mother's infidelity, or my father's gambling addiction, and I'm going to have a good night with them. The way things were B.E—Before Edgar. I was oblivious, but I was happy. And that's what I'm going to be tonight.

Tonight… no Edgar.

Well… hopefully.

Chapter 9

WE HAD A GREAT TIME LAST NIGHT. MOM AND DAD TOOK ME TO this quaint little restaurant they like to go to, and we had the best food ever. Everything was delicious, and Mom and Dad talked and had so much fun. They held hands, and kissed, and nothing seemed to be weird with them.

When I got home, I left my phone off, took a shower and got into bed.

I refused to allow Edgar to have so much power and control over me. So, I didn't turn my phone on until now.

I'm up and out of bed, ready to go to school. As I'm eating my cereal, I power up my phone. It takes a moment, but it starts dinging with several messages.

None from Edgar and all from Kristen. In each message the excitement builds of her telling me all about Brad. I smile at how into him she is, and by looks of things, he's really into her too. Another pang of jealousy for Kristen and Brad goads me. I want a boyfriend of my own to care for, and to care about me.

Once breakfast is done, I grab my bag and start heading

toward the door, when there's someone bashing on it from the outside. "What the… " I open the door to find Edgar standing there. He's not cleanly shaven, he has a black eye and he appears not to have slept for over a week.

"Oh my God!" I say as I step outside. "What happened to you?" I touch his forearm.

"Bad night," he says as he hugs me, his hands resting on the top of my butt.

"What happened?" I ask again.

He kisses my cheek; his lips stay connected with my skin a moment too long. "I need to hold you, kitty," he says as he squeezes me tighter to his body.

I don't know what to think, or what to do. "Do you need a doctor?" He shakes his head. "Hospital?" He shakes his head again. "What do you need? What can I do?"

"I just need to see my number one girl." He squeezes again.

My heart eases, and I feel at ease now I've seen him. "I didn't see you yesterday. You didn't reply to my message. I was so worried."

I feel his cheeks plump up, meaning he's smiling. "All I could think about was you."

"Tell me you're okay."

"I'm fine now." He lets me go and steps back. "You looked beautiful last night. Though I think that skirt was too short for you to be wearing out in public. I'd like you to wear it for me, and me alone."

"You saw me? But… " I point to his face.

"I had my people watching you, making sure you were safe. They sent me a photo. But don't wear that skirt again." It's not a request, it's a command.

"Okay," I respond. "I won't."

"I'll take you to school." He takes my bag, and carries it for me. We reach his car, and he opens the door for me. My bodyguard is already inside. He gives me a sideways glance, and rolls his eyes. I have no idea what his problem is with me. I'll ask him when Edgar's not around, though I doubt he'll answer.

The car starts in the direction of school, and I stare at Edgar and the bruising that's so dark around his eye. "What happened?" I ask. He shakes his head and lifts his hand at me as if to say, 'don't worry about it.' "Edgar, please tell me," I nearly plead.

He lowers his head for a moment, then looks back to me. "It was a misunderstanding," he says. My bodyguard sighs from the front. Edgar hits the back of his seat, and the sigh instantly stops.

"Promise me you're okay."

"*I'm* fine." He deliberately makes a point of indicating himself. "The other guy… " his voice trails off, letting me draw my own conclusion. The bodyguard chuckles.

A lump sits in my throat. I want to know, but I'm also aware, I *shouldn't* know. "Okay," I say, resigned to the fact he's not going to tell me. "As long as you're not seriously hurt."

"I'm not." He places his hand on my thigh and gently squeezes. "Now, about our date tonight. Be ready by five." Again, not a question, but a demand. He's not going to take no — or any variant of no — as an answer.

"Okay."

"Wear something cute, not slutty though."

I crinkle my brows at him, unsure of what he wants from me. "Like what?" I ask.

His lips draw up into a cheeky grin. "Something tight, but nothing revealing."

"If it's tight, then it's going to be revealing."

"I want your skin covered, but I want it so tight I can see the outline of your nipples."

Um… what? "That's not going to happen, because one… " I

hold one finger, then continue, "I don't have anything like that and two… " I hold up a second finger, "I wouldn't be allowed out of the house with anything that tight on and three… " I hold up a third finger, "I wouldn't feel comfortable in anything like what you want."

"But you wore a slutty skirt last night?" he counters.

I look away from him. He's got a point. "I'll see what I have."

"And wear red lipstick." Again, another command.

"Okay," I instantly agree, not even trying to fight him on this.

The car is quiet; it rolls on the street like a fine piece of machinery. Money buys everything, I guess. The tension in the car is almost unfathomable. Thankfully, we're at school sooner than I was expecting. The car comes to a stop, and my bodyguard steps out to open the door for me. "I'll be here to pick you up," Edgar says as I begin to slide out of the car.

"Okay." I offer him a smile, but I know he wants more. Like a kiss. I'm not going to give him our first kiss in the back of his car. How cliché. Although, this is anything but a rusty, dirty old car.

I turn to look at Edgar, he has an amused gleam to his eyes. "Kitty," he calls.

"Yeah," I answer.

"Tonight, you and I are going to have a lot of fun." The bodyguard chuckles. I'm not really sure what to make of that statement. I suppose, I'll see tonight.

"Okay," I reply again. The bodyguard closes the door and the car rolls away, disappearing down the road. The bodyguard is standing outside the school. "Can I ask you your name? I think it's weird I don't know it yet."

He crosses his arms in front of his chest and stares ahead, ignoring me.

"I take your silence to mean you don't have a name?" I smile trying to lighten his intensity.

"You don't need to know it," he nearly snaps at me.

"But if you're going to be hanging out around me, don't you think I should know what to call you?" I ask.

A few of the students are looking at me as they walk past. They're probably wondering why I'm talking to this guy who's at least six-foot-four, built like a tank, and wearing a designer suit.

"You don't need to know my name," he says again. I get the sense he's not really into doing this, but he has to. I wonder if Edgar has something on him, maybe a secret this guy doesn't want anyone to know. Something to keep him here, working for Edgar.

"Okay, then. Well... nice chatting with you," I say sarcastically as I walk away from him. What a jerk.

Heading into school, Kristen and Brad are at her locker, kissing. They're so into each other. He's a good head taller than her, and they're locked in a tight embrace. "Get a room," I grumble as I walk past them.

"Ohhh, how original," Kristen teases but smiles at me.

"Thank God you got your tongue out of his mouth before you said that. Could've been awkward."

"See you later." Kristen reaches up on her toes and gives Brad a kiss on the cheek. Brad gives me a nod, then leaves. "So, what's been happening?" she asks all excited.

"By looks of things, what you're doing is more interesting... or should I say *who* you're doing."

The hugest smile breaks out on her face. Her lips have a little bit of a red tinge to them from where she was kissing Brad. "I can't keep my hands off him," she squeaks with happiness. "We're going to prom together!" she squeals with a little jump.

"Congratulations. I'm happy for you." I give her a hug. "You seem happy."

"Oh my God! I am. So happy!"

"I'm glad it worked out for you both."

"But, what's happening with you? I know I haven't really

been around much because well… " Her face splits into the biggest, cheesiest grin ever. "I feel like we don't talk anymore. I'm sorry, I've been a bad best friend."

"Don't be dumb," I nearly snap at her. "You've got your hands full with Brad."

A mischievous smile spreads on her face. "They're full alright." She adds a wink.

Shaking my head, I get my laptop out of my bag, and close my locker. "Don't make me throw up on you."

"Come on, Hannah, what's going on with you? I know it didn't work out with Zac, and on that note, I'm sorry I called him. I was worried, that's all. But, tell me, what's happening. Who's the mystery guy who's been hanging outside the school. He looks scary."

I can't explain the bodyguard. I can't tell her about Edgar. Ugh, I can't say anything. She'll freak out, and then she'll call my parents, and tell them. And they have enough problems of their own without having to worry about me too. "He's no one." I shrug, downplaying what's happening.

"He can't be no one. He has to be *someone*."

I have to get her away from her curiosity. "I have a date tonight with a guy."

"Oh shit! Who? What's his name? Does he go to our school? What's he look like? Where are you going? What are you going to wear?" The barrage of questions makes me laugh.

"First, I have no idea what I'm wearing. Or where we're going. He's handsome."

"Handsome? As in he's old?" She scrunches her nose.

"No, he's not *old*. But he's a bit older than me."

"What's his name?"

I don't want to tell her the truth. "Braydon," I lie. Why did I lie? Because telling her his name is Edgar, and her telling Brad, might mean he knows who Edgar is considering what he told me about Zak.

"Braydon." She suggestively lifts her eyebrows at me. "Tell me about *Braydon*," she says his name in a sexy, low tone.

"He's a nice guy." I shrug my shoulders, trying not to say too much more.

"Where did you meet him?"

We walk slowly toward class, even though the bell hasn't gone off yet for the start of the day. I start to sweat. I hate having to tell her lies. But she really would freak out. "At the mall," another lie rolls off my tongue.

It's getting easier.

"Does he go to college?"

"Yep," I reply before really thinking this through. I'm going to have to remember the lies I'm telling, because they're going to be the same I'll have to tell my parents.

"What's he studying?"

"I don't really know. Something about astronomy or something." I shrug again. I'm doing a lot of that.

"That's cool. What are you wearing tonight?"

"I don't know." Something tight. "Maybe my jeans and a t-shirt." *Not my jeans and a t-shirt.*

"Want me to come over and help you? Pick an outfit out for you?"

NO! "Nah, it's okay. I'll find something."

The bell sounds for the start of the school day, and I breathe out a huge sigh. Phew, saved by the bell. "Promise me, you'll tell me everything that happens on your date."

"I will."

"Have you kissed him yet?" she asks as we hang around the front door. Kristen's class is three doors down, and my teacher hasn't arrived yet.

"Not yet."

Kristen smiles at me. "Yay! You have to tell me how the first kiss goes too. If he's sweet and gentle, or more the take-charge kinda guy."

The little I know of Edgar, I reckon he's the latter. More alpha and take-charge. "Okay, I promise I'll tell you."

"See you at lunch," she says before turning to head into her classroom.

I make my way into mine, sit at the back and take my phone out of my pocket. There's already a message there. It's from Edgar. **Thinking of you getting dressed up for me.**

I can't help but smile. I do want to look nice for him. I want him to look at me and think I'm sexy.

I open YouTube, lower the volume so it's on silent, and begin to search for smoky eye tutorials. My English teacher enters the class, and starts today's lesson. I keep flicking between what she's saying, and how to do the smoky eye effect.

I'm going to look hot for Edgar tonight, I hope he appreciates it.

Chapter 10

"WOW, YOU LOOK BEAUTIFUL, SWEETHEART," MOM SAYS AS I MAKE my way out to the family room, where she's sitting at the table with her laptop opened. "Where are you off to?"

"I have a date," I proudly announce.

She stares at me, blinking. "A date? Who with?"

"His name is Braydon, and he goes to college. He studies something to do with astronomy." That lie rolled off the tongue like silk. Easily.

"Do I get to meet him?"

Panic rolls through me, I don't want her to meet Edgar. Not yet. Maybe soon, maybe never. He's not exactly the type of guy who I can introduce to my parents. "Probably not today. It's just our first date. Maybe next time?" My heart thumps inside my chest, beating crazily, waiting for Mom's reply.

"Okay," she slowly says. "But next time, I want to meet him. Where are you going?"

"I don't know. He said dinner. We might go see a movie too. I have no idea what he has planned for me."

Mom's eyes narrow, she looks way more suspicious now. "Make sure you keep your phone on you."

"I will."

"And call me if anything happens, and I'll come pick you up straight away."

"I will."

"And your curfew is eleven."

"Mom, eleven? Can we make it twelve?"

"Eleven." She holds firm.

"Mom, how often do I ask you to break the curfew of eleven? And not to mention, how often do I actually break the curfew myself. Never. Please, just this once?" I plead.

Mom's eyes are boring into mine. "Only this once."

"Yay! Thank you, Mom." I lean down to give her a kiss, but I'm careful not to smudge my lipstick.

"Who taught you how to do that?" she asks as she makes a circular motion with her finger around my face.

"YouTube taught me. It's basic, but I like it."

"You look so much older than seventeen."

My phone rings from my room, and I run in to get it. "Hello," I answer, knowing it's Edgar because his name flashed up on the screen.

"I'm running a few moments late, wait for me outside."

"Okay," I reply and hang up. I tuck my phone and ATM card into my back pockets of the jeans I'm wearing, although they're so tight I'm not sure there's any room for anything to go in my pockets. When I get back out to the family room, Mom's rubbing her temples as she stares at the computer. "Everything okay?" I ask.

Mom looks up, frazzled that I caught her in such a stressful moment. "Just balancing our bank account." She smiles, but the smile doesn't reach her eyes. "Hang on." She pushes up from the chair, and walks over to her bag. "Here you go. Do you need more?" She hands me two twenty-dollar bills.

"It's okay. I still have the money from my birthday that Gran gave me."

"Don't use your birthday money. Save that for something you really want."

"Mom, she gave me five hundred dollars. I don't want anything. It's okay."

"Just take it, I'll feel better knowing you have cash on you if anything happens."

"Mom," I let her title out in more like a whine. "I don't need it." Not after I saw her stress from trying to balance the family bank account. *And knowing about Dad.*

"Take it." She's persistent.

"Okay, I will. But if I don't use it, I'll give it back to you."

"Deal." She gives me a more genuine smile.

I hug Mom, then I hear a beep from outside. "I'm going to go, okay?" I ask as I head toward the door.

"Okay." Mom follows, and when I reach the door, I give Mom another hug, then jog out the front.

"Bye Mom." I wave to her, as I turn to see the bodyguard standing with the door open. "Thank you," I say as I slide in the back. I'm met with silence from him. *How unusual.* Edgar isn't in the car. I'm in the back by myself. The bodyguard gets in the front, and I stare at him. "Where's Edgar?" I ask.

"He's waiting for you," the bodyguard replies.

"Where?"

Nothing.

I text Edgar. *Where are you?*

At the restaurant, waiting for you. His reply comes within seconds.

Which restaurant?

You'll see when you get here.

It's very mysterious, and quite intriguing and sexy. He's waiting for me. And I have no idea where I'm going. It's a rush. Thrilling and exciting. My stomach churns with anticipation. I'm hoping he does something romantic for me. Maybe he's bought me flowers, or maybe perfume. Man, how sweet would that be if he did something so perfect to try sweep me off my feet?

The huge smile on my face is an accurate portrayal of how I'm feeling. I'm giddy with anticipation.

The car travels fairly fast, taking me to Edgar quickly. Nervously, I wait to see what super romantic and beautiful gesture he's going to surprise me with. I'm sure, beneath that hard exterior is a man who's gentle and loving.

Time seems to drag on, but finally we reach a quiet street a few suburbs over from where I live. There are some cars parked, and the street is lined with young trees still growing to maturity. There's a lot of noise coming from about a hundred feet down the street. "Mr. Zaro is waiting for you." My bodyguard leads me to where he is.

I have to step down about ten steps, into a small, intimate restaurant. There's no name on the door. Nothing identifying it as a restaurant except for the delicious aromas, tables, and waiters. I see Edgar almost immediately. He's sitting in a booth at the back. He stands the moment he sees me. He's dressed in a tailored suit, his hair slicked to the side. He looks so hot. He could easily grace the cover of any scorching romance novel about a hot CEO. My mouth waters, and I become even sillier with excitement.

"Look at you." He holds his hand out to me, stands back and eyes me up and down. "You don't disappoint, Hannah. I knew I made a good choice in you."

That feels somewhat weird. Like I'm the prime cut of beef. "Thank you," I say carefully trying to decipher what he actually means.

"Umm-hmm." He licks his lips and stares at my body. "You

know I want to fuck you," he says brashly. He certainly doesn't mince his words.

"I…ah…" My shoulders slump forward. I'm not really sure how to respond to his crude words.

Thankfully, a waiter arrives, looks at me, and smiles. "What can I get for you?" His eyes are on me, and he's staring. This gives me mixed feelings. I'm uncomfortable because Edgar is sitting right next to me, but it also gives me confidence that I'm sultry and sexy.

"Um, I'm not sure," I say and look to Edgar for help.

He's staring at me, and at the guy. He's amused. I thought he'd be mad, but he's not. "She'll have a champagne, I'll have a whisky." Edgar flips his hand at the waiter to leave. The waiter looks at Edgar, and leaves, but not before turning around and staring at me again. "He was staring at you."

"I know. I'm sorry," I say.

"I like how he was staring at you."

"What?" I ask.

"It means he wants you." He nibbles on his lips, and my eyes go straight to his mouth. I swallow the lump and catch myself drooling at Edgar. His lips are plump and firm, and all I want to do is kiss them.

"Okay," I say after a few seconds. "But I can't drink champagne. I'm not twenty-one."

Edgar laughs. "You don't have to be twenty-one to have a bit of fun."

One glass of champagne can't hurt. "Only one," I say.

"That's all you'll need." The waiter arrives quite quickly with Edgar's whisky, and my champagne. He gives Edgar a nod and backs away quickly, not making eye contact with me again. "To us," Edgar says as he holds his glass up and waits for me to pick my flute up.

"To us." We clink the glasses together.

"I've gone ahead and ordered for you, I hope that's okay."

Drinking my champagne, a few bubbles get up my nose and makes it tingle. "It's very tart," I say about the champagne. "And thank you, for ordering for me."

"I'm sure you'll enjoy what I have for you. Drink up." He picks up my champagne flute and hands it to me the moment I place it on the table.

"I haven't had dinner yet. I don't want to get drunk and make a fool out of myself." I put the glass back on the table without taking a sip of it.

"Tell me about your friend Kristen," he asks, as he finishes his whisky off in one smooth motion.

"Wait… how do you know about Kristen?"

"I know about everything. Just tell me about her."

It really doesn't surprise me. "She's my best friend. And has been for a long time. She comes from a big family, and she usually likes hanging out at my place, because well… I'm an only child."

"Why didn't your parents have any more kids?" He seems genuinely interested.

"Mom nearly died giving birth to me. She has this condition, which is really rare. It's called placenta accreta."

"What is it?"

"The placenta attaches itself too deeply on the uterus wall, and instead of coming out after the baby–me – is born, they have to try to remove it. Mom nearly died when she was giving birth to me. Apparently, it's rare. Only a small percent of the female population has it. Mom's lucky. She nearly died; thank God she didn't."

"Is it hereditary?"

"Why, you planning on me becoming pregnant?" I chuckle and roll my eyes.

"No!" he says with more force than he normally would. "I

just want to make sure you can't die."

"I have no intentions of having kids until later. Waaaaaaaaay later. After college, *later*."

He smirks at me like what I've said is something he approves of. "You don't want any?" he asks while indicating to the waiter to bring him another drink.

"It's not like I don't want them. Actually, I haven't really considered them. They're not on the top of my priority list. I want to go to college first. That's what I'm working hard on."

"Hmm," he approvingly snorts.

I crinkle my nose. That's weird. But then again, there's nothing about this that's *not* weird.

The waiter brings over another whisky for Edgar, and another champagne for me. "Ah, no thank you." My parents will kill me if I come home drunk.

"One more won't hurt," Edgar says as he flicks his hand to the waiter, leaving both beverages on the table.

"Well, yeah it will. Just this one is making me a bit light headed, if I have two, then it might make me drunk. And I have no intentions on going home intoxicated."

"Then don't."

"I won't."

"I mean, don't go home. Stay with me tonight." He's deadly serious. There's no humor in his face. Nothing says… "just kidding." His dark eyes bore into me, and his lips are pressed into a thin line. He's staring at me as if he's expecting an answer. "So?" he asks, waiting for my reply.

"So… what?" I shake my head, not believing he actually thinks I'm going to say "yes" to such a ludicrous question.

"Stay with me."

"Let me think. Do I stay with you and die a slow painful death at my parents' hands? Or do I go home at midnight, *sober*, and live to breathe another day? Hmm, hard choice. *Not!*"

"I'm taking that smart-ass reply as a no, you don't want to spend the night with me?" His jaw tightens, and he turns his head away from me.

"I'm afraid so, Edgar This is a first date. If I do that I can tell you, this will also be a last date. My parents would be going insane. Actually, they would be beyond angry if I showed up tomorrow after spending the night with a man they have no idea about."

"Then move in with me," he casually says with a shoulder shrug.

I rub my temples, suddenly feeling a little light headed. "What?" I ask and look at the first flute of champagne to discover I've drunk all of it.

"Move in with me. I have an apartment near here, you can stay there."

Staring at him, I cock my head to the side. Huh? Is this guy serious? My fingers start tapping on the table, and suddenly the light-headedness is lifted and everything becomes much more focused and clearer. My leg bounces up and down beneath the table, making me move on the bench seat. "Um, no, I won't move in with you. I barely know you. And, there's the whole 'you're a drug dealer' thing too." I laugh at my own joke, a little too loud. Some of the other diners turn to look at me, then continue with their dinner.

"Are you okay? Do you need to go to the bathroom?" Edgar asks.

"No!" I shout, again too loud. "But I feel really energetic. Like I can't sit still. My leg is going crazy." I lift the crisply ironed tablecloth to show Edgar how my leg is bouncing. "I might um… " I look toward outside. "I think I just need to walk this off. Give me a minute, I'll be back before our food arrives."

Edgar smiles at me. "Here, have a sip of your drink." He holds out the second champagne flute, offering it to me.

I don't think I should take it, but my mouth is really dry. I need something to drink. I have a sip, just one little one, and then make my way out. My head is focused, and my legs are jittery. I think I have nervous energy. The whole 'move in with me' suggestion has spooked me. How bizarre! Edgar is weird. Like, who asks someone to move in with them on the first date?

Looking down toward the end of the street, I decide to go for a quick walk to burn off this nervousness. What's going on with me? Why am I so jittery? It has to be the 'move in' thing. Edgar is full-on, and doesn't like to take "no" for an answer. But he's going to have to accept it. I'm not staying the night, and I'm not moving in with him.

Before I know it, I'm at the end of the street and I still feel a buzz of adrenaline humming through me. "I should turn back," I say to myself. But my feet have other plans. They keep going.

The fresh night air should be making me chilly, but I'm so wound up that I can't feel the cold. I'm hot and strangely alive. Every nerve ending is awake and tingling with excitement. An unfamiliar feeling takes over my body, but it's so strong I can't do anything *but* act upon it.

I'm damned horny. So horny that I need to get back to Edgar right now.

My feet turn, and I break into a run back to the restaurant.

I don't know why I'm so lustful. I feel like I'm oversexed, starving for him, absolutely thirsting to have him devour me.

The moment I get back to the restaurant, I notice two things. One, is the number of men in here and the total absence of any women except me. Something about this turns me on even more.

The other thing I notice is Edgar, sitting back, his left arm up over the back of the booth, staring at the door waiting for me. He's nursing another whisky, and I see a new champagne flute sitting beside the previous two. Both of those are empty. Wait, did I consume them both?

"Here she is," he says with a sexy grin.

My heart hammers with a stuttering jump. Man, he's so sexy.

"Hey," I say as I sit beside him. But I need to get closer. I push the table back slightly, and crawl up on his lap, straddling him.

Lowering my head, I kiss him hard. My mouth overtakes his, and he lets out a sensual groan, that travels to every part of my body. I feel so alive. I crawl up closer to him. I can feel his erection pressing into me. Grinding on him, I try to find the friction I desperately need. "Slow down," he whispers. His hands snake up my back. The warmth coming from his hands is making me crazy.

"I want you," I say as I look into his dark eyes.

"We're going," he says, picking me up as he stands. "Wrap your legs around me," he commands.

Everything inside me is heightened. Every sense is overloaded with a crazy urgency I've never felt before. My sense of smell is craving more of Edgar's aroma. My sense of touch is tingling, eagerly awaiting a lick of his tongue, a brush of his warm hand. God, it's like I'm buzzing.

He carries me out to his car. The back door is already open. My bodyguard stands beside it, looking somewhat amused.

The hunger I feel for Edgar is staggering. I've never been so turned on, so horny, in my life. It feels like with every passing moment, my need for him intensifies.

The moment we're in the car, I straddle his hips again, this time rocking even harder. I can feel his arousal. He's getting bigger. And my God, do I want him right now. I attack his mouth, kissing him voraciously. My lips actually hurt from how hard I'm pressing against his mouth. Edgar's hands are all over my body. Under my shirt, on my breasts. He's pulling down my bra, and painfully playing with my nipples. It hurts, but the hurt feels amazingly good. Something I could definitely get used to.

I try to unzip his pants to get to what I really want. He's letting me while I allow him to violate me. Violate isn't really the word, because I *want* his hands on me.

I get to my prize—his hardened erection—and although I

have no idea what I'm doing, the sexually charged beast inside takes over. "Hmm," he murmurs as my hand strokes him.

"I can't wait until you're inside me," I whisper in his ear, before taking his lobe between my teeth and nipping on it.

Where is this coming from? Why am I so sexually charged? I don't know, and really, I don't care. This is feeling amazing. It's empowering, and sexy.

The car comes to a stop, and I don't even realize the bodyguard has opened the door. All I know is I want every part of me on every part of Edgar. I want him so badly it's hurting, it's insane how much. "Wait," he says, tucking himself away.

"Why do I have to wait?' I ask with a pout.

"Because I want to get upstairs before we screw out here on the sidewalk."

"I don't mind if people want to watch," I add with a sexy brow lift.

He chuckles and shakes his head while staring at my mouth. His own lips are drawn up in an erotic smirk. Carrying me inside, I move in for another kiss. "You are going to be my greatest achievement," he murmurs with a smile.

I don't even know what he means, and I don't care. I just want him. "Kiss me," I say.

Before I even realize it, we're inside an elevator and he's got me up against the back wall. His mouth is promising a sinfully delicious time the moment we're in his apartment. The energy bubble inside me is tightening. I can't wait for this. I can't wait to lose my virginity to him. He's sexy, and manly, and so damn alpha. He oozes sexiness. It pours off him, like he knows he has testosterone dripping from his pores.

He opens the door, and walks me down a few steps. I'm thrown on the sofa, like I'm nothing more than a ragdoll.

I lean up on my elbows, watching him undress. He even does that sexily. Slowly and languidly, as if he's putting on a striptease especially for me. "Hurry up," I say as I drink in his movements.

"You're such a greedy little kitty," he says in his sexy, deep voice.

He slows his movements, which sends me bat-shit crazy. I'm losing my mind. Jumping out of my skin waiting for him. His shirt comes off, and he has tattoos all over his chest and arms. They startle me, not the actual tattoos, but the fact he has them. My eyes drink up the site of the beautiful man standing in front of me. "Jesus," I whisper and nibble on my bottom lip.

Heat burns through my body, moisture pooling between my legs.

I can't wait any more, I stand from the sofa, and hurriedly strip my own clothes off. "In a rush, are you?" he teases.

"Yes!" I'm out of my clothes in a matter of seconds. Stripped bare for Edgar. I'm not even modest about my nakedness, I'm turned on and so proud that this luscious man wants me.

The next few hours go by in a blink of an eye. I can't get enough of him. When we finish the first time, I'm already on him trying to go again.

And again.

And again.

And again.

Until finally, I can't go on any more. I collapse beside him on the bed in a rumpled heap of exhaustion.

Closing my eyes, I fall asleep.

Chapter 11

WAKING, MY HEAD FEELS HEAVY AND I'M REALLY THIRSTY. MY memories of what I did with Edgar, are fuzzy at best.

Looking around me, I notice I'm not at home.

"What the… " I say as I sit up. The sheet slides off me, and I look down at my body. My very *naked* body. "What… ?"

I'm in an apartment, a small one, that looks more like a suite at a fancy hotel. Finding my clothes, I get dressed and grab my phone. Holy shit, it's Saturday afternoon. I stare at all the missed calls and messages. I didn't go home last night. My parents are going to kill me. They must be worried sick.

Dialing Mom's number, my rapid breathing and shaky hands can barely get under control.

"Hi, darling. Are you having a good time with Kristen?" Mom asks.

Huh? A few seconds pass. I try to wrap my head around what's happening. Why isn't Mom mad? "Um, yeah. I just wanted to let you know I'll be home soon."

"That's okay, she said you two were going out for most the

day. Will you be home for dinner?"

"Um, yeah, I should be." It almost feels like I'm in a parallel universe. As my head clears, I can only think of one logical explanation. Mom called Kristen searching for me, and Kristen covered.

I owe her big time.

"Okay, do you want me to come pick you up?"

"No, it's okay. Love you, Mom."

"Love you too."

I hang up, and read the several text messages from Kristen, and from Mom, and from Dad. First it was panic, then relief when they found me at Kristen's.

But I'm not at Kristen's, I'm at Edgar's after a sex-fueled night.

I jump up and make my way out of the bedroom and down a short hallway. I sit on the sofa to call Kristen. "Where have you been? Your Mom called me last night, absolutely panicking because you missed curfew. I covered for you and told her you came here because we'll be hanging all day today."

"Thank you so much. Oh my God, Kristen. This is crazy."

"Yeah, it's crazy. You've never done anything like this before. What happened? Where were you?"

I take a deep breath and let it out slowly. "I um… "

"What?" she snaps, clearly irritated with me. I get it. I'd be angry too if I had her Mom calling me and I had to cover for her.

"I'm kinda seeing this guy. He's older, and I stayed at his place last night," I avoid telling her about his questionable profession.

"Like you had a sleep over?" she drags out slowly.

"Um, yeah and other stuff."

"I knew it! It's that guy Braydon, right? Did you have sex with him, Hannah?"

A smile breaks out on my face, and my attention is drawn to

the pain between my legs. "Um, yes," I say "yes" in a small squeaky voice.

"You tart!" she says playfully. "If you were hooking up with him and staying the night, you should've told me so I could've lied better. Lucky your mom likes me and believed me. But, truthfully, I thought she was going to come over here and we both would've been busted."

I let out another sigh. Thank God for Kristen. "Thank you. I owe you a huge favor."

"Yeah, you do. And I'll be collecting on it."

"I'm going home soon, once I figure out where I am."

"Where you are?" she asks with concern. The lightness of her voice is replaced with worry.

I look around the small apartment. "Yeah, I think we're at his apartment, but I have no idea where it is, or even where he is."

"I bet it's dirty and stinks like a college guy's dorm room."

Everything is neat and tidy and within its place. There's nothing personal out. Honestly, it looks like a hotel suite. The generic prints on the walls, look more like something you'd find adorning the walls of a corporate office than something you'd see in someone's home.

"Yeah, kinda is. I gotta go, I'll text ya later. Thanks for covering with my parents."

We hang up, and I stay seated on the sofa, staring around the room. I search my messages, and there's none from Edgar telling me when he'll be back. I send him a text. **Should I leave?**

I've never had to do the walk of shame before. I've definitely heard about it, I mean who hasn't? But to actually do it, nope.

I get a reply within seconds. *I'll be there in a minute.*

Standing, I make my way down the small hall, and find the bathroom. I glance into the bedroom, and last night comes flooding back to me. I was insatiable. I couldn't get enough of Edgar. The moment we'd finish I wanted him again. The rumpled bed is stripped bare of any sheets or blankets. The pillows are strewn across the floor, and the bedside lamp has been knocked over. We were both adventurous, full of urges to be satisfied. The more he gave, the more I wanted. Both of us were wild and carefree, taking what we wanted from the other. We couldn't stop. "Whoa," I whisper as I touch my bruised, raw lips.

Everything was so clear last night. Every touch, smell, feeling was vibrant. We fed off each other. I remember how my skin tingled every time his mouth was on me. I craved him, starving for more, and my memory tells me so was he.

The front door unlocks, and Edgar comes in holding two paper mugs and a brown paper bag.

"Good morning, kitty," he says as he finds me staring at the disheveled mess where I lost my virginity.

"I didn't bleed," I say aloud.

"Because you were totally relaxed." He leans down, kissing me passionately. He takes control of my body, and I dissolve into a wanton mess. My head spins as he kisses me, everything sparking awake again.

A small part of my brain takes over, telling me to get home before Mom realizes what actually happened. "I need to get home," I say. I step away before his web draws me back in. He chuckles, and holds out one of the mugs. "What's this?" I ask before I take it.

"It's a mocha. That's what you were drinking the day I met you, so I assume that's what you like."

Awww, how sweet. He knows what I like to drink. "Thank you." I take it and sip on it, although it's not very hot, more like, lukewarm. He then hands me the paper bag. "What's this?"

"I didn't know if you like chocolate chip, or blueberry muffins. I bought you a blueberry muffin." He leads me out of the hallway, and we sit on the sofa. I tear the paper bag open, and break off a small piece of muffin, popping it in my mouth. "That mouth," he says, smirking. "What that mouth did last night..."

My face heats, and I retreat into myself. "I don't know what came over me."

"Well, I know what came inside of you."

I gasp. "Shit, I'm not on birth control."

"I know, which is why I bought this too." He takes out a foil-wrapped tablet out of his pocket, and hands it to me. "It's the morning-after pill. To make sure you don't get pregnant."

I take it and swallow it fast. "How did you get this? Don't you need a prescription?'

"Don't worry about it. But, I'll make an appointment with my doctor to put you on the pill."

"What happened last night was insane. I have never felt so alive, and excited, but that's not going to happen again for a while, and when it does, you need to wear a condom."

"I don't wear condoms," he declares.

I scrunch my nose in horror.

"Ugh." I nearly balk at that. "God knows how many diseases you have," I say too loud. "I have to get tested now. You might have given me something."

He looks amused. "I gave you something, alright. And you, you're a damn wildcat. You're not a kitty, you're a tiger. I would've never known you were so adventurous when it comes to sex. I can't wait."

Can't wait? For what? To have sex with me again? "This has to slow down. It's going way too fast." I stand and walk away from him. I need to clear my head.

"This isn't going to slow down, Hannah. In fact, it's going to speed up."

"Edgar." I place my hands to my head, trying to massage the stress building.

"What?"

Turning, I see how relaxed he is. "This is going too fast for me. I need some time. I can't do this."

"You could do it last night, and you were the one begging me for more."

"I have no idea what happened last night. It was like something overtook my body, and made me crazy horny. But now I have a clearer head, and I need some time. I… I… I can't… I don't even know… " I'm beginning to lose my control. Panic is etching its way inside me. I can't even think clearly.

"What?"

"I don't know!" I snap at him. "You're too much, too intense. You're not giving me a moment to breathe. You're demanding, and you want things I'm not sure I'm ready for."

"*You* were begging *me* last night, Hannah. *You* were the one who, the moment I gave you an orgasm, you were climbing all over me pleading for me to give you more. You were hot, and sexy, and exactly what I've been looking for."

What he's been looking for?

I take several deep breaths, trying my hardest to calm my frantic brain, and my agitated nerves. "What's happening to me?" I whisper, ashamed of myself for so many reasons. I never lose control. I'm never so aggressive in anything. But last night, I *was* forceful during sex. Insistent, even. "I need some time," I say again as I search around the room for my shoes. I stop abruptly, not being able to focus on any one thing in particular. "Is this where you live?"

"This is one of my places," he cockily replies. There's something more to his answer, but I'm in no mood to actually try to figure him out. "Can you take me home, please?"

Staring at me, I feel like he's assessing me. He pulls his phone out, and tells his driver to pull the car around to the front. His eyes stay on me. I can tell by his hard stare how unhappy he is with me for leaving. But I can't stay here. He does something to me, and when I'm around him I feel like all my willpower disappears. *Vanishes.*

He takes another moment or so, staring at me, before he stands and moves to stand beside me. "I'll see you later," he says as he kisses me on the cheek and leads me toward the door.

"You're not coming?" I feel so used. My heart breaks a little, upset that he's not coming with me in the car.

"I have work to do." He gives me another kiss, and holds the door open for me.

I step out into the corridor, where I take note of the numbers on the door opposite. "Is this a hotel?" I ask feeling even more shame creeping up.

"Yes," his reply is short and curt.

"Oh." I look around, unsure on what happens next. A huge lump of humiliation lodges itself firmly in my throat. Tears well up behind my eyes. Why do I feel like he's done with me? He got sex, and now that's it. I'm nothing to him. "Well done," I say holding onto every emotion inside my body.

"On?" he asks. His cold demeanor becoming icier.

"Conquering me," I say with a fake smile. "Well done." Turning, I walk away following the 'exit' signs.

The moment I get to the elevator, I press the button for down, and wait until it arrives. I know he's not going to come after me, he's not that type of man.

My stomach lets out a small rumble. I remember I didn't eat last night, and I left the muffin and mocha back in his room. "Good going, Hannah," I scold myself while holding back my tears. "Good going." I stare down for a moment, ashamed with myself.

The doors open, and I get in, pressing the button for the lobby. Thankfully, I'm alone and don't have to share the car with anyone. I couldn't handle the stares. The elevator quickly reaches the ground, and when it does, I falter in my step to leave the elevator. I can hear lots of people in the lobby, moving around, checking in and checking out.

My stomach tightens, and my pulse quickens as I leave.

So this is what the walk of shame feels like.

My cheeks flush with disgrace as I walk past the front desk and the concierge. I know no one is looking at me, but it feels like everyone's eyes are boring into me, and they're all laughing and pointing at me, because they know what I've done. I can see the black car waiting for me, my bodyguard waiting with scornful amusement. I make eye contact with him, and laughter is dancing in his eyes. He finds this highly amusing, which means I'm not the first girl Edgar has brought here, and I know I won't be the last.

I turn right, and head across the road where I can see taxis.

Bringing up the Uber app on my phone, I see there's an Uber near here. So, I book it, and wait near the cabs. I'd rather they look at me weirdly, than experience my bodyguard laughing at me, making me feel worse.

The Uber arrives, and I slink into the back quietly. Thankfully, it's an old lady, and she's chatty. I'm not really listening to her. Instead, I think about the peculiar night I had. What came over me? Why did I act like an insatiable animal?

I'm so grateful the night is over, and obviously, Edgar and I are over too.

Fine.

Anger rises.

Fine! What the hell, you're not going to let him get away with that, are you?

Hell no, I'm not. I take my phone out, and send him a message. **You're an asshole. I hate you.** There, take that! I give myself an internal high-five.

Immediately I get a text back. *Thinking of my mouth on you?*

It's like I have a switch inside me. He says these things, or I hear his voice, and I become instantly aroused.

Pieces of last night flash in my mind. All the *good* pieces. Where his mouth was, where my mouth was, what we did. How *hungry* I was for what we did. Without any warning, I burst into laughter. The Uber lady jumps a little. "Are you alright, sugar? You gave me a fright," she says as she looks at me in the rearview mirror.

"Sorry," I say as I regain my thoughts. "I just had a thought, and it made me laugh."

"Well." She forces a smile on her face. "I'm glad you're happy."

I turn to look at the scenery as we continue on home. So many thoughts and emotions are pulsating through me. I really can't understand why I was so horny and turned on last night. It makes no sense.

We pull up two houses away from home, and I get out, thanking the woman. I know I paid her, but courtesy costs nothing.

I run my hands over my still-sensitive mouth, and try to check myself without a mirror. I need to make sure I don't look like I've been having sex all night. I pull my hair back into a tight bun to hide the small birds nest on the crown of my head.

My heart rate escalates as I approach home, knowing Mom's going to ask me about last night. Damn it, I have no idea what Kristen told her; I should've asked her. But, if I avoid her, then maybe she won't ask me. I'll go straight to my room, grab my clothes, have a shower then back to my room and stay in there for as long as I can.

Yep, sounds like an awesome plan.

I head inside, trying to be quiet. Neither Mom nor Dad are anywhere. I don't call out. I don't want them to know I'm here. As swiftly as I can, I make my way to my bedroom, get some clothes, and head into the bathroom.

The moment I'm inside, I lock the door and take a deep breath. Phew, I made it.

Turning the shower on, I strip and get inside. Looking down at my body, I'm shocked to see bruises on my arms, legs, stomach, and thighs. "Jesus," I breathe, easily identifying the bruises as finger marks.

The water falls over my body, and I think about last night. Sex was amazing. Completely unlike anything I could have imagined it would be like. There was an insatiable beast inside me. Nothing Edgar could do was enough for me. I wanted it harder, faster, and I wanted *more*. I couldn't stop. It was almost like every emotion inside me was heightened, spiked to the maximum.

Another emotion creeps through me. It starts as a small bubble, and continues to build. Jesus, what the hell is wrong with me? I want Edgar again. Right now.

But he's not here.

I want that feeling. That endorphin high, so high I could fly past the clouds to the edge of infinity.

Yes! That's what it was. A combination of euphoric sex, mixed with sensual overdose.

God, this is insane, but I can't wait for it to happen again.

Chapter 12

I WAS WAITING FOR THE WRATH OF MY PARENTS BECAUSE I DIDN'T come home, but... I didn't get it. It made me feel even worse, because not only did I successfully deceive them, but I also stayed out with a boy. No, not a boy. A man who's eleven years older than me. And who happens to be a drug dealer.

The worst thing about this is that I'm planning to spend another night with him, because he's so damned addictive. Remembering what he did to me instantly makes me smile. He plays my body like a pianist plays the piano at Carnegie Hall for a sold-out audience.

He hasn't talked to me since I left his apartment, but I'm craving him. I know my need for him makes it inevitable I'll see him again.

I've been doing research, and I found sex releases endorphins to make you happy. So, maybe that's what it is and why I want to go back to him so desperately. My biggest worry is the lying. I really don't like lying, but I've done so much of it lately to everyone I love, that one more time won't really hurt.

I haven't texted or called Edgar since I got home on the weekend. And I doubt he'll be taking me to school today although I really want him to. But it might not be a good idea if he does, because I don't think I'll be able to keep my hands to myself.

Getting dressed, I head out to the kitchen, knowing both of my parents have already left for work.

Yesterday was a weird day. I was exhausted, but edgy. It felt like I had a hangover with an added effect of being moody too. Today's not so bad. I managed to sleep some, though I needed much more.

I'm feeling anxious. My hands have a slight quiver to them as I try and pour some milk over my cereal. My mind is jumping around, unable to keep one thought steady inside my head. Edgar is prominent though, but other snippets of thoughts and worries bounce around.

"Get it together, he only wanted sex," I say to myself. "I can't believe I was so stupid." I shake my head at my own stupidity.

Placing the cereal bowl on the counter top, I huff at myself in frustration. I'm such a dumb-ass. A cute guy says all the right things, does all the right things, and I fall for it. Hook, line, and sinker. Shame replaces all other emotions. I gave up my virginity to someone like him. My stomach churns with nausea. I knew all along nothing good would come of this. Edgar is not a good man. He admits it himself. Why on earth would I think he'd be different with me?

Neglecting my barely eaten cereal, I discard it, and rinse out my bowl. I head into my room, get my bag ready, shove my laptop into it and slip my shoes on. My head really isn't in it. I'm trying to focus on the now, rather than what happened. But putting something so monumental behind me isn't easy. He took my damned virginity, and he hasn't even bothered to call me. Do I really mean so little to him?

I open the front door, and my heart sinks even further. No car. No bodyguard. *No Edgar.*

Addiction | 121

The reality hits me so hard, I burst into tears. We really are over.

Slinging my bag over my shoulder, I start walking toward the bus stop. But my tears are bordering on uncontrollable, and I don't want anyone looking at me or asking me what's wrong. So I continue walking toward school, even though I know I'll be late by the time I get there.

I get halfway down the street and turn the corner when I see the black car approaching me. My tears stop immediately. He's here. My broken heart is now beating strongly. My pulse races as the black car comes to an abrupt stop just as it passes me.

I want to run to him, but I'm also conflicted because he's hurt me and I want him to work for my forgiveness.

I lower my head, pretending I didn't see him, and pick up my pace in walking. I hear the car turning around. I speed up, even though I know I can't outrun a car. I don't want to, either. I just want him to know I'm hurt.

"Get in," he says as the car rolls beside me.

"No," I reply, even though there's no conviction to my tone.

"Get in!" he says again, this time more forcefully.

I dig my heels in, now becoming aroused and excited at the potential outcome of my stubbornness.

The car drives ahead a few feet, and stops with a screech of the tires. Edgar gets out, comes to me, bends, and slings me over his shoulder carrying me toward his car. "Put me down!" I yell as I punch him on the back.

Secretly, I'm elated he's come for me, and even happier he's picked me up like this.

Seriously, Hannah, what the hell is wrong with you?

"You're acting like a spoiled brat," he says and throws me like a rag doll into the back of his car.

"You're being a jerk," I spit back. "You screwed me and then didn't even bother calling. You hurt me." The tears threaten again. I'm so damned emotional. One moment I'm crying, the next I'm angry, and then I switch to crazy turned-on.

"I got you a mocha." He holds the take-away cup out to me.

"I don't want it." I cross my arms in front of my chest and sulk.

"Drink the damn thing." He forces it further toward me.

Reluctantly, I reach out to grab it. "I haven't had much to eat and I'm hungry."

"Lucky I brought you a chocolate chip muffin then." He holds the paper bag out to me. Again, I slowly reach out, and take it.

"Why were you a jerk?"

He lifts one shoulder non-committal. "I had things I had to take care of."

"Like what?" I sip on my mocha. Yum, it tastes so good.

"Work."

The bodyguard chuckles. What is it with him? He's always chuckling when Edgar tells me things as if they have a double meaning. Anger suddenly spurs through me. "Were you with another woman?" I ask, sadness and anger both competing for the top emotion.

A smirk appears quite quickly. I'm not sure how to take that. Is it a yes, or a no? I want to clarify, but I don't want the answer either. I'd rather be in my happy place and not know than to ask and have my heart ripped apart all over again.

I feel like I'm on the brink of collapse. Not physically, but mentally. I can't figure this out, and I want to. But Edgar is holding virtually every card of the deck, and he's holding them close to his chest. I feel like his puppet. He pulls the strings and I jump at whatever he says.

How have I fallen so deeply, so quickly?

"No," he finally responds.

I let out a huge sigh. He wasn't with another woman, which gives me hope *I'm* his only woman. "Okay," I say with a smile. Sipping on mocha, the taste is divine, and the warmth traveling down my throat makes me feel all warm and fuzzy. Or maybe it's the fact Edgar wasn't with anyone else.

"Why were you walking to school?" he asks.

"I thought you weren't going to pick me up."

"Why didn't you catch the bus?" I lift my shoulders and lower my head. "Hannah, look at me." Slowly I lift my eyes, and find his dark stare intimidating. "Hannah," he says my name slowly.

It gives me chills. Small bumps on my arms. He's so sexy. "I wanted to walk," I say meekly.

"Why?" The authority to his tone sends me crazy.

"Because I was upset, and didn't want anyone seeing me crying."

"Why?" I lower my gaze again. Sipping on my delicious mocha, I try to avoid answering the question. "Hannah?" his dark tone crawls inside me. It claws its power over me.

"Because I thought we were over."

He lets out a small laugh. Not quite a chuckle, more like a snort. I can feel him rolling his eyes at my pathetic 'school-girl' ways. "I'm nowhere near finished with you."

The words tattoo themselves on me. They hold dominion and power over me. My skin springs to life. I want him to touch me, to tell me I'm his only girl, how there's no one else but me. I want to meld myself to him, and be everywhere he is.

The desire is taking over, the need for him is getting stronger by the second. But I don't trust myself not climb on top of him, and have my wicked way with him in the back of the car. So, I drink my mocha and count to twenty in my head. If I can stop this from happening, I'll be okay.

But the need is greater than anything I've ever felt before.

It's more than desire; it's more than want. The feeling is more urgent, more potent than any drug anyone can take.

This is insane. I'm in the car for all of ten minutes with Edgar, and I'm climbing out of my skin trying to contain the desire I have clawing inside.

I finish my mocha. The paper bag with the chocolate chip muffin is between us. I stare at the bag, but my eyes keep darting across to Edgar's sexy thighs.

My leg twitches slightly, and I feel the adrenaline spiking. My heartrate races, and my mouth dries from the exuberant hunger building.

My body is reacting to him. Everything is yearning for him. I look out the window, and see we're already parked at the school. Everyone's arriving, and I'm sitting in here seriously considering ditching school so I can be with Edgar.

I've gotta get my head on straight. I can't do that. I have to go in.

"Thank you for the ride," I say as I grab my bag.

He sits back, relaxed in his seat, staring at me. He looks like he knows what's going through my head. He's smiling at me, with one eyebrow cocked up. God, he's so sexy. "You sure you want to go?"

"I'm sure I *need* to go if I'm going to get into college."

"Such a shame," he says with a tsk. "I was hoping to spend the day with you."

"You could have done that yesterday, but you chose not to call." *Snap.*

"I was busy yesterday. But I'm not busy today."

The temptation is definitely there. I want to go with him, but I also know, the school will call my parents and find out why I'm not there. "I can't," I say in a pained voice. The pain is real though, I really, *really* want to spend time with him.

"Your loss." He rests his hand on his thigh, very close to his groin.

I climb back into the car, and over to him. All my inhibitions have totally evaporated. He does something to me that makes me do things I ordinarily would never do in public. "God, I want you," I say while grinding against him.

He grabs my butt, and squeezes tightly. I feel the car jerk

forward, and I know we're in motion.

My brain is struggling to fight the desire. The craving is winning. By a landslide. I don't even care that I'm going to get into trouble with my parents. I have no worry for what will happen. Only what's happening now in the back of the car.

Desperate, I undress Edgar. I know there are two guys in the front of the car; they're so close I can reach out and touch them. But my need for Edgar is insatiable.

I can't understand why this is happening, I've never been the type who likes being the center of attention, but something is building. It's screaming at me to let all my self-control go and be free. This feeling is euphoric and sexy.

"Wait," Edgar whispers.

But I can't wait, I need him, now. "No," I say as I greedily take his mouth with mine.

"Wait!" He pushes on my shoulders to set me away from him. The beast inside is hungry, it needs to be fed.

"Fine, if you don't want me, then one of them will." I indicate the two men in the front seat with a tilt of my head. I lean back, away from Edgar, and try to grope the bodyguard.

Hell! What am I doing? My sanity is slipping. My mind is being invaded by something dangerous, yet addictive. I shouldn't be doing this, but I can't help but feel intoxicated by my own sensuality.

Edgar stares at me, amused. "Let her," he says to my bodyguard.

That throws me for a second. He thinks I won't. He's testing me.

Lifting my chin, I gaze into Edgar's darkened eyes. "Really?" I playfully say as my hand slips further down the bodyguard's arm.

"Really," he says so assuredly.

I *feel* the bodyguard and for a moment I'm hit with a sickening dirty emotion. I shouldn't be doing this, but I want to show

Edgar how *I* have the upper hand. What I want, goes.

Edgar is enjoying the show way too much to stop me. I can feel his arousal growing by the second. He's getting turned on, and I'm getting more turned on that *he's* finding this sexy.

The car comes to a stop, and Edgar pulls me out of the car quickly. We're back at his hotel suite, and inside within a few moments. "Don't let me do the walk of shame again," I plead with him.

"Never, kitty." He leans down and kisses me. The kiss grows hungrier. I become more desperate. My mind is already skipping ahead, making plans for what I want to do with him.

We're up in the suite in a matter of minutes, but it seems like forever. I'm desperate for him.

I strip off as he's kissing me. Ready… waiting.

"Do you want to have a lot of fun?" he asks me as his gaze wanders my body.

"So much," I practically beg.

"Then wait here for a moment." He walks off to his room, and is back within a minute. He's holding a glass pipe in one hand, and a little bag with tiny rocks in the other. "This will make you go crazy," he says as he places a few of the rocks in the end of the pipe.

My senses overload. I think this is crystal meth. I step back. I'm no idiot. That shit is highly addictive. Crazy even. "I'm not doing that," I say as I step back.

"It's not addictive," he replies as he holds the pipe out for me.

"I don't want to do drugs, Edgar. That's not something I'm interested in."

"Why? It's something you can use once, we can have a lot of fun, and you don't have to use it again."

"Then why don't you smoke it?"

"I already did, this morning."

I'm still shaking my head, not wanting to touch that shit. "No, Edgar." But my head is fighting with me again. It's telling me, 'once won't hurt.' He steps forward, holding the glass pipe closer to me. "Edgar," I say with a sigh.

"It's not like you're injecting anything. I wouldn't let you do that. But this, this is okay. Come on, kitty. I'll look after you." I look down to my toes, not sure what to do. "Do you remember how much fun we had the other night?" Lifting my head, I slowly nod. "Do you know why we had so much fun?" Where's he going with this? Crinkling my brows, I shake my head. "Because I gave you some liquid meth in your champagne."

"What? Why would you do that?"

"Just to relax you. You were so uptight, and I thought you'd have more fun if you relaxed. It wasn't a lot, just a little bit. Like now, this isn't a lot. It's barely anything. Look." He holds the pipe out for me to see what he's put in there. He's right. There isn't a lot in the pipe.

"I don't know," I say, my stomach knotting with anticipation. A part of me wants to try it because he said it's not addictive, but another part is screaming *no* because I know it has the potential to screw me up.

"If you don't want it, that's okay. We'll have regular boring sex, but if you do have it again, we'll have all the fun you want to have. Think how it was on our date. Do you remember what it felt like?"

"It was mind-blowing," I say with a smile. The things we did were out of this world.

"It just won't be as good for you."

Reluctantly, I step forward. "Just once. No more after this," I say to Edgar.

"Just once," he says with a smile.

"What do I do?" I ask.

"I'll teach you, kitty."

I smile at Edgar and trust in him to look after me. Wrapping my lips around the pipe, I inhale.

Chapter 13

Two weeks later.

LYING IN BED, MY BRAIN HASN'T STOPPED. I NEED SOME. SO BAD.
Edgar gave me a little bit yesterday before school, but I need
more. I can't seem to think straight at all. My head hurts.

"Good morning, sweetheart. Want to come to the mall with
me?" Mom asks as she enters my bedroom.

"God, Mom. Get out!" I scream at her.

Ugh, stop it, Hannah. I just need a little bit, then I'll quit. I just
need a bit to get me through.

Mom's eyes widen, and her mouth falls closed. I've made her
sad. Who cares, she deserves it. She shouldn't be coming in here
without knocking. "I'll go fix you some breakfast," she says in a
small voice.

"Not hungry," I snap at her. She closes the door softly behind
as she leaves. She can't give me what I need. Only Edgar can.
He's been giving me a little bit every day before school, and it's
enough to get me through to the next day. But today's Saturday,

and I'm not going to see him until Monday again. He said he's busy, got a few things on. *Whatever that means.*

I lean over to pick up my phone, and notice how my hands have a slight tremor to them. I probably need something to eat. I ring Edgar's number. It rings out, so I dial it again. "Hey," he says in his sultry tone.

"Hey, can I see you today?" I ask.

"No, I'm busy."

"I know… but I really need a little bit."

"Hannah," he huffs frustrated. "I can't keep giving it to you. It doesn't grow on trees."

"Please?" I beg. "I'll do anything you want."

He chuckles. "Yeah, I know you will. But no, I don't have time."

"Please. I have money. Come on, please?" The begging is painful for me to hear. But I need some, just a little bit. Enough to get me through the day, that's all. I can quit, but I don't want to. It makes me feel so alive. I love it. It sends me somewhere so high, I know no one can touch me. "Please?"

He's quiet for a moment. My need grows hungrier and more desperate. "I'll meet you down at the bus stop in an hour."

"Yes!" Jumping out of bed, I quickly get dressed, and head out to the kitchen to find Mom making scrambled eggs. Crap, I need money, and I only have my ATM card, so I need cash. "Hey, Mommy," I say as I walk over to her and give her a huge hug. "Sorry, I snapped at you. I'm just stressed from school, and an assignment I have due."

Mom lets out a breath of relief. "That's okay. Do you want to come to the mall with me, or would you rather stay here and do your assignment?"

Running my hand up and down my arm, I notice how sensitive my skin has become. "I'll stay here," I say to Mom. "When do you think you'll be going?" I look around the kitchen, and see her handbag sitting up on the counter.

"I'll eat breakfast, then finish getting ready. I won't be long out, maybe an hour or two."

Perfect. "Okay." I keep an eye on her bag. It's my beacon. I know she'll have money in there. I'll wait 'til she's getting ready and take fifty dollars. I'll go to the bank and take fifty out of my account to replace it.

The annoying little voice in my head screams. *Don't steal, Hannah!*

I'm repaying it. It's just for now.

Mom's talking, and all I can think about is getting some more into me. I so can stop.

"Huh?" I ask Mom when I catch her staring at me.

"You've lost weight, you need to eat." She offers me her eggs.

"It's stress, from school." My mind is formulating how I'm going to take money out of her purse without her seeing.

Mom's still talking, but other than money and meeting up with Edgar, nothing else matters. Until I see Edgar, my head will remain jumbled and unclear. It's like a huge fog bank has nestled its way into my brain, and I can't get out of it.

As I watch Mom's mouth moving, and I vow to myself to stop after today. I just need one suck of the pipe. That should be enough to take the edge off and then I'll stop. I promise.

"… ready now," Mom cheerfully says as she comes in to give me a hug. She sniffs toward my hair and steps back. "You need to wash your hair."

Why? Can she smell something? No, impossible, I'm being overly careful.

I think back to the day I ditched school; the school called her and asked her where I was. I got home before she did, and was out of it from what Edgar and I had done, so faking being sick was easy. She believed me. I mean, she had no reason not to.

Guilt burdens me and a deep sorrow forms in the pit of my stomach. I shouldn't lie to my parents, but then again, they're lying to me. Edgar showed me more emails from Mom to the mystery man, and it made me sick.

Mom's concerned stare brings me back to the now. "What?" I ask.

"Are you okay? You zoned out." She reaches over to feel my forehead. "You don't feel warm, are you feeling okay?"

Crap, I don't want her to stay home. I need her to go out, so I can meet Edgar. "Yeah, I'm fine." I smile at her to show how terrific I am. "Need any house work done?" I ask as I turn toward the sink to look if there's anything that needs to be rinsed and stacked in the dishwasher.

"If you can vacuum while I'm at the mall, that'll be a help."

"Sure thing. When's Dad coming home?" I ask just to make sure he's not here when I leave to meet up with Edgar.

"Don't you remember? He's got that trip to Las Vegas this weekend," Mom replies. Her tone is tinged with concern. "Are you sure you're okay?"

Pull it together, Hannah! "Yeah, I'm okay. I just forgot." He's probably gambling the rest of their money away.

"Okay, I'm going to get ready."

I hang around the kitchen, watching as Mom disappears down the hallway and into her bedroom. She closes the door, and I wait for a few seconds to make sure she doesn't return.

My heart is beating fast as I open her bag, reach in, and grab her wallet.

I shouldn't be doing this. I shouldn't be taking her money. The guilt overtakes the need, and I place her wallet back in her bag. But my need screams again. It's a tug-of-war between the two of them. I take her wallet out, and flip the top up. Inside the bill compartment, there's a few twenties, tens, and fifties. I count it quickly. There's over four hundred dollars in her purse. By the time she notices a fifty gone, I would've put it back already. Problem solved.

No, I shouldn't take it.

Come on, Hannah. It's the last time you'll use any. You're quitting.

Just cut loose and have fun.

No. This is so wrong.

The money tempts me. It's just sitting there, waiting for me to take it.

I'm a good daughter, I don't ask for much. I nearly always do everything they want me to do. And it's just fifty dollars.

Don't take it.

Take it and have a bit of fun.

I swallow the lump sitting in the base of my throat, and pull out a fifty-dollar bill. Maybe, I should take another, in case fifty isn't enough. *No, stop. Enough.*

Okay, just one more. One hundred should be plenty.

I shove the money in my back pocket, close the top of her wallet and place it back in her bag.

The guilt is still there, but it's outweighed by the excitement of what's going to happen over the next few hours. I can't wait for Edgar to pick me up. I run to my room, and hide the money. Checking my phone, I see there's a message from Edgar. **Wear something sexy, I'm taking you to a party.**

Giddily, I ruffle through my drawer for a pretty underwear and bra set, then I search my wardrobe for something cute to wear. I'm so excited. We're going to have an amazing time.

He was right. Using meth and having sex afterward is mind blowing. Every inhibition dissolves and it takes you away to the highest of places. I love it.

Maybe, instead of quitting, I can have a tiny amount of crystal meth when I'm having sex. You know, I really don't like the name crystal meth. I prefer the term ice. Whenever I use it, my body covers in goosebumps, and a bolt of ice courses through my veins. It's exhilarating, and so damned liberating.

No rules. No exams. No teachers. No parents. Just me and the high of ice.

My mouth is parched and I do a small dance as I get my

clothes ready. I head into the bathroom to shower. I'll wash my hair, and make sure I'm looking extra good for Edgar.

I'm in the shower when Mom opens the door. "I'm going now, sweetheart."

"Okay," I say happily. Happily, because I know Edgar's coming over soon. Like a light bulb moment, something flashes warm inside of me. I think I love him. He looks after me, treats me well, and he's super sexy. Despite the fact, he's considerably older than me, he thinks I'm sexy too. He doesn't treat me like I'm a schoolkid. He treats me like I'm a sexy, desirable adult. And I love that.

"Be back soon."

"Okay, have fun." Cause I know I'll be having the time of my life. But I also know I have to tell Edgar that I'm going to quit. I think he'll be okay with it. I'm sure he loves me like I love him, so he *should* be okay with my decision.

I quickly finish washing myself, turn the water off, and jump out of the shower with a spring to my step. Heading into my bedroom, I check the time, and see Edgar will be here in the next twenty minutes. I towel dry my hair and body and get changed into my cute bra and underwear. I've found something to wear, but it's conservative and not seductive enough for a party or for Edgar.

I know Mom has a red mini skirt she wore to a party once, so I pad down the hallway to her and Dad's room, and open her closet. Ruffling through her wardrobe, I find the mini skirt and slide it on. It's a bit big around the waist but it barely covers my butt. Mom wore it with stockings and knee high boots. She went as a go-go dancer to the party and she looked awesome. I also find a tank top with thin spaghetti straps hanging behind the red mini-skirt.

I put the tank on, and it barely covers my midriff. Paired with the skirt, I look hot and edgy. Edgar's going to lose his shit the moment he sees me. I head back to my room, and find my pair of black high heels. When I wear the outfit as a whole, I know

I'm looking good.

I tie my hair back in a severe ponytail, and apply red lipstick. "Yeah, you look good," I say to my reflection in the mirror.

I do notice though, my collar bones are protruding a bit, and I scrunch my nose at the site of that. I'm petite by nature, but now it looks like I've lost a few pounds. I make a mental note to eat more, because I don't want to look like a skeleton.

Checking the time again, I get more excited knowing Edgar is on his way to me. I take the hundred dollars from where I hid it, and grab my phone. Heading outside, I walk to the bus stop to where Edgar said he was meeting me.

I don't have to wait long before a black limousine pulls up in front of me. The back passenger window slowly drops, and I see Edgar sitting inside. "My my my," he says as his gaze drops down my body. "We're going to have a lot of fun tonight, kitty."

"Eeeek!" I squeal with excitement.

"Get in." The door opens, and he moves over. I climb in, and over to him straight away. I sit on his lap, and start kissing him. "Your breath stinks, did you brush your teeth?" he asks.

"I'm sorry." I duck away, embarrassed by my breath. "Have you got gum?" I ask.

My bodyguard, who hasn't been at school for a week, chuckles. "It's started," he says to Edgar.

"What's started?" I ask.

"Nothing," Edgar says and takes a glass pipe out of his pocket.

Exhilaration bursts through me. "Yes," I shriek with delight. "Oh my God, I missed you," I direct my statement to the rocks he's putting in the glass pipe.

"You miss this more than me?" Edgar asks.

Lifting my head, I smile at him. "I miss you most of all. Followed closely by my little friend." I tap the pipe, and wait 'til he's prepared it so I can smoke.

"Naughty kitty." He offers the pipe to me.

Taking it between my lips, I inhale as he lights it.

Instant relief.

"That feels so good," I say slowly as I let the smoke sit in my lungs, filling them up, giving me a high so powerful and delicious. I let out the smoke, and open my eyes to see Edgar smirking at me. "Tell me about this party we're going to." I lean in and start kissing the column of his neck. He smells so sweet, like sunshine mixed with rain.

"It's a party a friend of mine is putting on. Actually, it's been going since last night."

"Sounds like a lot of fun." I unbutton his shirt, and make my way down his chest.

Grabbing my hair by the ponytail, he forces my head lower.

I know what he wants, and I have no problem in giving it to him.

I'm not sure where the party is, because I wasn't exactly paying attention to my surroundings in the limousine.

But the car has slowed at the entrance to a long, winding driveway. I look around, trying to figure out where we are. I can't see the house, and all we're surrounded by is tall trees and the mountains. "Where are we?" I ask.

"Fix your top." Edgar points to my tank top, and I giggle as I notice my breasts are exposed.

"Oops," I say and tuck myself back in to my bra.

"Here, have this." He holds the pipe out for me again, this time putting in some more rocks.

"If you insist," I say taking in another breath. He tries to take it away, but I inhale once more, getting as much into me as I can. The feeling is unbelievable. I feel invincible, like no one and nothing can touch me. My body dances merrily to the song playing in my head. "I feel so good," I say as I close my eyes and sway to the music.

"Kitty," Edgar draws me back to him.

"Yeah," I dreamily reply, still moving my body from side to side.

"I want you to have fun, okay?"

"I'm having the best time." I open my eyes, lean in, and kiss his cheek. "Thank you," I whisper. He's looking after me so well.

The car winds up the long driveway, and when we reach the top, I see a mega house sitting high and proud. The house looks like a movie star would live in it. It's white and airy, and has an ocean feel to it, even though there's no ocean near here.

Edgar gets out of the car, and holds his hand out to me. "If you need some more, come find me, okay?"

"Oh, before I forget." I take the hundred dollars out of my phone case, and hold it out to Edgar.

He looks down at the money and shakes his head. "It's okay, I think I have another way you can pay me." He winks and smirks. And I giggle again, because I know what he wants.

"Okay," I say. "Sounds like a good exchange."

We head into the house, and the first thing I see is men standing outside holding big guns. Man, what type of movie star needs men with guns?

"Now, I want you on your best behavior," Edgar whispers.

"I won't let you down."

"Edgar," a man in a very expensive suit greets us. He looks me up and down and smiles. "She's cute," he says as he steps forward, and kisses me on the mouth. "What's your name, sugar?"

"I'm Hannah," I say as I look past him and see the pool sparkling in the sunlight. "You have a pool!" I nearly yell.

There's a bunch of girls in there, swimming around naked. "Yes, I do."

I turn to Edgar, "Can I go?" I ask already unzipping my mini skirt.

"Go, have fun."

"Eeek." I kick off my shoes, take off all my clothes, dropping them where I am and run out to the pool. Jumping in, I make a huge splash. The girls in the pool, all about my age or a bit older, look over at me. "Hi!" I say once I've come up.

"Hi," they respond happily in unison.

One of the girls swims over to me, and touches my hair. "Your hair is so pretty," she says.

"Thank you." I smile to her. She looks like she's having a good time. Her eyes are glassy, and she's smiling at me. She leans in and starts kissing me. I've never kissed a girl before. It's different from kissing Edgar. Her lips are softer, and gentler. She moves close to me, I can feel her breasts on mine. It's not a bad feeling at all.

I look around and find Edgar and the suit guy sitting in chairs on the patio, watching us. There are a few other guys too. They've all got drinks in their hands. But all eyes are on me and this other girl.

I like it.

I like how they're watching us.

I like what it's doing to me.

And I like how Edgar is watching us.

Before I even realize, more guys gather around the pool. The other girls are giggling, and some of them are kissing, too. This is so much fun.

I'm so free.

I put on a show, and I love how the men are watching us. They're talking in low voices, and some have moved quite close to the pool to watch. I watch Edgar watching me. I'd do anything for him. Anything.

Chapter 14

STUMBLING THROUGH THE FRONT DOOR, MOM AND DAD ARE pacing back and forth.

"Hannah, what the hell happened to you? Where have you been?" Mom asks as she comes straight over to me.

"What?" I ask, still high from the pipe I sucked on in the car coming over here.

"Hannah, are you high?" She aggressively holds my chin and stares into my eyes.

"No, Mom," I respond, and giggle.

"Your pupils are huge, and your eyes are bloodshot. You're barely looking at me."

"I'm just tired," I say and giggle again.

"What's so funny?" she asks as she lets go of my chin and steps backward.

Shrugging, I look around not really able to tell them about the best time of my life. "Can I just go to my room, I'm tired," I laugh again.

"No, you can't." Dad steps in front of me and crosses his arms in front of his chest.

"What? You think you're going to stop me?" I laugh in his face.

"Hannah, you've been gone since yesterday. It's Sunday night. Where have you been?" Dad asks.

"It's not Sunday, it's Saturday. And why aren't you on your 'business trip'?" I air-quote *business trip*. What I wanna say, is why aren't you gambling away everything you've worked for.

"What's that supposed to mean?" he asks.

Mom looks to Dad, surprised. "Oh yeah, I know about you…" I point to Dad, then point to Mom and add, "…and I know about you too." I let out another laugh. "You're both fucking jokes. You're lecturing me about going out today, when both of you are fucked in the head."

"Hannah!" Mom yells at me. "What has gotten into you? You disappeared for nearly two days, we tried calling you, and Kristen, we tried everyone we know to ask if they'd seen you, and no one had. And now, you've shown up, high as a kite, and rude. What is going on with you?"

"You wanna know what's going on with me?" I lean into Mom. "I've been having sex. Lots and lots of sex. Dirty sex, rough sex, sex with a lot of other men, and a heap of women too." Mom's mouth falls open. "Yeah, I've been doing that too." I wink at her.

"Hannah," Dad says, clutching at his chest.

"Hannah," Mom follows, lifting her hand to cover her mouth.

"That's my name, don't wear it out." I laugh at my stupid joke. "Oh, and I had the time of my life. Drank a bit too."

Dad's demeanor changes, he straightens his back and lifts his chin. "Who did this?" he asks me.

"I did this, and man oh man, was it fun. You should've seen me, Daddy, you would've been so proud." Dad slaps my face, and Mom gasps. "You don't like me anymore cause I'm dirty?"

I blink rapidly at my Dad.

"That's it, we're taking you to the hospital and getting you help." Dad grabs me on my upper arm and starts dragging me out the house.

I turn and punch him in the jaw. He goes flying backward. I never knew I had this strength. "Don't fucking touch me, you pervert," I yell. Mom's standing by the front door, and moves to restrain me. I shove her hard and she hits her back on the door jamb. "Don't fucking touch me." I hold my finger up to Mom, warning her. She winces. I laugh at her. "Yeah, thought so." I take off down the road, and take my phone out of my bra. Dialing Kristen's number, she answers on the second ring. "Kristen." I say as I burst into tears.

"Oh my god, Hannah. Where have you been? Your parents have been looking for you, and they called me. I can't keep lying for you. I told them I hadn't seen you. Where have you been? You've been missing since yesterday."

Her response angers me. "Great. You're such a self-righteous bitch. Why didn't you just cover for me, Kristen? I thought you were my best friend. Obviously, you're not."

"Hey, that's not fair!" she shouts into the phone. "We are friends, but you've gone all weird on me, not telling me anything, and being moody at school. What's happening with you, Hannah?"

"You know what?" I snap at her. "You're a bitch, and I hate you." I hang up on her, and keep stomping down the street. What a bitch. I can't believe she didn't cover for me. I thought we were friends, what an ungrateful and unreasonable cow. I hate her so much.

Dialing Edgar's number, his deep gravelly voice answers immediately. "Kitty," he says into the phone.

"I had a fight with my parents, can you come get me please?"

"I'm not your personal Uber."

I burst into tears, and beg him to come. "Please? I've had a huge fight with my Mom and Dad, and a huge fight with Kristen. I've got nowhere else to go."

He huffs as if he's irritated. "It'll cost you," he says after a moment.

His tone changes to husky and deep. The fight with my parents is now forgotten. Just hearing his voice makes everything better. "I'm good with the price." I smirk into the phone.

"I'll be there in a few minutes."

"I'm walking toward school."

"Okay, I'll find you."

Hanging up, I get excited at the fact I'm going to see him again, and hopefully, he'll give me some more ice. Mom and Dad have killed my buzz. I was so happy and high, and then they went and screwed it all up. It's all their fault, if they'd just left me alone when I got home, then I'd be in bed, high and happy. Not to mention that bitch, my ex-best friend. God, I hate her guts. Shaking my head, I'm internally fuming at her and the way she's acting. Like she's the perfect friend, who's never done anything wrong.

Mumbling to myself about Kristen, I see Edgar's car turn the corner. It slows as it approaches me. When he stops, I run across the road, straight to him. "Hey there, need a ride?" he asks once the window is down.

"Don't know, sugar, where you going?" I like this make-believe world of ours. It's fast, really sexy, and fun.

"How about you move that cute little ass of yours and get in the car?" I wiggle my butt and Edgar's eyes move straight to it. "Yeah, now get in and sit on my lap," he says.

Chills cover my body. I love how he's so controlling. It does something to me. My nerve endings spark awake and my heart pumps quicker for him. I get in the car and sidle up to give him a kiss. He turns his head, and I end up peppering kisses down his strong jawline, all the way down the column of his neck. "I had a fight with my parents, they killed my high." I pout but continue kissing.

"Poor baby, do you need some more?" he asks. I nod my head, desperate for another puff on the glass pipe. "What are you going to give me for it?" he teases.

"What do you want?" I ask.

"I have some friends coming in from out of town tomorrow, and I want you to help me entertain them," he says as he takes the glass pipe out of a small compartment in the rear console beside him. "Do you wanna help me entertain them?" he places a couple of crystals in the pipe, and lifts his lighter.

"I'd do anything for you," I say as sincerely as I can. I honestly would. Edgar's shown me a way of life I never thought was possible. It's liberating and free. It makes me want to spread my wings, and soar through the open sky.

"Would you really?" he asks as he pulls the pipe back before I have a chance to inhale.

"I love you," I say. "There's nothing I wouldn't do for you."

He places the pipe to my lips and holds the flame from the lighter under the glass bulb where the rocks are. Inhaling deeply, I feel the smoke fill my lungs. Closing my eyes, I let it take me away to the clouds. Floating high, every problem I have has been erased by the intoxicating rush from the crystals.

"Are you flashing?" Edgar asks.

"Huh?" I respond and open my eyes to find him fondling my breasts.

"Are you flashing?"

"What's that?" I push my breast further into his hand, wanting him to be rough with me. Everything in my body is on overdrive. The highest of highs.

"It's the highest of rushes."

"YES!" I exclaim. "I've never felt anything like this before. It's better than any other you've given me. Why does it feel so good?" The rush peaks, and starts to settle too quickly. "Can I have more?" I ask. "Please?"

"You're such a good kitty. Here you go." He holds the pipe out, and I suck it in as deeply as I can. The high is back just as quickly as it began to disappear. It's amazing. "You're a good girl, Hannah."

I smile at him and ride this one out. "Thank you." The car jolts to a stop, and he opens the door. I look around, but don't actually recognize the place. It's not where he's taken me before, it's somewhere new. "Where are we?" I ask.

"This is for you."

It's a motel, not as nice as the one he lives in, but at least it's somewhere for me to stay. "It is?" I ask, delighted and happy he's taking care of me.

"All for you."

I jump on him, and wrap my legs around his waist. "Thank you, thank you, thank you." I kiss him over and over again. He really looks after me.

"You need to pay me though, Hannah."

"How?" I ask.

"I told you, you have to help me entertain my friends."

"Okay." *Kiss.* "I love you." *Kiss.* "Will you stay with me tonight?" *Kiss.*

"Not tonight, but I'll come by in the morning."

He walks me into the motel, past a guy who looks like a serial killer staffing the front desk. He's fat, and wearing a shirt that's at least two sizes too small for him. His hair is oily and stringy and it hangs limply around his face. "Boss," he says to Edgar. Edgar acknowledges him with a small head nod.

"You know him?" I ask.

"Yeah, he works for me."

"Huh." I think about it for a moment, but I catch the aroma of someone smoking ice and I forget what I was thinking about. "Yummy," I say as I try to follow the scent.

"No more tonight, Hannah. I'll bring you some tomorrow."

"That's not fair," I whine. "Just a little bit? I don't even know what time you'll come by tomorrow, what if I don't see you 'til late. You can't let a girl starve," I say in a cutesy voice.

"I won't let you starve. And I'll be back early tomorrow, because I need to take you shopping."

"Yay, what are you buying me? My very own pipe?" I clap my hands together.

"No, I'll be buying you some clothes, and shoes."

"Boring... " I roll my eyes. "I can just go around naked, I don't mind." I start taking off my top right here in the hallway he's walking me down.

"Keep your clothes on." Edgar places his hand to mine, stopping me from taking my clothes off. "You can strip off once you're in your room." We approach a door, it's got a wonky number 6 and a straight number 9 on it. I start giggling. "Here you go." He opens the door and I step inside.

The room is small. It has a single bed, and a door that leads to the bathroom. It's darkish, but at least it's clean. The bedding is ancient; it's got big orange flowers all over it. "Can't you stay? I'm going to be so bored if you go."

"Turn the TV on." Edgar points to the dated television in the room.

"It doesn't have cable," I whine again.

"Read a book."

I look around the room. "There are no books. Please, stay with me?"

"No," he says with authority. "But, tonight, take a nice long hot shower. Everything you need is in there, so enjoy it. There's some snacks in the bar fridge." He points to a cupboard, then walks over and opens it, showing the small fridge in it. "I'll be here early tomorrow. Set your alarm on your phone and be ready by eight."

"Maybe, I should go to school." I kinda really should.

"That's fine," he nearly snaps at me. "If you don't want to spend time with me, then fine, go to school. I just thought... " He runs his hand through his hair and sighs deeply.

"What is it?" I rush over and hug him, trying to comfort him.

"I thought you loved me like I love you."

"You love me?" My heart fills with even more love for him. "You really love me?" I could climb the Empire State Building and scream it for the world to know. I've won the jackpot with him. I can't believe he loves me. I'm the luckiest girl in the whole wide world.

"Of course, I do." He leans down, and places a kiss to my cheek. "Now, be a good girl and stay here tonight. Tomorrow, we've got a big day of shopping."

"Okay." I hug him tighter. "For you, I'll do anything."

"I know, because we love each other." He hugs me even tighter. "And just because I love you... " He takes the glass pipe out of his suit jacket pocket. "Because you're my special girl." He lights it, and I get so excited, I nearly jump him right now.

Chapter 15

I DIDN'T SLEEP THE ENTIRE NIGHT. NOT ONE MOMENT. MY PHONE kept ringing. It alternated between calls from Mom, then Dad, and even Kristen. I ignored each call. My phone kept ringing, until finally, it ran out of charge and died. They're all dead to me now. No one understands me.

This is the real me. Not that shy girl who would stay in the shadows and let people boss her around. Nope, that was never me. I like the way I feel now. Except for *right* now. I'm edgy and angry and pacing the room. My head is going at a hundred miles an hour, and all I can think about is seeing Edgar. I hope he brings the pipe with him. I keep staring at the time; it seems to have stopped. There's a digital clock by the bed, and every time I look at it, the numbers don't move. Six-forty-eight. Ugh, hurry up. I need to see Edgar. He said we're going shopping today, I hope he gives me a little to help me out. I only need a small amount. Just enough to take the edge off.

"Where are you?" I scream as loudly as I can. My voice is so angry, it even scares me.

Someone bashes the other side of the wall on the other side of it. Crap, I hope I didn't wake them. Who cares if I did? I need my Edgar, and a little suck on the pipe.

"Hey," I say to myself as I pace back and forth. "Where do you think you're going shopping?" I try to distract myself, but I can't. The glass pipe consumes every thought. I look at the clock, six-forty-nine. "Are you kidding me?" I grumble, remembering to keep my voice down.

"I can't just stay here, I'm going to go mad." I slip my feet into my shoes, and open the door to the room. Wait, did Edgar leave the key? I look around the room and can't see it anywhere. Shit, if I leave, I won't be able to get back in again. But I have to get out, I'm going stir crazy. I just need to walk outside. Get some air into me, and that should make me feel better.

No, Hannah, *that* won't make you feel better. You know what will.

It's true. Walking outside won't help. Not unless I find some ice. Ugh, no, I can stop anytime I want. I'm not addicted. I'm not stupid. Only dumb people who aren't careful get addicted to shit like that. I can stop. I just don't want to.

Six-fifty-two.

This has got to be some kind of joke. It's not seven yet. This isn't right, there's gotta be something wrong with the clock. I walk around to check the cord, and see it's plugged in right. I continue my pacing, stressing myself out of my own mind.

Grabbing the remote, I turn the TV on and start flicking through the channels. *Boring. Boring. Boring.*

Nothing is keeping my mind satisfied. All I can think about is my need to see Edgar. As I'm mindlessly staring at the TV, I notice an ashtray sitting on the table. Picking it up, it has some weight to it. So, I open the door, and jam the ashtray between the door and the frame, and step back to see if it keeps it open. Yes! Success. It stays ajar enough for me to able to come and go as I please. I leave the room, and head down the hallway. I think this is the way Edgar and I came in. I'm not sure, though. I was kinda high.

I see the fat guy from last night. He lifts his head to glance at me, then lowers it again. Not even a second later, he comes out from behind his desk. "Where are you going?" he asks as he stands in front of me. His shirt looks even smaller, and dirtier than I remember from last night.

"For a walk." I try to side step him, but he moves in front of me again.

"No can do. The boss won't be too happy about that if I let you go."

I take a step back, clarity pushing forward in my brain. "What? You're keeping me here, like a prisoner?"

"Nah." He panics, I can hear it by the pitch of his voice. "Boss told me to watch out for ya, that's all."

It doesn't feel like that's all. It feels like more than what he's saying. "I'll deal with him when I get back." I manage to avoid him, and run out the front door. I can hear him shuffling behind me, like he's chasing me, so I run even faster. I'm thinner than him, I can outrun him.

I make it outside, and quickly try to think which way we came in. Truthfully, I was high, and I can't exactly recall the details. I turn left and run down the side toward a street where I can hear noise. The building itself is seedy, with plenty of graffiti adorning the grimy brick wall. It looks dodgy. Like something you'd see in a low-budget movie.

Yuck.

I walk out on the street, and immediately I notice how it's bustling. Lots of cars and trucks zoom past, and there seems to be a lot of people out and about too.

Looking around, I know I'm in a crappy part of town. The road is a thoroughfare to get from one end to the other, and it's used on a daily basis by a lot of cars, but the area itself isn't particularly appealing to anyone.

A lot of prostitution happens here, and lots and lots of drug dealing.

Hmmm, I wonder if I could find someone to buy a quarter of a gram from. Just a bit to get me through until Edgar comes to pick me up.

I don't have any money. Damn it. I'm going to have to wait. But I know he won't be here for hours. What am I going to do?

Staring at the building as I walk down the sidewalk, I walk into something. "Sorry," I mumble as I turn to face a police officer walking the beat.

He's young. He can't be any older than twenty. *Oh no, act normal, Hannah.*

"Are you okay?" he asks me as he steps back to access me.

"Ah, yeah. I'm fine." *Act normal, act normal, act normal.*

His eyes take me in, looking me over for a long minute before he says, "Are you lost?"

"What's that supposed to mean?" I snap a little too angrily.

"Hey," he asserts while standing taller. "Don't talk to me like that."

Instantly I drop my eyes to the ground, staring at nothing but my shoes. I feel so embarrassed for talking to him like that. "Sorry," I mumble.

"What's your name?"

"Hannah," I reply in a small voice.

"Where do you live, Hannah?"

Panic rushes through me. "A street that way." I point in the direction of where Edgar's put me up to live. God, I love him so much.

Another police officer joins the one who's talking to me. He's much older, and much more suspicious. "Martin, leave her. She's a junkie," he says tapping the cute cop on the shoulder.

"I am not!" I nearly yell at him.

He huffs at me, and turns to walk away. But the younger one, he stays to keep talking to me. "What are you doing out here?"

"I'm waiting for my boyfriend."

"He told you to meet him down here?" He looks around at the sketchy part of town.

"Nah, I um wanted to get some fresh air, so I came out for a walk."

"Where did you say you were staying?"

There's something oddly familiar about him. Like he's a friend from way back, but I know he's not. I've never seen him before, but I feel really relaxed around him. It's weird. "Just over that way." I point again but don't actually tell him.

He stares at me for a moment. His eyes doing that whole 'cop' thing. But surprisingly, it doesn't freak me out. I feel comfortable with him. "Hannah, I want you to tell me the truth with my next question."

"Okay."

"Are you in some kind of trouble?"

"No!" I say with more force than is warranted.

"Is anyone doing anything to you that you don't want them to do?"

"No, he loves me," I reply.

"What's your boyfriend's name?" It's starting to feel a bit like an interrogation.

"I've gotta go. Nice talking to you, Police Officer Martin." I salute him and smile, hoping to diffuse the unusual tension. He's showing a lot of interest in me, when all I'm doing is minding my own business and walking on the sidewalk. "Bye." I turn to run, but look over my shoulder to see if he's following me. He's not, thankfully.

I try to remember where the motel is, knowing the general direction of it. Going through the front door, I see the fat guy behind the counter again. He sees me, and a smirk slowly drags across his face. "Nice of you to come back," he says and chuckles while shaking his head.

Oh shit. I can tell by the evil glint to his eyes, I'm in trouble. I run down to my room, and find the door wide open. Edgar's sitting on the bed, beside him is the glass pipe. The bodyguard is standing beside him. "Hey," I say. My gaze is fixated on the pipe. Yes, relief. "Is that for me?" I ask with excitement.

"It was," Edgar replies with an expressionless voice.

"Was?"

"Was." My heart sinks, and I suddenly feel sick. "You left after you were told not to."

"I just needed some air. I was going stir crazy in here. And my phone died, and I don't have a charger for it, I can't even play any games on it. I… I… " I struggle to make an excuse, I'm grasping at straws. "Please, can I have some?" I look to the pipe, and to Edgar.

"No," he says with authority. My heart breaks further.

"I didn't do anything wrong," I plead. "That's not fair."

He picks the pipe up, and my fixated gaze travels with it as he moves it around. "You want this?" he asks.

"I'd do anything for it." I nod my head.

"Then get on your knees and crawl over to me." I get on my knees, and crawl over to him. "Go get Simon." Edgar flicks his head to the side, talking to the bodyguard.

The bodyguard laughs. "You're a cruel man, but I love it." He chuckles again.

"Stay there, Hannah." He halts me when I'm close to him. My stare is on the pipe, I can't look away from it. It's calling me, begging me to take it and to inhale every morsel of rock that's in the bulb of it. Exhilaration takes over. I can smell it, almost taste it. It's right here, in front of me. He's teasing me with it. I can't wait to have it.

I hear footsteps coming down the worn hallway carpet. Turning, I see the bodyguard, and the fat guy from the front desk. Oh, his name is Simon. Both are staring at me. Fat guy licks his lips while he stares at my butt. *Yuck.*

"Thank you, gentlemen," Edgar says. "Now, you're both here because someone needs to be taught a lesson for not listening to me. Don't you, kitty?"

I drop my head in shame, but I nod. I shouldn't have gone outside, I should've stayed here and waited for him like he wanted me to.

"And you really want this, don't you?" He waves the glass pipe in front of my face, and I nearly pounce on it. But I nod my head again. "I asked you what you'd do for it, and you told me, and I quote 'I'd do anything for it.' Isn't that right, kitty?" I nod again. "Lick my shoe." My head lifts to stare at him. He wants me to lick his shoe? Like, for real? "Didn't you hear me?"

"I... " I swallow the spit in my mouth, unsure of what I actually *did* hear. "I'm not sure," I say after a few seconds.

"If you want this, and if you love me like you say you do, you'll lick my shoe."

The need for the pipe is great, but licking his shoe. That's disgusting. "I... " I struggle to say anything, because all I can think about is the pipe.

"You told me you love me. Do you not love me anymore, kitty?"

"Of course, I do. But licking your shoe?" My brain is fighting with the temptation in front of me. God, I really want some, but how can he ask me to do something so vile as licking his shoe?

"Kitty?" He snaps my attention back to him. "I understand if you don't want to... but I love you."

My mind cracks, it's all I need to hear. Smiling, I lean down and lick the top of his shoe. I lick it again, to show Edgar how devoted I am to him. I sit back on my heels and smile at him, pleased with myself. "I love you," I say with sincerity.

"I know you do. Now come get your reward." I crawl over to him, place my lips to the pipe, and inhale the moment he lights it.

"Wow, you've got her trained well," the bodyguard says

from behind me.

I have no idea what he means, and in this moment, I don't give a rat's ass either. The smoke fills my lungs, my eyes close as every thought in my head disappears. I'm flying, up in the clouds. I'm free as a bird, with her wings open while she skyrockets through the air. "Yeah," I mumble to myself.

Chapter 16

EDGAR HAS KEPT THE SUPPLY OF ICE UP, AND I'M TAKING IT. EVERY bit he offers to me. We've been out shopping, buying me clothes. I'm kinda too wasted to know what he's been buying, but I think it's bras and panties. Skimpy ones. I don't mind, I don't have anything to hide.

At the moment, he's taken me to a beauty salon. I stumble in attached to his arm. "Sit," he says and points to some chairs.

He walks over to some woman who looks like she's staring at me, and gives her instructions while looking at me, then back to her. She touches him on the arm, and this gesture spikes my anger. "Hey, don't fucking touch him!" I yell at her as I stand and charge over.

"Settle down, petal. I have no interest in your man, I like the women." She smirks at me.

"Ewww," I say. "You're not my type," I sassily reply.

"Don't worry, I like mine sober."

"What's that supposed to mean?"

She stares at me for a second too long, then turns to continue talking to Edgar. He grabs my shoulders to swing me around so he can look at me. "Be nice to her. If you complain, or she tells me you've been a bitch, you know what I'm not giving you anymore of."

My shoulders sink at his warning. "Okay," I respond.

"Now, go with her."

I follow the woman and promise myself not to say anything to her at all. Regardless of what she says and does, I'm going to be quiet and be a good girl for Edgar, because he wants me to be.

She takes me into a room and closes the door. Her face is impassive, and somewhat bored as she eyes me. "Strip," she instructs me. I have no idea why, but I'll do it. Once I'm naked in front of her, she looks at my heaped clothes on the floor in disgust. "Get on the bed and lie on your back. First, put your arms over your head." I do what she wants. She wears gloves, and starts applying something warm to my armpits.

Closing my eyes, I make sure to remain quiet. I don't want to get in trouble with Edgar.

Rip!

Mother… that hurt like hell!

"Other arm," she says warning me she's about to do the same thing.

Warmth, a few seconds… rip.

Ouch!

"Keep your arms up, I've missed some."

I scrunch my eyes more tightly closed and get lost in my head. I don't want this. It hurts. But Edgar wants it, so I'll do it.

"Now your pussy."

What? She's going to wax my vagina? "No way," I say way too forcefully.

"Fine, I'll go out there and tell him you're not cooperating."

She steps back toward the door. "No!" I yell at her. "I'll do it."

"Lie back and open your legs."

It's not like I'm ashamed of my body. Actually, I really love it. I love how I feel when I'm touched, and when I have sex. It's spectacular. Everything inside me comes alive, from my nerve endings to my blood. My skin tingles with excitement, and my heart races when I'm having sex. It's the most satisfying thing I can do. I love being high and having sex. It's almost like an addiction.

Of course, I'm not addicted to either, but I love doing both.

I don't have a problem. I *can* stop anytime I want.

I feel the warmth of the wax, and I push past the anticipation of what's about to happen next.

Warmth, a few seconds… rip.

Ouch!

I cringe as the stinging feels like fire is touching the most sensitive part of my body. "I have more to do, don't move," she murmurs in a tone filled with disgust.

I want to get up and smash her for her hurting me. *She likes hurting you*, my brain tells me. I crank an eye open to see her smirking. Bitch, she does like hurting me. "What have I done to you?" I ask as she applies more wax on my vagina.

"Pardon?" She turns her head slightly to look at me.

"What have I done to you? You look like you're having way too much fun… " I move my eyes to where the wax is and add, "… down there."

"I'm just doing what I've been paid to do. You haven't done anything to me." She continues waxing me.

"Yeah, right," I grumble to myself. Bitch. She's trying to goad me into a fight. I will. I'll smash her if she continues pretending she's better than me. I lie back down, close my eyes, and try to push her out of my mind. Instead, I think about the party Edgar's going to take me to, and the reward he's going to give me for being a good girl in here.

I'm not sure how long it takes, but when she's done, I'm

totally smooth all over my body. Other than my mid-length brown hair, and my eyebrows, everything else has been waxed off. Everything. Every little bit.

Getting dressed, I head out to find Edgar sitting at a bench seat. The bodyguard is standing beside him, his arms crossed in front of his chest.

"I'm done," I chirp happily because I know I'm going to be rewarded for being good. And the reward will be delivered in a beautiful, clear glass pipe.

"Yes, I heard you behaved yourself."

The high of my last lot has been on the decline since that bitch started waxing me. But, I hung in there, behaving myself because I know what the prize will be.

"Now, when we get you back to your room, I need you showered. I'll place your clothes on the bed, and that's what I want you to wear."

The bodyguard is a few steps ahead of us, and he arrives at the car before us, opening the door. "Okay," I say to Edgar. I'm so excited. "What kind of party is it we're going to?"

"The best kind. You're going to have so much fun."

"Do I know anyone there?"

The door closes, and Edgar brings out the exquisite pipe. My eyes light up, and I know he knows he has something I want. "You'll know me." He chuckles, places a couple of shards in the bottom, and offers it to me.

"Thank you," I say. I inhale nice and deep, making sure the smoke touches every part of my lungs. The rush is alluring. The tingling starts from the top of my head, and surges all the way down to my toes. Like a floodgate that's been opened, the high flows in quickly, sparking every nerve ending awake. "Yeah," I mumble as I lie back, dazed and content.

I don't hear anyone talking, I don't even feel the car traveling on the road. All I know, is I'm airborne, and I love it.

"Hey," Edgar shoves me on my arm. Opening my eyes, I

know we're back at the motel, where my room is. "Let's get you inside, so you can get ready." He waves the pipe in front of me, it's a silent promise. Go with him, and I get more. *Yay!*

"Okay," I obediently reply.

He grabs hold of my upper arm, and leads me inside. The fat guy is gone, but another guy has taken his place. "Hi!" I wave to him. "I'm Hannah," I say as I giggle.

He looks me up and down, and scrunches his mouth at me. That makes me laugh even more. I'm not sure why, but his face is funny. A cross between a hamburger and the Roadrunner. But the Roadrunner was cute. I laugh some more. "What are you laughing at?" Edgar asks as we head down the hall to my room.

The moment we're in front of the door, I giggle even more. "Sixty-nine. That's so funny." I point to the lopsided six. "Get it... Sixty-nine." I lean into Edgar and kiss his neck. "Can we sixty-nine each other?" I whisper.

He opens the door with his key, and pushes me in. "Go for a shower, kitty. I'll have your clothes ready for you when you come out."

"Okay." I don't bother looking to see who's in here, I know Edgar's here, and I think the bodyguard too. Stripping bare, I leave all my clothes on the floor, and walk into the shower. Turning the water on, I get in and start washing myself.

It feels like I've been in here for a second, when Edgar barges in, rips the flimsy plastic curtain back and stares at me. "Will you hurry up, you've been in here for over twenty minutes."

I burst into laughter again. How funny. Twenty minutes. "Yes, sir, Mr. Bossy." I fake salute him.

He turns the water off, grabs a towel and wraps it around my body. "Hurry up," he snaps again.

"I'm hurrying." I giggle.

"Stop laughing, it's getting annoying." That makes me laugh even more.

"Shut her up, will you?" the bodyguard yells from in the

room.

"If you can be quiet until you're dry, I'll give you a special present," Edgar says.

"Yay, a present." I clap my hands like a giddy school girl. I purse my lips together, and pretend to zip them up. But the laughter inside wants to break out. Edgar roughly dries the water off me. I do my best not to laugh when the towel touches my vagina. It kinda tickles, in a good way, even though it's also sensitive from where I've been waxed. But I like it.

"Okay, you're done, now go get ready." He turns me and smacks me on the butt. I jump and giggle again. Heading into the room, on the bed, there's three things. "Is this what you want me to wear?" I point to the little bra and panties.

"Yes." Edgar takes his phone out of his pocket, and scrolls through it.

"Oh, can you get me a charger so I can charge my phone? It's dead." I look around the room for my phone, but I can't see it anywhere.

"What phone?" the bodyguard asks.

"Oh, I thought I had one." I shrug. "I don't know. Maybe I didn't bring it with me."

"You were a good girl in the bathroom. Would you like some more?" I turn to see Edgar holding the pipe.

"Just a little bit. Not too much." I'm still naked, but when Edgar offers you a treat, you take the damn treat. Man, this is so good. I love it. I suck in all of it, and grab hold of his hand so he doesn't take it away. "Little bit more," I say sucking in the last breath's worth.

"That's enough for now. Get dressed." He stands back to watch.

I feel myself stumble a step, but I catch myself before I fall flat on my face next to the bed. That would've been so embarrassing. I pull on the panties, the string goes straight up my butt crack, and I try to pull it out. "This is annoying," I say as I move on the spot. "Do I have to wear them?" I keep fidgeting because of the thin piece of material itching my butt.

"Yes, you do," his reply is definite. Which means, I have to wear them. "You'll get used to it."

I huff and try to stop pulling them out. Then I pick up the bra, and put it on. It's one of those push-up bras, it makes my breasts look plump and nice. "I like this. Can I keep it?" I ask as I fondle my breasts. I keep playing with myself, and Edgar's quiet, not having answered my question. I look up and see him staring at me. He's got a deviant smirk on his face. "What?" I ask. His eyes go to the bodyguard, and I turn to look at him, too. He's got an erection, and he's watching me. Then I turn back to Edgar and push my boobs out so I have a curve to my spine. "Do I look nice?"

"You are by far my greatest… " He intakes a sharp breath before he continues. "… girl," he finishes. "My greatest."

I giggle again. I'm not even sure what's so funny this time, but I laugh.

"She certainly is," the bodyguard says. "Good choice."

"Thank you," I reply as I wiggle my butt at him. There's a men's long-sleeved white shirt left on the bed. "Do you want me to wear this?" I ask.

"Yes, I do." I pick it up, put it over my shoulders and begin to button it up. When I get to the button above my navel, Edgar's hand stops me. "Just to there."

"Okay." I smile at him, happy to make him proud. "What shoes should I wear?" Not that I have a lot.

"These ones." Edgar holds out a box, and gives them to me.

"Where did they come from?"

"We bought them, today. Remember?"

My memory must be going, because I don't. Opening the lid to the box, I see a pair of really high heels. "I've never worn anything so tall before." They're red and strappy and are cute as hell. "You might need to walk beside me so I can hold on to you," I say.

"I will, don't worry."

Sitting on the edge of the bed, I slide the heels on, and fasten the strap on the side. They make my legs look long and awesome. "These are so cute. Did I pick them out?" I ask looking to Edgar.

"You did. You said you wanted them."

"Oh yeah, I remember." I don't, but that doesn't matter. Standing, I find my balance. It's actually pretty easy. I wobble a bit, but once I get the hang of them, I'm okay. "Are we going to your party now?" I ask, ever so keen.

"Yes, we are."

We head out, and once we get to the front desk, the hamburger guy looks up at us. He can't take his eyes off me. "How much?" he asks Edgar.

"How much for what?" I ask.

"Nothing, kitty. Just keeping walking." He shakes his head at hamburger guy and tightens his hold on my upper arm.

We get into the car, and Edgar pours himself a drink. "Can I have one?" I ask.

"No, but you can have some water." He opens a bottle of water and offers it to me.

"I'm not thirsty," I say. "But I would like a bit more of that pipe." I flutter my eye lids to him.

"No, that's enough for now. I need you awake, not overdosed."

"You're no fun." I sit back and cross my arms in front of my chest, pouting like an infant who's about to throw a tantrum. "I'm not going to overdose, because I don't have a problem," I reply with considerable snark.

"I'll give you some when we get to the party. And while we're there, you can have as much as you want."

A smile spreads across my face. *Yay!* "Okay."

Leaning my head back against the leather seat, I close my eyes and look forward to an awesome night.

"A promise is a promise. Here you go, kitty. Now, promise you'll come back to me when you want some more."

I open my eyes to see Edgar offering me the pipe. "I will," I say before guiding the pipe toward my lips.

"Good girl."

Once I've gotten the highest I've ever flown before, Edgar opens my door and takes my hand. "Wow, you gave me more than normal."

"I want you super relaxed for this. Just have a lot of fun. And do whatever you feel like doing."

"Whatever?" I waggle my eyebrows at him. "Or should I say… whoever?" I laugh at my joke. But this is real, I'm so turned on right now, I think that if Edgar just touched me, I'd be exploding with pleasure.

"Whoever, and whatever."

I look at the house. It's not as big as the one from that other party we went to, but it's still pretty big. It's nice and neat on the outside, with gray siding, and big white windows. There's another four cars here, and a big black people mover too. "There's not many people," I say looking at the cars.

"This is a more intimate party," Edgar says and gives me a kiss on the cheek. "Now, you can take off the shirt if you want." I unbutton the shirt, and he takes it from me, slinging it over his arm. "I love you, Hannah," he says. This makes me smile even more.

The door opens, and we're greeted by a really handsome man. He's older, maybe in his early thirties, and he's wearing just jeans with no shirt. His chest is rippled with muscles, and he has a tattoo over his heart. "Cute tattoo," I say as I reach out to touch it.

"You're friendly." He looks to Edgar, "This'll work well." He gives Edgar a small nod.

I don't know what's happening, all I know is I'm super horny and I can't wait to get Edgar alone. Hell, even in front of everyone. I don't mind.

"This way," Edgar says as he takes me by the hand and leads me toward the back of the house.

At the back, there's a huge open room, with a heap of cameras set up. All of them are pointing in different directions. There's a sofa, and beside it, over a bit further, there's a giant bed that's made up to look all pretty with pink and white bedding. There's also a fake kitchen with a dining room table and chairs. "Oh!" I say as I gravitate toward the pink fluffy bed. "What's happening here?" I jump on the bed, and giggle as one of the pillow ruffles tickles my nose.

"We've got a few friends coming over, I hope that's okay?" the guy who answered the door says.

"Yes! I love making new friends," I say. "Do you have a pool?" I sit up in bed and cross my legs.

His eyes go directly down between my legs. "Nice," he says and turns to Edgar smiling. "She'll do really nicely."

"I told you," Edgar proudly responds.

"You told him what?" I ask Edgar.

"I told him how pretty you are."

"Thank you."

Just then, another girl walks in. She's got long blonde hair, and she's wearing only a tiny thong. She's got nicer boobs than me, and I feel like I'm ordinary in comparison to her. A guy walks in behind her. He looks scary. I don't like him. But I like her. She's pretty, much prettier than me.

The guy and Edgar shake hands, and she walks over to me. "Hey," she says in a bit of a slur. She touches my hair, then gently strokes her hand down my face.

"Hi. I'm Hannah. You've got such nice boobs." I reach up to

feel them.

"They were a present from Charles." She points to the guy she came with. "He wanted me to get them, so I did." She leans down and her blonde hair falls into my face, it smells so nice. "He paid for them." She starts to laugh.

I can't help but start laughing too.

"Okay, girls," the guy who answered the door starts. Both me and the other girl turn to stare at him. "Ginger, this is Hannah, Hannah this is Ginger. And I'm Nate. There are a few more people coming a bit later on, but for now, why don't we get to know each other?"

"Edgar," I call.

He's standing by the sidelines watching. "What is it?"

I just smile at him. "I love you," I say.

"I love you so much it hurts." The smile on his face tells me this is true love. "Will you get to know our new friends?" I nod my head eagerly. "Do you want a bit more?" He's already taking the pipe out of his pocket.

I want to say yes, but I'm not feeling like I should have any more right now. "Not yet."

"Okay, it's here for you when you want some."

"Can I have some?" the girl asks.

"Ginger, you've already had yours. Don't be greedy," Charles says.

"Yes, sir." She smiles at him like she's seen the first rainbow of the year.

"I'll give you something else a little bit later."

"Okay." She turns back to me, and starts playing with my hair. "Have you ever done heroin?" she asks me. While gently dragging her fingers through my hair.

"No way. I don't want needles. That's too hardcore for me." It's all over if I start doing needles. "Besides, I don't like needles. They're scary."

"Oh, my God, you should try it! It's the best feeling ever." I look at her arms, and notice the lack of track marks. She notices me looking and says, "Charles doesn't let me inject on my arms. I have to do it between my toes. It's different."

A small moment of clarity beams through so forcefully that I actually pull back from what's happening. For a second, a moment in time, I turn to look at Edgar who's talking to Charles. He gazes at me, and notices something different in me. "What's wrong?" he asks as he comes over and sits beside me on the bed.

"What's happening here?" My high is beginning to crash, and fast. I'm hurtling toward rock bottom, somewhere I don't like.

"We were invited over to hang out with some new friends."

I look at the girl, Ginger, and notice she's kinda high. "But what am *I* supposed to do here?" What is happening inside my head? A whirlwind of emotions is taking over. "Why am I here?" I stand from the bed. Confusion is the strongest of emotions coming through.

"Kitty, come here." He hugs me close to his chest. This feels so nice. "I know what you need." One hand falls away from the small of my back. It disappears into his suit pocket, and he brings out the pipe. "This'll make you feel better."

"What? No, it won't." *Just have a bit, you just need a small amount and you'll feel heaps better.*

"Not even a little bit. Look." He shakes a crumb of a rock into it. "It's not a lot, just enough to take the edge off. You're nervous about making new friends. That's all this is."

Oh yeah, that's it. Makes sense. "I don't know," I say skeptically. He's right, it's just that I don't know who Ginger is, and her boyfriend doesn't look very nice. "He scares me," I whisper to Edgar about Charles.

"Oh, kitty. Charles and I have been friends for years. He won't hurt you."

I peer around his shoulder to Charles, who smiles as he's staring at me. "You sure?" I ask.

"Here, let me introduce you." Edgar turns me around, and Charles hasn't moved. "Charles, this is the love of my life, Hannah. You're not allowed to hurt her, or you'll have me to deal with."

Charles does a double-take toward Edgar, then nods and smiles. "I wouldn't dream of messing with your number one girl."

"See, kitty. He won't touch you, 'cause he's too scared of me."

"That's right," Charles echoes from behind. "Besides, I know how much he loves you."

Everything settles down, and I feel happy knowing Edgar's always going to protect me. God, I love him so much. "Okay," I say in a small voice.

"Now, you know what would make me so happy?" Edgar says in a kind and gentle voice.

"What?"

"If you have a little bit of this and go over there and talk to Ginger and Nate. There's also going to be someone over there taking some pictures. Is that okay with you?"

Awww, he's asking my permission. How sweet. "Will it make you happy if I do what you want?"

"It'll make me so happy that I'll stay with you tonight."

"You will?" I ask with so much enthusiasm. "Do you promise?"

"Of course, I promise. I love you so much, Hannah." He offers the pipe again. This time, I take it and smoke it. "You're such a good girl. Now, Nate, why don't you come over here and make Hannah feel comfortable?" Edgar offers my hand to Nate. He saunters over to me, the top of his jeans are unbuttoned. There's a small trail of hair leading down beneath the jeans.

"You sure are beautiful, Hannah. Ginger was just telling me how gorgeous she thinks you are."

"Really? I'm ordinary compared to her."

He leans down, and whispers in my ear, "But she's a junkie. You're not and that makes you so much more desirable than her."

Something inside me snaps. My erotic need takes over. All my nerve endings spark alight, my heartbeat increases, and I become the wanton girl I love being. I push him down on the bed, undo his zip and pull his jeans all the way down. Straddling his hips, I sink down on him.

Ginger, moves so she's over his face, and we begin to kiss.

Yeah baby, this is what the pipe feels like.

Bliss.

Chapter 17

THE DAYS HAVE BLURRED TOGETHER, AND I'M NOT SURE WHAT DAY it is. Or month. I have no idea.

I open my eyes, and a hunger burns inside me from the moment I wake. I know Edgar said he'll be here early today, because he has another party for us to go to. I hope he'll be here soon, because I need the pipe.

Scrubbing my hand over my face, I go to the bathroom to take a shower. Hopefully, that'll wake me up a bit. Turning the water on, I feel for the temperature. It's hot against my skin. Man, I feel like crap.

Once finished, I go over to brush my teeth. Edgar told me my mouth has been stinking really bad, so he hasn't been kissing me. I want to try and not have bad breath, so I've been brushing as often as I can. Looking in the mirror, I notice how my face is covered in acne. I've never had so many pimples in my life. Even before I get my period. I've never had such horrible skin. I don't get why.

My face is starting to look gaunt too. My eyes have sunken in, and my angry skin does nothing for my looks. Because I've lost a ton of weight, I can now fit into size zero clothes. Not that I like clothes. They scratch against my skin. I'd rather be naked then have something on me.

I finish looking at my ugly face, and go to sit on the bed.

My stomach is hurting. My lungs feel like they're about to collapse and I catch myself shaking. God, I hope he hurries up.

I get up and start pacing. I don't have a key, so I can't even go outside without locking myself out of the room. "Screw it," I say to myself.

Getting dressed in some tracksuit pants, and a t-shirt, I slip on my runners and head out the door. I know Edgar will be here soon, so no use in trying to prop it open.

I hurry past the guy at the front desk, the fat one, and try to look as inconspicuous as possible. "Hey," he says as I start to run. "You know he won't be happy," he calls after me.

I turn and give him the finger.

When I've run as fast as my legs can carry me, I find myself out on the busy thoroughfare. There are a few stores lining the road, nothing too fancy. A corner store, a laundry, and a few small burger places.

My stomach rumbles, but the blood pulsating through my veins has a bigger thirst. Something I can't legally buy. Problem is, even if I could buy it, I don't have any money. Edgar doesn't give me any, and I've never really thought to ask. I suppose I better ask him for some, in case I need it. Like now.

I want both food and the pipe. The pipe more.

I walk along the street, trying to think how to get money so I can buy some… things. I can't call my parents, because I don't even know where my phone is, I can't remember bringing it with me. I don't know, that's all kinda hazy. I don't have anything I can sell at a pawn store, the only things I can do is either steal or sell myself, and neither of those are an attractive option.

I walk past the corner store and look inside. They have some fresh fruit, like bananas, apples, and oranges. It's not busy, which means I can't waltz in and try to take one. I turn around, and stare inside.

I'm really hungry.

"Ugh," I mumble to myself. I don't want to steal. But, I might have to. I don't know how long it's going to be before I see Edgar for some food, or the pipe.

"Hannah, is that you?" I turn toward the deep voice, and a police officer is standing in front of me.

"Yeah, who's asking?" I snap.

"I met you a few weeks back, just over there. Remember?" He steps closer, and I back up.

I stare at him for a moment, then another, before I begin to piece together the blurred memory of meeting him. "Oh yeah, um... Marvin?"

"Close, Martin." His suspicious eyes cast a gaze down my body, then back up. "Are you okay?" he asks. "You look like something's bothering you."

Duh, Einstein. I need the pipe. "I'm just a bit hungry." I rub my hand up and down my arm. My skin hurts. How's that possible? For your skin to physically ache. It's so tender, that touching it is making me hold in the screams.

"Do you need something to eat?" He steps closer.

"I just need some money to buy food." Yes, maybe I can get enough from him to buy some rocks. Yes!

His skepticism doesn't ease up. He's still staring at me. *Just give me the damn money already.* "Let's go buy you something to eat." He steps closer to me as if he's going to walk me somewhere.

"No, it's okay. I'm sure you're busy. If you give me the money, I'll go buy something." Come on, buddy. Take the hint.

"Hannah, I'm not handing over the cash I've worked hard for so you can go and smoke it, or inject it. I'll buy you something to eat, but I'm not supporting your drug habit."

I laugh out loud. "Goes to show what a great cop you are, because I don't have a drug habit."

"Really?" he says as he places his hands to his hips in an intimidating stance.

For a second, I retreat into myself. But I don't have a drug habit. I don't have a problem. "Yes, really." I mimic his stand.

"Is that why you're virtually a skeleton? Your skin looks infected. Your hair is mousey and limp, and your eyes have no sparkle to them. Is that because you're not an addict? I can help you, Hannah. Get you the help you need."

I laugh again. "You're a joke." I shake my head at him. "You think you know me. Well guess what? I don't have an addiction. I'm just hungry." I step closer to him.

"You're a drug addict. In just the few weeks since I first saw you, you now look like death warmed over."

"I'm not a drug addict!" this time I scream it so loud, it brings attention to us by the few passing pedestrians.

"Do your parents know where you are? I'm sure they're sick with worry."

"You wanna save the world? Start with someone who needs saving. I'm fine." I turn on my heel, wanting to get out of here.

My hunger is increasing. And I can feel myself slipping into emotions I don't want to feel. Martin's making me mad, and without the pipe, I can't cope with what he's saying.

"Hannah," he calls and grabs my upper arm. Turning, I make my hand into a fist, and smash him on the chin. I don't even know what came over me, but I just hit a police officer. Before I can get my head around what's happening, he's got me in handcuffs and is reading me my rights.

"What are you doing?" I shriek at him. There's a crowd gathering which makes my blood boil. "Let me go!"

He's pushing me down the road and from one of the stores, his partner comes out. "What did this one do?" he asks with a short, yet impassive tone.

"She hit me."

"Assaulting a police officer. I see a jail stay in her future," the other one says with a smirk.

"I won't do it again. I'm sorry. I'm just hungry... I don't know what came over me," I beg for leniency. "Please. Please. I'll just go back to my room."

Martin's now in front and has a grip on my shirt, the other guy is holding the handcuffs behind me. "I'm taking you back to the precinct," Martin replies.

"I'm sorry." I burst into tears. I don't want to be arrested. "I'm really sorry. Please, don't do this."

We get to the police car, where Martin opens the back door, and pushes me in, placing his hand on my head to make sure I get in safely. For a police officer, he's fairly gentle. The other guy though, he looks like he's over it and over me.

"Please, I'll be good."

"Shut up," the other cop says as he closes the driver's door and starts the car.

"I'll... I'll... " I don't want to say it but I will if it means not going to jail. "Do you two like to party?" I say in a seductive voice.

Martin and the other guy look between themselves, then Martin slowly turns in his seat to stare at me. "You're willing to sleep with us both just to let you go?" I nod my head furiously. The driver shakes his head. Martin looks like I've stabbed his dog in the gut. "I'm going to do something I usually wouldn't do."

Finally, he's going to take me up on my offer. "Yeah," I say in a husky voice trying to make him excited.

"I'm going to find out who your parents are, and I'm going to insist they put you in rehab."

The hope drains away from me. He's going to send me back to them. They don't understand. "I'm not a fucking junkie," I spit toward him. I try to move my arm so I can hit again. If I'm going to jail, I may as well go for beating the shit out of this cocky bastard. But I can't move them. They're secured behind my back. "I fucking hate you. You're like everyone else."

"What? Trying to help by getting you clean?"

"I'm not addicted. I don't have a problem." I literally spit at him. Disgusting pig. I hate him so much.

"You can't see it because you're in the deep of it. But I can tell you, you're an addict. Your arms are clean, so I doubt it's heroin. Judging by your skin, and how bad you look, I'd say it's meth. Right?"

I attempt to sit back in the seat, proud of myself for spitting at him. "Filthy pig." But I can't sit back, not with the handcuffs biting into my wrists. I try and maneuver them off, maybe I can be a magician and wiggle out of them. Then I can make a run for it when they get me back to the police station.

But I can't make them budge. If anything, they're getting tighter.

"This will be the best thing for you, Hannah," Martin says as I fight the cuffs.

"How would you know? You're probably from some rich family who loves you."

"You have no idea where I've come from and what I've gone through. You'd best not speak unless you know all the facts."

"Great, send me back to *them*." The them is my parents. "You have no idea the huge mistake you're making."

"Why? What's so bad about your parents?"

I can't go back there. They won't understand how much I love Edgar and how he looks after me. They'll treat me like a kid, and God damn it, I'm not a kid. I'm a woman, someone Edgar loves and cherishes. "My father beats me," I say without a quiver to my voice. "And my mom, she tried selling me to her boyfriend for sex. Yeah, great family."

"Your parents are divorced?" he asks.

Oh shit, I just lied again. Shit, I have to follow through with this. "Yeah." My voice trembles. "And they don't have time for me. Dad has a new girlfriend, and he hates me, and Mom is the drug user, not me." The rest of the lies follow so easily. Too easily. "I'm not going back there."

"Well, I can tell you right now, you're under age. And unless you have a relative who can come down and bail you out, you'll be going to jail."

I don't want my parents here. There'll lecture me, and tell me how disappointed they are in me, and that Edgar is a bad influence. They'll try to stop me from seeing him, and they'll put me under house arrest. "Call my grandmother, she'll come and get me."

The car rolls to a stop at the police station, and Martin helps me out of the car. Regardless of the fact that I spat at him, he's still being gentle with me. He takes me down a cold, long hall, and pulls me into a cell before he closes the door behind the both of us. "Who's your supplier, Hannah?"

"My supplier? I don't have a supplier. And as I've told you, I *don't* have a problem. I *can* stop any time I want."

The shakes are setting in, and my stomach is roiling with nausea. "I might be a while calling your grandmother. Which means, you're going to start hurting soon, if you're not already."

"Why are you doing this? Do you get off on locking up pretty young girls?" I smirk at him, knowing how good I look.

"To me, you look like a junkie. There's nothing pretty about you. Not now. But there can be, if you get clean."

"I'm not a junkie," I say through a clenched jaw. "I told you already."

He nods his head, and his face mellows. He looks like he feels sorry for me. "Tell me about whoever gives you the drugs."

"There's nothing to tell. He loves me."

"Of course, he does. That's why he keeps giving you more drugs. Does he ask you to do anything for him?"

"Like what" I ask with clear distain. "He doesn't ask me to do anything."

"Does he ask you to have sex with other people."

I lean in and whisper, "He doesn't have to ask, I love doing it."

He shakes his head again. "You're not in too deep yet, Hannah. You can get out of this before you end up dead. Or with some disease you can never get rid of. At this moment, you're a statistic, and not a good one."

"Fuck you," I say to him, roll my eyes and look away. "You have no idea about me, but you're all for judging me. Isn't that a bit of a double standard, considering you told me not to do that to you?"

"Really?"

"Whatever, just leave me alone."

He stands and makes his way out of the cell. He then instructs me to stand, turn around and back up to the bars, where he takes the cuffs off my wrists. "And by the way Hannah, the only thing I've believed that's come out of your mouth, is that your name is Hannah. Everything else I know is a lie. Your father doesn't beat you, your mother hasn't tried pimping you out. You've probably got good parents who are worried sick about you. I bet if you call this boyfriend, and call your parents, your parents will be here in a heartbeat, but the boyfriend won't. He doesn't care about you. To him, you're probably a commodity, and nothing else."

"Goes to show how much you know, because Edgar, loves me." I stroll back to the bench seat in the cell and sit down. "Call him, get him on the phone. He'll be here so fast. Unlike my parents."

"The biggest shame about this is not how you think other people see you, but it's how you see yourself." And with those words, he leaves.

I hate him so much.

But one thing he's said is a hundred percent true. I'm hurting. And soon, I'm going to need a small hit from the pipe so I stop hurting. Just a little one. Not too much. Because I'm not an addict.

I can stop anytime I want.

I just don't *want* to.

Chapter 18

"Sweetheart!" Mom cries when she sees me. She steps in for a hug, but I push her away. "You look so different."

"Hannah?" Dad mumbles as he stands back, assessing me.

"Yeah, whatever." I roll my eyes and push past him and Mom. "Have you paid my bail, or what?"

"We did. But, what's happened?" Mom asks.

"I'm just living my life. Sorry if it disappoints you."

Mom gasps, and tears fill her eyes. "I'm concerned and worried."

"Whatever," I say again. Martin is standing beside my parents, he has a smug look on his face. "Can I go, or what?" Pain is torturing every part of me. My skin is so sensitive I feel like it's about to erupt into flames. My eyes hurt. Even my hair hurts. I've never felt so much pain in my life as I'm in right now.

"No. You have to go to rehab before your appearance at court."

"What? That's bullshit, and you know it. You tried to grab

me, and I was defending myself. And we all know I don't have a problem. So why do I need to go to rehab?"

"Thank you, Officer York, we'll get her into rehab first thing tomorrow morning. But tonight, she needs a shower, and something to eat. Thank you, again." My Dad shakes his hand, and then Mom does too.

"I don't want to see you like this again, Hannah."

I roll my eyes and make a gesture that mimics jerking off. "Whatever." Then I stick my middle finger up at him.

"Hannah!" Mom scolds.

And this is the reason I don't want to go back to their house again. I don't fit in there anymore. I can't express who I am with them trying to crush me.

Dad goes ahead, and by the time Mom and I are out the front door, Dad's pulled the car around. Mom opens the back door for me and I slide in. I'm already formulating a plan to get out. I just need to call Edgar to come and get me. He'll be worried sick about me. I know I'm stressing out because I'm worried about him and what he's going through.

Dad and Mom are talking in the front, and I'm holding on to the hope of seeing Edgar. It's bordering on exhausting listening to these two idiots go on about how much they missed me, and how everything's going to be different now I'm home.

The darkness outside tells me I've been in the jail cell for too long. The shakes and the sweats confirm it. I need the pipe. Just a little bit. Not enough to get me high, just enough to get me through the next few hours.

When they go to sleep, you can sneak out.

Perfect, I'll wait 'til they're in bed, and leave. Wait, I need money in case Edgar doesn't want to come pick me up. I know he loves me, but he does have a life other than me. I'll get some cash out of Mom's purse. I've done it before, I can do it again.

Yep, wait 'til they're asleep, take the money, and run. But how will I call Edgar? I'll take Dad's phone. He usually leaves it out on the kitchen counter charging overnight.

The car pulls into the garage at home, and I drag my feet heading into the house. "Do you want to take a shower?" Mom asks.

"Why? Do I stink?" I retort sharply.

"Hey, don't speak to your mother like that. She's just asking if you'd like a shower."

"We're so happy to have you home," Mom says as she sidles up next to Dad. He hugs her, and I roll my eyes at how fake they are.

"Really? You two are going to stand there and pretend everything is all 'happy family'?"

Dad narrows his brows, and Mom tilts her head to the side. "What are you talking about?" Dad asks.

"Yeah, you're going to pretend you don't have a gambling addiction." Dad's face looks puzzled. "And you're going to tell me you're not screwing around behind Dad's back. But yeah, I'm the one with the problem." I stomp down the hallway toward my bedroom. "Great fucking family we have! A gambler and a whore. No wonder I ran away." I slam the door to my room and pace inside it.

Looking around my old room, even this nauseates me. Everything is so bland. The bedding, the walls... everything. "Ugh, no wonder," I mumble to myself.

"Hannah, come out so we can talk." Dad knocks on the door.

"Go away. I want to be left alone. Don't you get it?"

"No, I'm not going anywhere until you come out and talk to us."

Shit, if he doesn't go anywhere, that means I can't make a run for it tonight. Okay, you can do this Hannah. Tell them what they want to hear, then when they're asleep, you can get out of here. I pull my shoulders back and open the door. "Fine, talk."

"Come to the kitchen. We can have something to eat and drink."

I just need the damn pipe. That's all I need. Nothing else. But remember, tell them what they want to hear, put them at ease, and you can get to the pipe. "Fine." I close the door behind me, and follow Dad into the kitchen, where Mom's already made me a sandwich. There's a glass of juice beside the plate. She has a mug of coffee for herself, and one for Dad. I sit in front of the plate, and stare at it. "Thanks," I mumble, even though I don't pick it up to eat it.

"Where have you been?" Mom asks once we're all seated.

"At a friend's."

"Do we know this friend?"

"Nope." I pick half the sandwich up and nibble on it. If I eat, I can't answer their stupid questions, and it'll take my mind off the pain.

"Hannah, you've been gone for nearly two months. We've been everywhere trying to find you. We even filed a missing person report. That's how they found us when you were arrested."

Huh? Wait, that's right, I didn't give Martin their phone number. Oh man, I must've been seriously messed up if I can't remember that. "Whatever. I'm back now. What do you want?"

"We want you to be accountable for your actions. You might end up going to jail because you punched a police officer in the face. Do you know how serious that is?"

"Whatever." I shrug.

"You're saying that a lot. Don't you even care?"

"Why would I when he was trying to molest me? I had to punch him to get him off of me."

Mom sighs and looks to Dad. "We know what happened, and that's not the truth."

"Yes, it is!" I shout at them. "You believe everyone but me." I shake my head and cross my arms in front of me. "This is bullshit. You're full of shit."

"Stop that." Dad slams his hand on the table, it makes Mom

and me jump. "Can't you see what you're doing to yourself?'

"Me!? That's a laugh, coming from you." I stand and tip my chair over in anger. "And don't bother trying to stop me. You may have hit me before but I won't let you lay a hand on me again," I scream at Dad while pointing my finger in his face.

"Hannah, what are you talking about? I've never hit you."

"Really? How convenient that you forgot the time you punched me in the side of the head because I didn't get your coffee to you the moment you woke up. And you... " I stare at Mom, "... you're just as bad as him. You tried to molest me when I was in the shower. You're both scum. At least Edgar loves me. You two, you're pathetic." I run to my room and slam the door shut.

Cowards and liars. That's all they are.

I can hear Mom crying from my room. I don't even feel bad. Why should I? They've tried doing some horrible things to me, and they want me to feel bad? No way. Not gonna happen.

I grab a change of clothes and go for a shower. The hot water on my skin is irritating. I hate the pain I'm feeling. I can't wait to get out of here. These people are liars and not good people.

When I finish in the shower, I open the door to find Mom standing out in the hallway. "What do you want?" I grumble as I walk past her.

"I wanted to tell you that grandma passed away last month."

Turning to look at her, I notice how she's in dark clothes. Tears are spilling down over her cheeks, and she looks really sad. "She was old," I reply. "That's what happens to old people."

Mom cries some more. God, she's really turning it on. "Hannah, what happened to you?" she asks in a small voice.

"I woke up and got away from this house of hell."

I go straight into my room, and slam the door so hard, it vibrates the wall. I hate being alone, especially here. It reminds me of what I'm missing back in my motel room. Edgar lets me have a smoke of the pipe before he leaves, and that keeps me going until I see him again.

I start to pull my hair. "You're such an idiot. Why did you have to leave? You should've stayed where Edgar told you to stay, you wouldn't be here if you had." I tug on the ends of my hair and pull my fists back to discover tufts of hair in them. *You have to get out of here.*

Suddenly, I get a brainstorm. I can pack some clothes, open the window, jump out and run. But that still leaves me with no money. Or any way of getting in contact with Edgar. Worry overtakes me, he must be so anxious. I bet he's searching everywhere for me.

Packing, I keep listening to the voices talking in the kitchen. When I can't hear them anymore, I place my ear to the door to make sure they've gone to their room. I open it, and I can't hear anything except my own heartbeat in my ears, and the scream of the voice in my head telling me to get out of here and back to Edgar.

I poke my head out, still listening. They've moved from the kitchen and are now in their room. Good, this gives me a few moments to get out in the kitchen, take what I can and make a run for it. There's a small night light in the family room; it's giving me just enough illumination to see what I'm doing. I look around for Mom's purse, and see her bag sitting on one of the kitchen bar stools. I rifle through it, and find her wallet is missing. But my hand does touch something cold and metallic. I bring it out to find it's Grandma's engagement ring. Yes, I can give this to Edgar in exchange for picking me up. I just need Dad's phone. It's charging overnight on the counter, just like it always is.

Taking it off charge, I see it has three bars of battery. That's enough. I only need it long enough to call Edgar.

I stuff it in my pocket, along with Grandma's ring, pick my bag up, and sneak to the front door.

"See ya later, fuckers," I whisper, then giggle as I open the front door, close it quietly and run down the road.

When I'm a few streets away, I start laughing. Yes! I did it. I got out of there, and they have no idea I'm gone. Instead they were too busy in their room, probably having sex and not caring about me anyway. I could hear them talking, but that was probably noise of them having sex.

It's full dark now, and it won't be light for a long time. I need to get back before Edgar gets any more worried about me.

Dialing his number, I wait for a few seconds before he answers the call. "Yes," he snaps into the phone.

"It's me, Hannah."

"Where the hell have you been?" he roars into the phone. "You disappeared, and I had no idea where you were."

"I got arrested."

"What!" he screams louder. "Where are you?"

"I'm near my parent's house. Down past the bus stop. I'm so sorry I've worried you."

"Wait there, we're on our way."

He hangs up, and I burst into tears. I can't believe how worried he sounded. I'm so ashamed of myself. I vow to make it up to him any way I can. I hide behind a car parked in someone's driveway and wait for Edgar to come and get me. I keep peeping around every time I hear a car approaching. One car passes, and it's Dad's. He's driving slow, and must be looking for me. I'm never going back there again. Not after all the horrible things they've done to me.

I can't believe my Mom hit me tonight. She slapped me so hard, and then Dad pulled my hair trying to drag me inside the house. What is wrong with them? Why do they have to be so horrible?

Another car whizzes past, and I peek out to see if it's Edgar. It's not. *Hurry up, I miss you.*

I sit, cradling my knees, just waiting for the love of my life to show up. I hear another car approaching, I look out and see it's

Edgar's. I make sure no one else is nearby, then jump up, grab my bag, and run toward the car.

It stops abruptly, and the back door opens. I dive in so fast because I don't want my Dad to find me. The car takes off quickly, and the force of it makes the door close on its own.

"I'm so sorry," I cry when I see the anger on Edgar's face.

"Didn't I tell you not to leave your room?" I nod my head then drop my face in shame. "What have you been doing?"

"I got arrested."

"Don't lie to me, Hannah. Were you out hooking so you could get drugs?"

My head shoots up to look at him. The anger on him is fierce. His nostrils are flared, his jaw is tight and his hands are made into fists. "No! I promise, I haven't done anything like that. I love you, I wouldn't do that."

"Bullshit." He slaps me across the face. The sting of his hand shocks me. "How much money did you earn?"

"I didn't do that." I keep crying while cradling my face. "I promise you. Look… " I take out my grandmother's ring and give it to him. "My grandmother died, and she left me this ring. I was going to give it to you for looking after me."

He keeps turning it over in his hand. Gauging it from all angles. "Your grandmother died?" he asks in a calmer tone. I nod my head. "Oh, kitty. Come here." He shoves the ring in his pocket, then pulls me toward him. "Sorry, baby. I just missed you so much." He places gentle kisses on my head. "You just made me so mad. I was worried about you when you weren't in your room."

"It's okay," I huff in relief.

"When was the last time you had some?" He reveals the pipe, and instantly every part of me sings with joy.

"When you gave it to me."

"Oh, baby, that was yesterday. Here you go." He empties a few small rocks in the bowl of the pipe, and holds it out for me.

When I inhale, the high takes over immediately.

Yes, old friend. Here I am, in your company. God, I missed you so much. It feels so good being at the top. Flying so high I can almost feel the air rush beneath me. My body trembles, but not because I'm craving more. Because the rush is so great.

"Hannah, are you okay?" Edgar nudges me.

"Yeah," I say slowly.

"You've gotta get out of the car. We have to get you inside."

"Okay." I follow him out, not forgetting the bag of clothes I brought with me.

"When you called me, where did you call me from?" he asks.

"Oh." I begin to giggle. "I stole my Dad's phone."

"Do you still have it?" I try to focus on unzipping the bag I brought, but my hands and my brain won't coordinate. Edgar places his big palm over mine, and moves my hand away. "What's in here?' he asks gently.

"I brought some clothes with me. I think I stuck the phone in there too. You know, after I called you."

"I'll have a look when we get inside. Come on, kitty. I missed you today."

Aww, he's so sweet. He takes me by the hand, and has my bag in the other hand, and we walk past the hamburger-looking guy. I start laughing again, unable to stop. When we get to my room-room sixty-nine- I continue laughing. "That's so funny," I say as I collapse on the bed and stare up at the patchy ceiling.

"What's funny?" Edgar asks.

I turn to look at him. Why's he asking me what's funny? I'm not laughing. "Huh?"

"Never mind." He sits on the edge of the bed and unzips my bag. "What have we got here?" He takes out some clothing. "You brought this with you?"

"Hey, that's mine. Where did you get it?"

"You brought them with you. From your parent's house."

"Oh yeah, I did," I say remembering. Man, what's wrong with my brain? "I think I'm having a brain fart." I start to laugh again. "Brain fart. That's so funny. Like farting, but it's my brain." Edgar takes something out of the bag and slides it into his pocket. "Hey, what's that?" I ask.

"You know what I think you need?"

"What?" I ask sitting up on the bed cross-legged.

"I think you might need a bit more of this." He takes out the pipe.

"Yay!" I squeal with delight.

He places some rocks in it, lights it, and holds it out for me. As I'm inhaling, he's talking to me. "Tomorrow we'll need to go meet some people. I'll be here early."

"Can't you stay with me tonight? I miss you so much."

"I can't tonight, I've got some work to do. But, tomorrow I'll be able to." I give him a pout as I move to my knees on the bed and he stands to leave. "You're such a good girl. Now, don't leave until I come back in the morning."

"I won't. I promise." I cross my heart.

"Good girl. Try to get some rest, because tomorrow we're going to have a lot of fun." He pats me on the head.

"Yay!" I can't wait to see what tomorrow will bring.

He leans down and kisses me on the cheek. "Remember, don't be naughty, and tomorrow I promise to reward you."

"I love you," I call as the door closes behind him.

I hear him faintly replying, "I love you, too."

Oh, life is so good. What could go wrong when the world is so high?

Chapter 19

I DON'T FEEL WELL.

My stomach is rolling, and I think I'm going to throw up. Maybe I've been overdoing it lately. Edgar's been taking me to lots of parties, and I've been having the best time.

Since I ran away from home — for the second time — I've kinda been smoking the pipe a bit too much. Maybe, that's why my body is reacting this way today.

Edgar took me to another party yesterday, I was introduced to so many people, but I got to see Ginger again. Man, she looked wasted. She was so off her face, I could barely talk to her. But then again, we didn't need to do a lot of talking, we were doing other stuff. Edgar likes it when I'm with other men and women. He says it turns him on. He says he likes it so much, which is why he records it. I don't mind. I don't have anything to be ashamed of.

Oh, crap, my stomach. Yep, definitely going to throw up. Lunging up off the bed, I run to the bathroom and hug the toilet bowl. I must be coming down with something. I vomit another time, and then once more.

Standing, I flush the toilet, and wash my mouth out. Yuck. Spew. I hate being sick.

But surprisingly, I feel better once I've thrown up. I head back out to my bed, and grab the pipe Edgar's left for me. Last week he told me I'm now responsible enough to have my own pipe. But he still rations out how much ice I can have.

I think he was so worried he'd lose me if I left the room that he decided to leave me a pipe so I had no need to leave. It's only because he loves me.

God, I love him more than my own life. I'd literally do anything for him. *Anything.*

Lighting the crystals, I inhale and immediately feel so much better. I lie on the bed, letting the crystals take me wherever they want. "Oh man, this is the life."

Oh shit. I think I'm going to throw up again. I run into the bathroom, and repeat what happened a few minutes ago. Maybe I'm just hungry. I rack my brain, trying to think the last time I ate. I think it was yesterday, after Edgar brought me to that party with Ginger and that other girl... what was her name? I can't remember, but she was weird. Ginger and her got it going on, and Edgar had a camera there, recording them. I don't know.

Standing, I flush the toilet again, brush my teeth and go straight for the pipe. I need some more to get through this stomach bug I have.

I lay down, turn on the TV and flick through the channels. I'm spaced out, so nothing is catching my attention. I wish Edgar would hurry up and get here. I'm bored. And lonely. And I think I've caught something.

My eyes droop closed, and I'm dozing, bordering on sleep. The high from the pipe is quickly dwindling. But I also know I'm on rations. And I know I have to make this last 'til Edgar returns.

Oh crap, I'm gonna hurl again. I run to the bathroom, and

huddle over the toilet. I hear the front door open.

"Kitty?" Edgar calls. My head's in the toilet, vomiting. This is how he finds me. "Shit," he says.

"I'm sick. I think I have a stomach bug."

He turns to look at the bodyguard and gives him a small nod. The bodyguard is gone in a matter of seconds. "Get up," he says quite frustrated with me.

"Sorry I'm sick."

"Just get up."

Standing, I brush my teeth again, then head to my bed. He's pacing back and forth, while he's on his phone. I listen to the conversation. "Did you bring me some more? I think that's all it is. Or I'm hungry."

He turns his back to me. "Yeah, today's shoot is off."

What shoot? Who's shooting who? Does he have a gun? Can I see it?

"I think she's knocked up."

"Who is?" I ask.

"Stupid bitch."

"Who is?" I'm becoming more and more frustrated with him.

"Yeah, I've got someone else. She's not as good, but she'll do."

I wish I knew what he's talking about. Wouldn't be me. He loves me, and he wouldn't talk about me like I'm nothing to him. He hangs up, let's out another sigh and turns to look at me. "What's happening?" I ask.

"Nothing." His face is impassive but bordering on anger. "I can't stay long, I have somewhere to be."

"Oh, I thought we were going out today."

"I'm going out, you're staying here."

"Is everything okay?"

He runs his tongue over his teeth, and stands over me. "Not

really. But I'll make it okay."

I smile, happy to know he's going to make everything better. "Okay." I reach for the pipe again. He stands back, and watches me light it up.

"You need to calm it with that." He pointedly looks at the glass pipe in my left hand.

"Are you saying I have a problem?" I snap at him. "Because I don't. I can stop anytime I want."

He smirks at me. "Of course, you can. But I'm saying you need to calm it down before you overdose."

I roll my eyes and take another breath.

The bodyguard returns. His cheeks are pink, like he's been running, and he hands Edgar a package in brown paper. "What's that?' I ask. The bodyguard closes the door and stands in front of it. Guarding it. My gaze travels between Edgar and the bodyguard. "What's happening?"

"I need you to go and pee into this." Edgar opens the packaging and holds out a small cup.

"But I don't have to pee."

"Get up!" he shouts at me which makes me flinch. "Get up, now."

My skin covers in goosebumps, and my heart leaps into my throat. "Okay."

Tears brim in my eyes, but I stand and take the cup. "Leave the door open," he commands as he paces back and forth. I go and sit on the toilet and try to pee. I manage to get a few drops out. "Done?" He barges into the bathroom, taking the cup from me. Ewww, it's got pee on the side. But he takes it from me, not caring about the pee, and sets it on the counter. He places a white stick in it, grabs me off the toilet by the upper arm and pushes me out and onto the bed. "You better not be pregnant," he says to me through a clenched jaw.

"I'm not." How could I be?

He keeps pacing, and I'm too terrified of him to get up and

go hug him. The bodyguard has been quiet the whole time, but now he clears his throat. We both look over to him, then Edgar disappears in the bathroom.

"Shit!" he yells angrily.

"What?" I ask.

I look to the bodyguard, and he shakes his head at me.

"You're fucking pregnant." Edgar emerges from the bathroom.

"I'm what?"

His steps are long and deliberate. He comes straight to the bed, grabs me by the shoulders and pulls me up. He slaps me hard across the face. "You stupid bitch, you're fucking pregnant!"

"How?" I start to cry.

"Really? You're so stupid you don't know how the hell this happened?" He smacks me again across the face, then again with the back of his hand, and once more.

"Stop!" I cry as I try to cover my head so he stops hitting me.

"You're no longer a worthwhile investment for me, you stupid pregnant bitch."

"Stop, you're hurting me." He punches me in the stomach. I collapse to the floor and try to bring my knees up to protect myself. But he's angry, and his anger is driving him. "This is your baby!"

"We haven't had sex since I moved you here. You stupid, dumb bitch." He keeps hitting me. I try to move my hands to protect the parts he's striking, but if I move them to my head, and he lays into my stomach. If I move my hands to my stomach, his shoe connects with my head.

My crying is doing nothing to stop him. "Stop! Edgar, I love you!" I struggle to say as he keeps beating me.

"Edgar, enough," I hear the bodyguard finally say.

Edgar backs away from me. The pain throughout my body is

extreme and much worse than the pain from not having the pipe. Every part of me hurts. "You are by far my biggest disappointment," he says and spits down at me.

"We've got to go, we'll be late to the shoot," the bodyguard says.

Something lands next to my head, it's a small bag with a lot of rocks in it. "That should be enough for her to kill herself with," Edgar says.

I'm huddled, trying to hold my stomach, which is seizing in pain. My head is about to burst open, and there's a stabbing pain in my back. Every part of me is hurting. The pain is so extreme, I can barely move for fear that I'll tear open.

The door slams shut and I'm left crying and in pain. "Come back," I try to say. "Please, I love you."

I don't hear anything more. Instead, my body spasms with what feels like hot sharp knives being driven, over and over again, into every part of me. I'm hurting. No, it's more than hurt, it's agony.

"Please, Edgar." I try to reach for the bag he's thrown by my head, but my arms won't cooperate. The pain is on a level I've never felt before. Moving slightly, I look down and notice the blood seeping onto the ragged carpet. Something thick drips from my temple, into my eye, running down and across the bridge of my nose. "Help," I try to call. My voice is small. I'm losing the battle to stay awake. The pain is so great, I don't think I can cope.

Please…

Chapter 20

"FUCK, SHE'S STILL ALIVE," EDGAR'S VOICE SAYS. I CATCH A TONE OF disappointment.

"Look at her, you nearly beat her to death. What do you want to do?" I know it's the bodyguard. I can tell by the deep drawl of his voice.

I'm not sure how long they've been gone, but I do know I'm hurting.

My body is aching from how Edgar hit and kicked me. And I'm hurting because I can't get to my pipe. If I can have just a little bit, I'll feel so much better. Just one inhale. That's not unreasonable, is it?

"I'm not leaving her here; I need the room. I've got another girl nearly ready."

"Dump her?"

"Yeah, I think so," Edgar replies.

"You love me," I say as I try to hold onto hope.

"Did she say something?" the bodyguard asks.

"I don't know. But look at the mess she's made. What a joke. She lasted all of five months. I thought I'd have her at least two years before this shit happened."

"Should've gotten her fixed when she first got here. Then you would've had her 'til she died." The bodyguard laughs as if what he's saying is funny.

"Bring the car to the back exit, and open the trunk. I'll bring her out."

"On it."

I try to move my head so I can see what's happening. But as it turns out, I don't have to move much. Edgar squats down in front of me. He looks so handsome in his suit. His hair is brushed back, and his dark eyes are staring right at me. I blink and try to talk, but nothing is coming out of my mouth.

"I can't believe you, Hannah," he says and tenderly wipes a few strands of hair away from my forehead. "You've brought this on yourself. All you had to do was not get pregnant, and now… " His gaze travels the length of my body before he chuckles. "… well, let's put it this way, I highly doubt you're still pregnant. But you're also damaged goods. You're not worth anything to me now."

"I love you," I plead with him as a tear falls from my eye.

"My biggest disappointment to date." He shakes his head at me, then lifts his chin when he hears someone at the door. "What is it?" he asks.

"Sorry, I thought you were out. I was coming in to clean the room and get it ready for you."

"I won't be long." Edgar stands, and searches around the room. "Grab her pipe from over there," he instructs someone. I hear the footsteps, but don't know who he's talking to. Edgar grabs me like a rag doll and holds on to me. "Jesus, look at the mess she's made. Shit, I'll have to get the carpet replaced. Can you rip it up and burn it? There's too much blood for me to have it cleaned."

"Yeah, I can do that." The unknown guy walks past me, and I notice it's the hamburger guy from the front desk.

The door closes, and I'm carried down the corridor. Where's he taking me? I want to protest, but I'm so tired, not to mention the intense pain all over my body. I close my eyes and try to let the gentle motion of Edgar's walk soothe me.

It's not long before the cold air hits my body, causing my skin to erupt into goosebumps. "Cold," I moan in pain.

"Shut up!" Edgar spits toward me.

He heard me! Yay, he heard me. "Please, I'll be better. I won't get pregnant again, I promise I'll do better." I'm thrown with a thud, the back of my neck hits something hard.

"What's she saying?" the bodyguard asks.

"Who knows? It just sounds like mumbling to me. Like I care." I open my eyes and realize I'm in the trunk of the car. The trunk lid closes, and I'm surrounded by darkness.

The lullaby of the car's motion settles me. I'm not freaked out, or scared, I'm actually enjoying the solitude. Weird, huh? I should be terrified because I have no idea where I'm going, but I know Edgar will keep me safe.

But I do wonder why he has me in the trunk. I don't know. Maybe he's taking me to a surprise party, and he doesn't want me to see where we're going.

I don't know.

I wish he'd let me see a doctor. I'm really not feeling well. My head is thumping like crazy. I try to move, but my movements are restricted by the way I'm lying. My left arm is behind me, and my right arm is squashed under me.

The car finally comes to a stop.

The trunk lid opens, and both the bodyguard and Edgar stare down at me.

I smile at Edgar, like he's the sun after a long, difficult night.

"Look at her looking at you," the bodyguard says as he gently slaps Edgar on the shoulder. "She loves you so much."

Edgar shrugs. "She'll learn to unlove me."

What? "Don't you love me?" I say.

"It sounded like she asked you if you love her." The bodyguard chuckles again.

Edgar rolls his eyes, and steps back. "Just get rid of her. She's costing me too much in meth, and she's not worth it anymore." He leaves. A second later, I feel the car dip, and I know he's sitting inside.

"Right, let's get rid of you." The bodyguard leans in, grabs me under the arms and pulls me out of the trunk. He hoists me up and over his shoulders in a fireman's carry. "Thank god you're a skinny bitch." He walks a few steps and drops me to the ground. He retrieves my pipe, and a bag of rocks from his pocket and throws them by my head. "Good luck." And with those final words, he turns and walks away.

"Wait!" I try to yell.

I watch as the tail lights of the car become smaller and smaller.

Lying out here, I try to look around, but the pain is really preventing me from moving. The night is dark, and the stars are twinkling above. I want to get up and start walking, but there doesn't seem to be anywhere to walk to. Maybe, if I close my eyes, I'll wake up and realize this is all just a bad dream.

Yep, that's what it is. A nightmare.

Edgar would never leave me. He loves me. He told me he loves me. We're going to have this little baby, and we're going to be a happy family. I'm caught up in a nightmare, but it feels so real. I know it's not though.

When you wake, Hannah, you'll see how perfect life is.

Chapter 21

THE HEAT IS WHAT WAKES ME. OPENING MY EYES, I TRY AND MOVE. I'm in a lot of pain; everything is hurting. But thankfully it's not as bad as I imagined it would be. Slowly, I sit up, and look around me.

Beside me is my pipe, and a bag of crystals. Yes, I need that right now, because I have no idea where I am. What a crazy-ass dream I've been having. I take the pipe, open the bag, and pour some crystals into the bottom. There's a lighter in the bag, and I use it to get my first hit of the day.

I inhale deep and the smoke travels through me.

When the high takes over, I'm finally able to relax.

Looking down at my body, I notice that my shorts are drenched with blood around my crotch area. Lifting my hand to my face, I feel several places where I'm hurting. I try and not focus on the pain; the pipe will help with that. I just need to find a way to get back to the motel. I don't even know where I am. I can hear some cars, but there really isn't any other native sound.

Carefully, I stand, and start making my way toward the

sound of the cars. I'm in the scrub along the shoulder of the road, but not too deep. It doesn't take me long to get to the road's edge. I try to stay back, so the cars whizzing past don't see me. God, they'd probably call the cops if they saw me. I can't go back to Edgar in a police car. He'd lose his shit. I duck down behind some larger shrubs and have another hit of the pipe. It gives me the courage to keep going. I don't need it, I just want it. There's a big difference.

I try to stay behind the tree line so people don't see me, and I can't walk too fast either. The pain radiating through my body prevents me from moving fast. But thankfully, I have my pipe, and that helps me though when the pain gets too much.

I keep walking for what feels like days, but I know it's only been a few hours. The sun has passed from high in the sky, lowering closer to the horizon. I'm not sure where I can sleep tonight. I'll need to find somewhere. Considering I have no idea where I am, I'll have to make do with what I have. And all I have is my ragged clothing, a massive headache, a sore body, and my pipe.

As I continue stumbling through the scrubs, I step on something crunchy. It's a few pages from a discarded newspaper. Yes! I can try to find some more for warmth. The sun is setting, and it's getting darker, so I'm going to have to find more soon if there's any chance of me being able to get out of here.

I manage to find a few more sheets of newspaper, and I head further into the trees. I can still hear the cars, although a lot of them have disappeared now, probably because it's getting later. I find a small clearing, no bigger than a dining room table, and I try to gather some sticks.

I'm not a camper. I never have been, but right now my survival instinct is kicking in. As long as I can stay warm and safe, I should be okay.

I'm sure Edgar is sick with worry and probably out looking for me. I have to get back to him. I can't leave him alone. He'll be lonely and heartbroken without me.

Taking my pipe out, I check to see the residue on the bottom. It's not enough to keep me going all night, but at least it's enough for right now. Since I don't know where I am, or even how long it'll take me to get back to Edgar, I'm going to have to make this work.

Panic sets in. What if I get lost out here? What if I never get back to him? Oh my God! I should flag a passing car down and ask them to take me back to him. But I know other people aren't like us. They'll try to take me to the hospital or the police. Raking my hands through my hair, I rip the hair out as I try to contain my stress.

All the "what ifs" are killing my head. I can't deal with this. I load my pipe up and have another hit. Yes, the pipe makes everything better.

Edgar's the sweetest man ever. He really looks out for me, everywhere I am. I can't wait to see him again. The thought makes my heart warm, just knowing how much he loves me and looks after me. I wish every woman in the world had their very own Edgar.

I collect a pile of twigs and use my lighter to make a fire. I have no idea what I'm doing, but I just need to get through the night. In this instance, my pipe isn't going to be enough.

The fire isn't lighting. The twigs aren't catching. "Ugh," I grumble. I'm going to have to use a piece of newspaper to help it. I crumple the newspaper and stick it under the collection of twigs I've gathered. I light the paper, and hope it works.

By some miracle it does, and the twigs catch alight. At first the fire is angry and red, but it quickly dwindles down and I place a bigger branch on it to continue the heat.

I wonder what Edgar's doing right now. I bet he's searching the streets for me. He's probably not leaving any corner unsearched. "I'll be home soon, baby." I smile, and my body sparks with a nervous energy. I can't wait to see him. I'm going to run into his arms, and never let him go.

I sit staring at the fire, not really thinking about much other than Edgar. He's in every thought. Well, nearly every thought. The pipe is a close second.

As the night gets darker, and the temperature drops, I try to get closer to the small fire I've got going. It's the only thing I can do until it becomes light and I can start walking again.

Happiness feeds my soul. I'm hoping tomorrow is the day I get back to Edgar. I just need to get to my room, and I'm sure he'll be there, worried sick.

Opening my eyes, I know today's the day. Reaching for my pipe, I inhale a crystal, and it fills my body with warmth, and love. It's such a good friend to me. It never lets me down. It always looks after me. Exactly like Edgar. He's by far the best thing to ever happen to me. I just need to get home to him.

My body may not like it, but I'm going to push on and get back to my room. Standing, I see the fire has gone out, but I'm okay with that. I don't need it anymore. I follow the sounds of the cars whizzing down the highway, peek out from behind the shrubs and see a huge street sign up ahead. I walk toward it, being very careful not be seen. My entire body is aching. But thankfully, the pipe lets me escape the pain for a while.

I look down my body and notice the number of bruises I have on my legs and arms. I can only imagine how I look. But it's not how it looks.

I'm hazy how I got these bruises or how I got here, but it's okay. I don't need to remember. I just have to get back to Edgar. Once I do, I know everything will be fine.

I walk until I get to the huge sign, and sigh with relief. I'm not that far from the motel where my room is. I should be able to get there by sundown if I continue walking. But how will people react to my clothes being so bloody? What do I do? Ugh, this is annoying.

My feet are hurting, and the pain is returning everywhere else. I take a few minutes to have another hit of my pipe. It takes the edge off, and I know I can keep going with help from it.

I'm not exactly sure how far I've walked or how much further I have to go, but I'm getting thirsty. Near that big sign, there was a discarded bottle with some water in it, I should've taken it and drunk it. My mouth is parched, and my head is becoming lighter and lighter. I need water. I need something to drink.

I stop for a while and sit on a big boulder. I'm getting sorer and now I'm thirsty. But, I know I'm close to the motel. The trees aren't as dense, and there are more cars speeding past. I have to cross the highway and head toward the left, then I should be able to get to the bridge on the east side of town. Then all I have to do is cross the bridge, stay in the shadows, and the motel is only about another hour's walk from there.

"Okay, Hannah, you can do this," I say to myself.

As I cross the highway, I'm super careful that no one sees me. But a brilliant idea crosses my mind. Kristen lives close to here. I'll go to her house and ask to use her phone. Maybe she'll give me some money too.

Now, running on adrenalin, I try to move as fast as I can toward her house. I can't wait to see her. She's going to be so happy to see me.

I know it's out of the way from the motel, but I really can't show up looking like this.

I have to look good for Edgar. Have to.

Walking the streets, I finally arrive to Kristen's house. I fix my hair and straighten my clothes, and knock on her door.

I hear her laughing before she gets to the door. I know it's her. She opens it, and looks at me. For a moment, I don't think she's happy to see me. "Hannah?" she shrieks, staring at me.

"I've missed you," I say as I step forward to hug her, and she steps back.

"Oh, my God," she mumbles. Her eyes keep wandering my

body. "What has happened to you?"

"What do you mean?" I ask, suddenly angry at her judgement. She's looking at me like she's better than me. She's not. If anything, I'm better than her. I cock my hip to the side, and cross my arms in front of my chest.

"Hannah, you've been gone for nearly six months. And you've shown up now, looking like this?" She waves her hand over my body.

"What's wrong with me? Am I too hot for you, *Kristen?*" I spit her name with distaste.

She stares at me, shocked. "Hey, I'm worried," she says in a gentler voice.

I take a moment to stare at her and decide she's not a threat. "Look, can you lend me some clothes? I fell over and hurt myself, and I've been bleeding."

She looks my clothes over. Her eyes widen as they notice the huge bloody stain on my crotch. "Are you sure you're okay?" Her question has an underlying tone to it. I don't like it.

"Yeah, never been better. Look." I smile at her. Her sharp intake of breath drags me back to her shocked face. "What now?" I wanna smash her. She's looking at me like I'm shit.

"I'm so worried for you. You've lost so much weight; your skin is filled with scars. Your arms look like you've been clawing at yourself. Are you on meth?" she asks.

"Oh, now you're Little Miss Perfect? I'm not a drug addict. I *can* stop whenever I want."

She shakes her head at me. Tears sparkle in her eyes as she holds in a cry. "Who are you?"

"I'm Hannah, your best friend," I say with so much venom. Who does she think she is?

"That's not what I'm asking. And you know it."

"Look, can you give me some clothes, or what? And can I borrow five dollars?"

"Borrow? Like you've got any plan to give it back? Like your grandmother's engagement ring? Do you still have that?"

"What? What are you talking about?"

"What happened to your grandmother's engagement ring? Your mom called me, in an absolute state that you left the house, and stole her mom's engagement ring. Not to even mention you stealing your dad's phone."

"I've never stolen anything. Did they also tell you that Dad's a chronic gambler, and Mom's a whore? I bet they didn't tell you that. Did they also tell you they tied me to the bed and refused to let me go to the toilet? I had to pee on the bed."

"Hannah, everything you're saying has never happened."

"Really? I bet Dad didn't say he beats the shit out of me. How do you think I got these bruises?"

"You haven't been home in months. How's he been able to beat you?"

"You don't know anything!" I turn to leave, but remember I need some clothes. "Are you going to give me clothes, or what?"

"Of course, I am." I take a few steps toward her, but she shakes her head at me. "You have to stay out here. I can't have you inside."

"Kristen, what's going on?" Her mom appears at the door. "Oh, my God," her mom says when she sees me. "Hannah. What… ?" Her mouth is open as she stares at me. "What have you done to yourself?"

I roll my eyes. Great, another judgmental bitch. "Can I have the clothes?" I snap at Kristen, totally ignoring her bitch of a mom. She has no idea.

"Sure. Just wait." Kristen steps back, but her mom keeps staring at me. "Mom," she urges her to go back in the house.

"Want a taste? Twenty bucks," I say to her mom as I grab my crotch.

Her mom stares at me horrified, her mouth gaping even wider. "I hope you get the help you need, Hannah. For your own sake."

"Whatever," I spit at her as the door closes.

I can hear them talking, and I know they're talking about me. As I pace the front yard, I see someone peeking out the front window. I poke my tongue out and stick my middle finger up at them.

"She looks like shit. I bet she's hooking," I hear her mom say.

"Mom, she's probably blown half the state," Kristen replies, then laughs.

"More like all of it. I always thought she'd amount to nothing," her mom continues.

They both laugh.

The front door opens, and Kristen is standing there, holding a plastic bag. "Hannah," she calls.

I walk over to her, ready to smash her pretty face in. "I can't believe you think I've had sex with half the state!" I snatch the bag out of her hands, and rifle through it.

"What?"

"I heard you and your mom. She said she always thought I'd be a hooker, and you said I've probably had sex with half the state. I can tell you I don't hook."

Her face falls. "We didn't say anything like that? If you heard, I told Mom to call your mom and let her know you're here. Nothing else was said."

"Bullshit! Why are you lying? I heard you with my own ears."

"You heard wrong, Hannah. You must be hallucinating. I'd never say anything like that. I'm worried about you. You look terrible, like you've been on the streets and haven't had a shower in weeks."

"You know what? I'm the happiest I've ever been. Edgar takes care of me."

"Who's Edgar?"

"He's the father of my baby." I rub my stomach to show her

I'm pregnant.

She stares at me, then looks away for a second. "Hannah, can I take you to the hospital?"

"No! I'm fine."

"You're covered in blood and bruises. You need help."

"I don't have a problem, Kristen. But I bet you do." Turning I walk away from her. "Thanks for the clothes," I say as I flip her the bird. What a bitch.

"Hannah!" she calls. I stick my middle finger up further.

Heading to a nearby alley, I rummage through the clothes, and take out a pair of jeans and a t-shirt. Taking my clothes off, I drop them to the ground. Sliding the jeans on I zip them up, and notice how big they are on me. Man, Kristen has put on so much weight. These are barely staying on me. I dig around the pockets just in case there's any money in them. There isn't. "Ugh, stupid bitch," I yell toward her house.

Then I look in the bag and find a thick jacket, something I can wear when the temperature drops. She's also put in some tissues, and antiseptic hand wash. "What am I supposed to do with these? You could've given me money. God, you've always been so selfish."

I leave the plastic bag, the tissues, and the hand wash behind, and make my way back to the motel.

God, I'm so excited. I get to see Edgar soon. I can't wait to run into his arms, and give him a hug. I won't be able to run, because I'm still hurting, but I'm gonna try so hard.

I take my pipe out of the pocket of the jacket, shake a couple of rocks into it, and take a huge breath.

I'm coming, Edgar. I can't wait to see you.

Chapter 22

WALKING THROUGH THE STREETS AT NIGHT IS PRETTY SCARY. NOW I understand why Edgar didn't want me to leave my room. It was my safe haven, and he knew I'd be kept safe.

I know I'm going in the right direction, but my high is starting to fade. The jitters are setting in, and I'm grinding my teeth together as I walk. I have more crystals left, but I want to see Edgar as sober as I can. It's not like I have a problem or anything, but I want to get the full effect of how happy he is when he sees me. He's going to be so relieved. I can feel it in my bones.

"Hey," someone calls.

I turn my head to see a car crawling beside me. It's an old crappy car, and looks like it's been used in a ram raid. "Yeah," I say as I slow and face it.

"How much?" he calls out the window.

"How much for what?" I ask, perplexed.

"How much for a blow-job?"

"What?" I nearly yell at him. "I'm not a hooker."

"Come on, babe. No need to pretend," he yells and adds a laugh. "I promise, I won't tell on you."

"Screw you!" I stick my middle finger up and keep walking toward the motel.

"That's what I'm hoping for. A hundred should do it."

"For a blow-job?" I ask, suddenly stopping.

"Yeah, babe. Hundred dollars. And if you let me go bareback, then I'll throw in an extra twenty."

Am I actually entertaining this thought? No, I can't. Edgar would lose his mind if he ever found out. "I'm not a hooker," I say once more.

He shrugs his shoulders and drives off.

He leaves me alone, and this gives me the drive to keep going 'til I'm at the motel. But a hundred dollars, man, that could buy me a gram, and that could last me a couple of days if I'm really careful.

No, I can't bring myself to do that.

But… a hundred dollars. If I do two a day, then that's two hundred a day, and that could buy me an eight-ball, which could last a week if I'm careful. No… no… no. Edgar would be so mad. I can't do that to him, not after how good he's been to me.

I round the corner and see the long walkway to the motel. Yes, I'm nearly back home.

Entering the motel, the hamburger guy is at the front desk. He looks at me, looks away, then quickly turns his head back to me. "What are you doing here?" he asks.

"I'm going to my room," I snap. The low is really starting to take effect on me. I'm really angry, and in no mood for his shit.

"You don't live here no more," he says.

"What? That's bullshit. Call Edgar, I bet you he's worried sick about me."

"He's the one who got rid of you."

I burst into laughter. "Yeah, right." I shake my head at him. "He's probably worried about me. Call him." I stand with my hands to my hips.

He's already on the phone. "There's a problem," he says into the phone, not even trying to hide what he's saying. "The girl, she found her way back." He listens and nods his head. "Okay."

He hangs up, lifts his head, and smirks. "See, told you."

I turn to make my way down to the room, and he calls after me, "I was told to tell you to wait here."

I roll my eyes and stop walking. "Fine. But Edgar's going to kick your ass when he arrives. He loves me, and nothing comes between us." I place my hand to my stomach and start rubbing in a circular motion. "We're having a baby, and he's going to marry me. He said he's got a ring."

The guy nods but seems unconvinced by what I'm saying. "Yeah, sure," he grumbles.

"He loves me!" I shout. The anger is taking over, and I hate when I'm like this. I take my pipe out, and shake a bit more into it. I was hoping I'd be sober, but it's okay, I'm only having a little bit. Just enough to take the edge off. God, I hope Edgar arrives soon, I don't have much left, and I'm going to need some more soon.

"Stay there, and don't move." He points to the spot I'm at. I stick my middle finger up at him. What a jerk! The giggles take over. A hamburger jerk. Hamburger jerky. How funny.

I stand, staring at him, and he does his best to ignore me. I huff, and walk around the foyer, waiting for my guy to show up.

And I wait.

And wait.

And wait, some more.

"What the hell are you doing here?" His voice is my drug. It's the only thing I need. He's here.

Turning, I see him walking toward me. He looks so beautiful

in his tailored suit, a long black coat over it, and looking like the perfect Prince Charming. "Edgar!" He takes my breath away. He's my perfect.

"What are you doing here?" he says again. He reaches me, grabs me by the upper arm, and squeezing hard, starts dragging me out of the motel.

"Ouch, Edgar you're hurting me. It's bad enough I was beaten by my father, I can't have you hurting me too."

"What are you doing here?!" he yells in my face. Spittle hits my nose, as his hand tightens even more around my arm.

"I love you," I say.

The bodyguard is behind him, casually leaning on the car. "She has no idea. You have to break it down for her." He chuckles and shoves his hands in his pockets.

"We're going to have a baby." I grab his hand and put it to my stomach. "See? Can you feel this?"

"Man, she's a fucking idiot," the bodyguard says shaking his head.

"Don't talk to me like that!" I yell at the bodyguard, who's now laughing at me. "Are you going to let him get away with this? You love me, and you're letting *him* speak to me so badly?"

Edgar raises his hand and backhands me. "I'm going to tell you what you are to me."

My cheek explodes with pain, but I turn to look at Edgar with nothing but love in my heart for him. "Tell me, baby. Tell me how much I mean to you." My pulse quickens, and all I want is for us to live happily ever after.

"You've never been anything more than an investment to me. I saw an opportunity and took it. A cute girl with a hot body, nice tits and a pretty 'girl next door' face and I knew I'd make a ton of money on you. That's all you've ever been. An investment. But now you're a liability, and like any good businessman, I cut what costs me money without giving me a profit. And you're nothing more than a money pit. You've made me a lot of money, I'm going to start losing it all if I keep you around. And I'm not prepared for that."

Tears spring to my eyes. What is he saying? "But, I'm carrying your baby." I lift my hand to protect my unborn baby.

"You were pregnant, but I got rid of it. And even if I didn't, that ain't my baby, and that ain't my responsibility. Good luck with it. But you and I are nothing to each other."

"But you sent me flowers, and had him looking out for me." I point to the bodyguard.

Edgar laughs and shakes his head. "He wasn't looking out for you, Hannah. He was protecting my investment, making sure nothing came between me and my money. He looks after me, not you. He doesn't give a rat's ass about you."

"Couldn't give a shit if you live or die," confirms the bodyguard from behind Edgar. "I get paid to look after his assets."

Standing still, I blink at his words. No, he can't mean that. "I don't believe you. You love me."

"Words. That's all they were." He checks his watch and steps back. "Gotta go. I have someone I'm breaking in." He winks at me. "She has potential, but nothing like you did."

He steps further away from me toward his car. "Wait!" I call, trying desperately for him to come back. "I can do better. I can be anything you want me to be."

"What I want you to be is gone, never to return. You're worthless to me." He shrugs, then smiles. "Off you go. And don't bother coming back here because the next time, I'll dump you as a dead body." He flicks his wrist at me, as if discarding a piece of trash. He gets in the back of his car and the bodyguard closes the door.

"Wait," I try again.

"Here, this should be enough. Consider it your severance pay." The bodyguard tosses a bag of rocks at my feet. Not even a full bag. I bend to pick it up and stuff it in my pockets.

They leave, and I'm left completely alone, with nothing more than a bag of crystals and my pipe.

At least my pipe won't ever disappoint me. It's the only true thing in my life. What am I going to do?

My Dad beats me and my Mom tries to sexually abuse me. My best friend thinks I'm nothing but a cheap whore, and I have nowhere to go.

Crying, I turn and head out to the road.

What a night. But it's okay, because I know Edgar will be back. After all, he loves me. And we're going to be a family soon.

Chapter 23

"Is Edgar here?" I ask hamburger guy at the motel.

He rolls his eyes, walks around from the counter, and starts walking me out. "Even if he is, he's not going to see you." He huffs as he removes me again from the motel.

"But he told me last night he'll meet me here."

"No, he didn't. The drugs are screwing with your mind, girlie. He hasn't seen you in nearly a week. And he told you if you come back here again, he'll kill you."

I slap him across the face. "Edgar would never say that. We're having a baby together." I rub my hand on my concave tummy and hum in happiness.

"You have to go. If he sees you, he *will* kill you."

"You don't know what you're talking about. He came to me last night, and told me how much he loves me, and to meet him here."

"No, he didn't. And please, don't make me tell him you're here. I don't want to see you hurt." He pushes me out the front door, and points toward the end of the alleyway. "Please, leave." He's not angry with me, which makes me believe what he's saying is a joke.

"Okay, I'll leave." I turn and wink at him. "I'll leave forever." I wink again. "Be back later," I whisper to him pretending it's a secret. He knows Edgar loves me. He'll be so happy to see me.

The sun is shining, and the day is beautiful, so it's a great day to go for a walk. I'm really lucky 'cause my body hasn't been hurting me as much. Dad really did a number on me when he beat me. He was vicious, and I think if I didn't fight back he would've killed me.

I head down to the bridge I've been sleeping under and sit by the river's edge. At night it gets cold, but luckily, I've been collecting newspapers and keeping warm with them. There are other people who congregate beneath the bridge once the sun goes down, but I don't talk to them. They're all drug addicts or alcoholics. I don't associate with people like that.

"Hey," a girl says as she sits beside me.

I stare at her suspiciously. She looks terrible. Her hair is all limp, her face is filled with spots, and her teeth are nearly rotten. And, she smells really bad. "Hey." I discreetly move a few inches away from her.

"Have you got a pipe? Mine broke."

I cast a cynical stare over her. "Maybe but I don't got no rocks," I say. I do, but I'm not giving any to her. What I have is all mine.

"I got some from my dealer. Had to suck off a couple of guys for it." She holds out the small clear pack, and my eyes light up. "You can have some if I can use your pipe," she offers.

Sounds like a great deal to me. I've been really careful not to smoke all of mine, because I'm waiting for Edgar to give me more. "Okay." I stick my hand in my jacket pocket, and get the pipe and the lighter. "How much does your dealer charge?"

"The more guys I can service, the more he gives me."

"How many for that much?" I eye her little plastic sleeve.

"Three guys. I'm pretty good at it, so I can get them to cum within a few minutes."

"Yeah?" I ask intrigued.

"Yeah. Want me to set you up?"

"Nah, my boyfriend will be back soon. We're gonna be a family." I rub my stomach to show I'm pregnant.

"Yeah?" She takes my pipe, places a nice round crystal in the bottom, and lights it up.

My jealousy grows immediately.

I want to be able to smoke whenever I want, but until I see Edgar again, I'm going to have to be conservative. But hey, this chick is offering. I may as well have some.

"Yeah. I can't wait for this baby."

She inhales deeply and I yearn for it to be my turn. She hands me the pipe, and like a greedy child inhaling all the candies at a party, I light it up, and take the biggest breath I can. I use up the crystal in the bottom. There's nothing left, and I crave more. "Good, huh?" she asks as she lies back on the embankment.

"Yeah, I love this stuff." I lay beside her, flying from the pipe. "Don't you love it when you feel like you're up with the birds?" I watch as the clouds rapidly move through the sky. It's like they're playing with each other. Chasing the one in front. I start to laugh. The girl next to me laughs too.

I don't know what she's laughing at, but we both find nothing funny.

"Have you ever had heroin?" she asks.

"Nah. I don't do hardcore drugs. I sometimes have a puff from the pipe, but I'm not a junkie," I reply.

"You should try heroin. Man, the high it gives. I'd say it's better than this." She feels for the pipe, which I've already moved to the other side of me.

"I'd never do needles. Once you do needles, that's it, there's no turning back from it." I start laughing again. Not sure what's funny, but something is making me laugh so hard, I nearly have tears rolling down my cheeks.

"I'm Sky," she says as she moves to prop herself up by her elbows.

"I'm Hannah." I keep looking up at the sky. "I haven't seen you around."

"I just got here about a month or so ago. How about you?"

"I'm waiting for my boyfriend."

"You said that before." Did I? I can't remember having this conversation with her. "What's your boyfriend's name?"

"His name is Edgar. He's the love of my life. And he loves me, too." I add in the last part in case she gets any ideas about him. He's mine. And there's no chance in hell I'm going to share him with a skank like her. I'm sure she's nice enough, but she's also a junkie. And he's too good to be with a drug addict.

"I think I know him."

"No, you don't," I nearly scream at her. "You don't know him." I sit up, ready to smash her face in.

"Yeah, I know Charles and Ginger."

"Who?" Who's she talking about. "Who?" I ask again.

"Ginger. Really pretty. Charles was looking out for me for a while, but then I decided to leave. You know, I just wanted to be on my own."

It hits me, I know who Ginger is. "Oh yeah, Ginger. I know her. Charles scared me and I didn't like him. But I liked Ginger. I wonder if she's okay?"

"Yeah, Charles asked me to act in a couple of movies." She starts giggling. "You know, with Ginger."

How lucky is she. She got to be a movie star. "You're so lucky," I say dreamily. "I wish I could be in movies."

"They were fun."

"Yeah?"

"Yeah."

"Hey, how old are you?" I ask Sky.

"I'm seventeen, how about you?"

"Me too. But I turn eighteen soon. In like, six weeks. I'm hoping Edgar proposes to me. We're going to be a family. Did you know that?" I rub my hand on my stomach again.

"Yeah, you said."

I feel the urge to pee, so I stand and say, "I need to pee. I'll be back in a minute." I walk a few steps and hide behind a small shrub. Pulling down my jeans, the first thing I see is there's red in my underwear. "Oh no," I say. I pee, then stand and do my jeans back up. Walking over to Sky, I have tears in my eyes.

"What's wrong?" she asks.

"I'm spotting. I think I'll be okay. But I don't have any tampons."

"Sorry, neither do I."

"Wait, I have some newspaper, I'll use that." I head back to where I've been sleeping and find my newspapers and the bottle I've been using for water. I grab a sheet of newspaper, then head back to the shrub. Pulling my pants down, I line my underwear with the newspaper and then pull my jeans up.

"Hey, are you okay?" Sky calls.

"Yeah, I'll be there in a second." I walk down to the creek, squat and wash my hands in the shallow water. When I get back, I sit beside Sky and cross my legs. "I know this baby is okay. I'm just spotting."

"That happens. But what if it's not okay?"

"I'm perfect, and so is this baby. I think it's a girl. I just have a feeling it's a girl."

"Will you call her Sky?" she asks.

I beam at her suggestion. "I don't have any friends, and I don't like anyone who uses the bridge at night. If you're my friend, then yeah, I'll call her Sky."

"Then that's settled. We're friends." She leans over and hugs me. Phew, she smells real bad. "Do you know there's a women's shelter just around the corner. They have limited spots, but if you get there early enough, they'll take you in. They'll also feed us, but we're not allowed to smoke or anything. Want to come with me tonight?"

"Yeah? You'd let me come?"

"Yeah, we're friends. But we have to leave soon if we want a bed for the night. Or we won't be able to get in. It fills up so quick."

"Do they have tampons?" I ask as I stand. The newspaper is itchy between my legs, and it feels like I'm walking with a surfboard stuffed in my pants.

"They have so many things. But I'm telling you, don't smoke nothing while you're there. They'll kick you out, and they won't let you back in. Like, ever."

"Okay, well before we go, want to have some more? That way they can't throw us out."

"The women who run the shelter, they won't put up with shit. So, you gotta be quiet, and not talk back or nothing. Got it?"

I cross my heart. Then pull out my pipe. "Just one more." I hand it over to her, and hope she sprinkles a couple more rocks into it.

"When we get there, we can have a shower. I'll watch your stuff, if you can watch mine."

"Yep," I say but I've actually stopped listening. I'm not even sure what I've agreed to. All I can focus on is the delicious rocks in the bottom of the pipe. She lights it up, and inhales.

My mouth salivates, and I can't wait 'til it's my turn. I want to snatch it out of her hand, but considering they're her rocks, I better not do that.

"I can introduce you to my dealer too. In case your boyfriend gets held up. He'll hook you up if you do a few guys for him. It's really not that hard. You suck 'em off, and my dealer gives you some rocks."

"I suppose," I say as she hands the pipe over to me.

Yes, bliss. This is definitely the high life.

Chapter 24

"YOU'RE INSATIABLE," JUSTIN, SKY'S DEALER, SAYS AS HE HANDS more rocks over to me.

"I can go another two or three guys," I reply. Greedily taking the rocks from him, I shove it in my pocket and can't wait to get back to the room we're renting. It's not very nice, but it's enough for me and Sky. We're sharing, and it works well for us.

She's always here, at Justin's place. I come and go. We get paid in either rocks or money. The rocks are worth more than the money, but the room we're renting costs a hundred a week.

"Well, off you go." He taps me on the butt as I walk out of his office. I suppose you could call this a brothel. I stopped bleeding about a week ago, and since then I figure I might as well try to make some money until Edgar comes back.

I head out to the reception area where a girl named Misty is working the front desk. "You're gonna go again?" she asks as she stares at me.

"Yeah," I snap at her judgmental gaze.

"Room three." She looks down at her phone and keeps

playing the game she's on.

I walk into room three, and there's a really fat young guy sitting on the bed. No time for politeness, I know what he wants. "Did they tell you that you have to wear a condom?" I say as I begin stripping the limited clothes I'm wearing.

"Yeah. But if I wanna go bareback, can I pay extra?" He stands and unzips his jeans.

"No bareback, I don't want your cum inside me."

"Okay." He shrugs as if he's saying, 'it was a worth a try.' "Bend over," he says.

I do what he tells me, close my eyes, and think of the rocks I'm about to get for having sex with him.

My steps are fast as I walk along the dark streets. I can't wait to get home so I can light these crystals up. I've been coming down for about an hour, but I really need the money, so I decided to do one more guy before I left.

"Hannah?" a deep voice calls from behind.

Turning, there's a police officer walking toward me. "Yeah?" I answer unsure on who this guy is.

"It's me. Martin. Remember?" He approaches me slowly, and I take a step backward. I'm racking my memories, and I don't recall ever meeting a cop. I don't cross paths with cops. I shake my head, not remembering who he is. "You punched me, in the face. I arrested you."

I straighten my back. The memory is vague, but something's in there. "Oh yeah," I say as more of the event floods back. "You tried to have sex with me, and I kneed you in the groin."

"No, that's not what happened. But I did grab your upper arm when you tried to run, and you turned and punched me." He rubs his jaw.

"No! that's not what happened. You and some other guy tried

to have sex with me." Yes, I remember exactly what happened. Why's he lying?

"Hannah, it's the drugs. They alter the truth for you. They blur the lines between reality and hallucination." He steps closer and I step backward.

"I'm not a drug addict. I can stop anytime I want."

"Yes, and you said that last time. And I'm positive you've said it a million times since then."

"You don't know what you're talking about." I'm getting edgy. I need the pipe, and this asswipe isn't letting me get back home. "What do you want?" I ask.

"I only want to talk."

"I'm not talking to you. You're a rapist. My Dad nearly beat me to death because you sent me back to them. I told you they're not good people. But you insisted. You were wrong."

"Your father didn't nearly beat you to death. He didn't even touch you. But you ran away again, and they came straight to the station. I've been looking for you."

"You're an asshole." Why does he have to make this shit up?

"Let's go for a coffee," he says and waits for me to follow him.

"I'm not going anywhere with you. You'll shove me in a car, and sell me off to a sex trafficker. Edgar told me about people like you. You're probably not even a cop," I taunt him. "Leave me alone."

"Hannah, if you don't stop, I'll arrest you," he says.

"You'll arrest me for not having a coffee with you, or for not having sex with you?"

He steps closer, and this time I don't move. I can see he's irritated at me. His lips are pursed into a thin line, and his eyes narrow. "Why are you talking like that? Is that all you think of yourself? Because I'm not thinking about that. I'm thinking about how I want to help you because I don't want you to continue being a statistic."

"You think I'm not happy?" I smile at him and jut out my hip. "I'm the happiest I've ever been. My boyfriend and I are going to have a baby together."

"Where is he?" Martin asks, taking me by surprise. "Your boyfriend, where is he?"

"He's out of town."

"When did you last speak with him?"

"I talk to him all the time."

"Do you have a phone?"

"Yeah." I reach in my pocket, but it's not there. "I must've left it at home. But I talk to him all the time."

"And he allows you to walk the streets at two in the morning?"

"He trusts me." I'm getting angrier and angrier at him. Why is he asking about Edgar? "He loves me," I say.

"I can see. A young girl, walking through the streets at two in the morning where anything can happen to her. He obviously cares about you so much, he's driving you." I go to tell him Edgar's car has broken down and that's why he's not here. "But he's out of town, right?"

"No, I never said that. His car's broken down. God, why are you being so horrible? Just leave me alone." Why does he think he's out of town? Edgar loves me.

"You can come for coffee, or I can arrest you. Which would you prefer?"

I huff and stomp my foot. "Fine, you can buy me a coffee. And something to eat 'cause I'm hungry. But I can't stay for long, because Edgar will be back soon. He's gone to take his Mom back to the airport." We begin walking toward the main street, where most of the stores are closed because it's late, but a few stay open twenty-four hours a day.

"What did you do tonight?" he asks.

"I worked," I respond before I think about what he's asking.

"How were the clients?" What? He knows?

"I'm not a hooker."

We walk down the block, and he opens the door to a small, spice-smelling diner. There's nothing appealing about this place. I wrinkle my nose and roll my eyes. "What, you're too good for this place?" he asks and chuckles.

"Actually, I am. I wouldn't be caught dead in here."

"The coffee is good, the pancakes are better, and they're both hot. When was the last time you had something to eat?" he asks and shifts his eyes suspiciously toward me.

"I eat all the time. This baby is super hungry." I place my hand to my stomach protectively.

He nods his head, his gaze dropping to my stomach for a second before rising again. "How far along are you?" he asks, but I can tell there's something more to his voice.

"At least… " I think back, and I become stumped with his question. "I don't know."

"Have you been to the doctor so they can check that you and the baby are fine?" He's not asking questions a regular cop would ask. If I didn't know any better, I'd say he cares. Don't know why though. This ain't his baby.

"No, not yet. But I'm sure everything's perfect."

"And what about the drugs? Don't you know the drugs will affect the baby?"

"I'm not a drug addict," I say through a clenched jaw. "I can stop anytime I want."

"So you've said. But, do you think about your baby and what you're doing to it?"

I slam a fist to the table, and stand. "If you're gonna lecture me on my non-existent drug addiction, then you can go to hell." I turn to walk away, but he stands and grabs on to my hand.

"Don't go. I just want to talk. Two adults, talking. That's all. And hopefully, you'll have something to eat. Sit down,

Hannah." He sits and picks the flimsy paper menu up. "I'm starving. I think I'll get pancakes with bacon on the side. What about you?" He looks up to me, waiting.

Hesitantly, I take my seat again. The rocks in my pocket are calling me though. I grind my teeth to stop the anger from coming through. I want to go home and light up the pipe, but I'll have to wait. "Pancakes too," I half grumble. "And a mocha." He looks to me and smiles. "And hash browns." He nods his head. "And some fruit." Man, I haven't had fruit in a while. Strawberries. My absolute favorite. I haven't had the sweet taste of a strawberry since... I sigh out loud. Since I was at my parent's house. That's a long time. But they wanted me gone. They told me to steal from Kristen, and if I didn't I was no longer allowed to stay at home. It's all their fault.

"Tell me about your boyfriend," Martin says. A smile immediately lights up my face.

"He's the love of my life."

"Yeah?" Martin looks over to the guy standing behind the counter and says, "Two stacks of pancakes, both with a side of fruit, bacon, and hash browns, one mocha and a coffee."

The guy nods to Martin and disappears out the back. There's another couple sitting up the other end, and they're giggling and hugging each other. I stare at them longingly, hoping Edgar returns from his business trip soon.

"Yeah, he's overseas. He had to go for some family business."

"Oh yeah? I thought you said his car's broken down."

"No!" I say way too forcefully. "I never said that. He'll be back next week."

"Yeah?" Martin asks.

"Don't you believe me?"

"Why wouldn't I?"

The guy from behind the counter brings over our coffees, and places one in front of me, one in front of Martin. "Anyway, I'm moving from here when Edgar gets back. He said he's taking me to Hawaii."

"When did he tell you this?"

"The last night we spent together, just before he left." The days are a bit blurred, but I definitely know he said Hawaii.

"Tell me about him. He sounds like a great guy."

"He is." I place my hand to my heart, feeling it beat rapidly beneath my touch. "He's got this bodyguard I don't like, but Edgar said he's going to get rid of him because he makes me feel uncomfortable."

"Wow, really? Getting rid of people who work for him because you don't like them. He sounds better and better. Have you ever been anywhere with him? Edgar, not the bodyguard?"

"Edgar used to take me to loads of parties. They were so much fun. I met so many nice people. They were all really friendly. Except this one guy, he freaked me out a bit."

"Yeah, who was that?" He picks his coffee up and sips it.

"Um, I don't remember his name. But the girl he brought over to the party, she was really nice. But she's a heroin addict, and I don't really associate with addicts. They make me look bad. Sky does ice sometimes, and heroin sometimes, but not a lot. She knows when she has to stop. You know, it's more recreational than anything else."

He looks down to his coffee, and a strained smile stretches his face. "I'm sure you can both stop anytime you want. That's a comfort to know. I'd hate for this to take over your life. I mean, I couldn't imagine what being a drug addict would feel like. How lonely they'd be, or what they'd have to do to get drugs. I've seen some turn to prostitution, stealing. And my God, the lies they tell. But the worst thing is that they actually believe the lies themselves. But, I'm glad you're not like that." He reaches over to squeeze my hand and quickly pulls back.

"No way. I couldn't do anything like that. It's just not in my nature."

"Drugs change people, Hannah. I've seen sweet girls who fall victim to drugs, and I've seen kids who come from drug-affected families. It doesn't discriminate. Once you start, it's hard to stop."

"Well, you're not describing me."

He nods his head, the same pained smile still stretched across his face. "Why were you walking in the middle of the night?"

"I just needed to stretch my legs. You know what I mean?"

"No, not really. When I'm home, I like to stay home."

"You must've had a good family upbringing. I didn't."

"Here are your pancakes. I'll bring your sides in a minute." The guy from the counter places our food down in front of us. My stomach rumbles with hunger. I could eat. I'll probably eat all of mine, and all of his.

"I had a great upbringing. Both my parents were in law enforcement, and my older brother is in law enforcement, and my younger sister is studying to be a lawyer."

"See, you're all smart. I got beat up by my parents often."

He nods his head, then it slowly turns to a shake. "I've met your parents, Hannah. And they've never raised their hand to you."

"What would you know? You didn't live with them."

I want to leave, but I'm also really hungry. If I stay, I'm going to have to hear his lies about my parents, but at least I'll get to eat. I'll gorge myself really quickly, then I'll leave. Ha! Sucker, I'll leave him with the bill too.

"I've met them," he says slowly again. "And I've been in contact with them often."

"They pretend to be great parents, but really they're not. Do you know, I'd go days without food? They'd turn the water off to the house and make me so thirsty, I'd have to sneak out to the neighbors and have a drink from the yard faucet? Do you also know, they'd chain me to my bed and leave me there for days before they'd come back? They're swingers, and they'd bring all types of people over to the house and let them do anything they want to me." Tears well in my eyes. They're the most horrible people I've ever met.

"And Edgar saved you?" Martin asks as he eats his bacon.

"Edgar is my light. Before him I was trapped in darkness, but he flicked a match, and suddenly, the world became good, not bad anymore."

"And when did you say you last saw him?"

"It was only a couple of days ago. He loves me more than his own life." I can't wait 'til I see him again.

"These parties he'd take you to, did you ever do anything you didn't want to?"

"Like what?"

"Were you ever forced to do anything?"

"Like sexually?" I giggle. He nods his head. "Everything I did, I did because I wanted to." I lean over the table and motion for him to come closer to me. He moves in and I whisper, "Sex is so much better with a bit of rock." I wink at him and giggle again. "So much better. You should try it."

"Not my scene," he says as he waves his hand in front of me. It's like he thinks it's addictive or something.

"You're so missing out. It's honestly mind-blowing."

"I'll take your word for it." He pauses and takes a few more bites. I'm inhaling my food, like I haven't eaten in days. Grabbing the fruit, I'm disappointed there are no strawberries, but the banana and apple pieces are nearly as good. "So, I'm thinking, why don't we try to get you into somewhere else to stay?"

"Like where?"

"A place that might be able to help you."

"Help me? What's wrong with me?"

"Maybe to teach you other ways to deal with things instead of drugs."

I throw my fork on the plate. He's gotta be kidding me. Here we go again, about the drugs. "This is the last time I tell you this, Martin. Get it through that stupid head of yours. I'm not an addict." Why is he insisting on attacking me?

"No, I know you're not. But wouldn't you want to get clean for the baby? Maybe, go back home with your parents?"

I burst into tears. "I can't go back there. I can't. They hate me," I say through the blubbering.

"I'm sure you'll find they're worried sick about you, and they'd do anything to help you."

"No, they hate me. They told me they'd kill me if I ever went back there."

"Hannah, I know that's not real. But I also know that *you* actually believe what you're saying. That's the drugs talking. It's not reality."

"I'm not a junkie."

"Yes, you are."

"I'm not. I swear I can stop… "

"Anytime you want," he finishes.

"See, you get it." I smile, suddenly forgetting what I'm actually angry about. That's right, I need to get back home.

"Why don't you let me help you?"

"Why do you want to help me so much?" I start laughing, like something's really funny. I'm not sure what, but I think he said something to make me laugh. "Did your momma die from a drug overdose?" I keep laughing, how funny would that be if she did?

"No, not my mother. But my oldest brother."

I know I should be concerned, but how can I be? That's one of the funniest things I've ever heard. "Really?" Tears start to form, and I wipe at my face with the back of my hand. "How?" I barely manage to spit through my laughing.

"He died with a pipe beside him. And I bet that's where you're heading." He takes his phone out of his pocket, and looks at it. He smiles then puts it back in his pocket.

"I would, if I was a junkie," I say slower in case his brain works slower than mine. How many times do I have to repeat myself? I'm not a junkie. They're dirty, and do all kinds of things for drugs. I'm so much better than *them*.

"Hannah, tonight is going to end one of two ways."

My laughter stops, and I shove more food in my mouth. "Yeah?" I seductively blink at him and lick my lips. "You want me?" I ask in a husky voice, pushing my chest out.

"Not like this."

"So, you do want me? This is why you're buying me something to eat. I'm sorry, but I have a boyfriend."

"No, you don't. You're delusional because of the drugs, and you actually do have a huge problem. You're addicted, and you're going to die."

I start laughing again. "You're so funny. So arrest me then, officer." I playfully stick my hands out to him, so he can handcuff me. "I like the bite of the cuffs. They're so much fun."

"I'm going to do something I never thought I would. But, I'm going to help you, and I'm not even going to say sorry for what you're about to go through?"

Huh? "What's that, officer? You going to tie me up, invite a few friends over and take advantage of me? You know… that's so kinky."

"Hannah… "

Martin looks behind me.

The voice sends chills down my back.

I can't believe he found me. Wait, did Martin tell him where I am? "Did you do this?" I ask, tears spilling over.

"I had to. They're the only ones who can save you from yourself."

A hand comes down on my shoulder. Turning, I see a man who's old and ragged-looking. Beneath his eyes are dark circles and he looks like he's lost a lot of weight.

"Hannah," he says again as he gasps in horror when he sees me.

"Dad," I whisper. Turning to Martin, I stare at him, I feel so betrayed. "I despise you," I say.

"I know," he replies. He doesn't look like he cares that he's about to send this lamb to her slaughter.

Chapter 25

Day two.

I'VE BEEN LOCKED IN MY ROOM FOR TWO DAYS. THE SHAKES HAVE set in, and I have a bucket where I've been vomiting. I tried to get out, but my parents have put bars on my window. My room is different than it was the last time I was here.

Everything but my bed has been removed. There's not even any clothes. "MOM!" I scream in pain. I can barely think.

She's in my room in a moment, and sits on my bed. "Have some water," she holds a glass out to me. I smack it out of her hands.

"I don't need water!" I scream at her. The moment I do, my stomach cramps, and I try to get to the bucket. My skin is hot, and feels like it's melting. "I just need a little bit, just a bit. Please, Mom, let me have my pipe. I promise to stop after a little bit."

I hurl again, and my stomach jabs me with another stabbing pain. Mom takes a face cloth she's brought in with her, and wipes at my mouth. "No," she says.

"I hate you!" I spit toward her. Her eyes fill with tears, but she lifts her chin and nods her head.

"And I hate what these drugs have done to my girl."

"Yeah?" She wipes at my mouth again. "Your little girl was having the best time of her life," I say trying to hurt her.

The muscles in my legs cramp, causing me to lock up and groan in more pain. "I can only imagine how hard this is for you."

"Fuck you." I start to cry. Every part of my body hurts. Everywhere. From the top of my head, to my toes. A throbbing ache is punching me repeatedly in the side of the head. "Please," I beg. "A little bit?"

"No." She stays strong. I hate her, so much. "Because, I love you and I want you better."

"No, you don't. You hate me. You want me to be a drug addict so you can tell all your perfect friends how you have a loser as a daughter."

"What you're saying, it's the drugs. We love you, so much. And we're so happy you're back home."

"I'm going to run away the moment you're not looking."

"You might, but we'll never stop looking. You're everything to us."

My stomach cramps again, and my body sweats like I've been drenched in water. I start crying again. Mom reaches out to touch me, and I scream at her to stop. "Go away," I say when exhaustion and pain have won this battle. "Leave me alone."

Mom stands, takes the bucket to empty it. When she leaves, Dad comes in right away, carrying another bucket. "Sweetheart." Dad sits on the bed, exactly where Mom was. "Have a drink of water."

"Stop trying to shove water down my throat. I hate you both so much."

"We're hurting as much as you are."

"Just leave me alone." I move to my side, close my eyes tight and try to fight through the pain. I can barely concentrate on my breathing, trying to not take such deep breaths, because even that hurts. The door latches shut, and I hear a lock

They've locked me in here, like I'm an animal.

My feet and hands decide right now is a good idea for them to tingle with pins and needles. Because having the shakes, sweating, cramping, and vomiting isn't enough for me to deal with.

"You can do this," I mumble to myself. I just need to live 'til the next minute. The pain will get better, I know it will.

Day four.

"How are you feeling?" Mom asks once she's inside my room.

"Like death." I grit my teeth, and hug my body. My mind is screwing with me. There are moments I'm disoriented and barely know where I am, then other moments of clarity push in and remind me exactly what's happening to me. I'm also going through bursts of sleeping, then being hit with insomnia until it hurts to keep my eyes open.

This is crazy, and not what I want.

If I could, I'd have a small taste of the pipe, just to get me through. But my conscience screams at me to keep going because the hard work is nearly over.

"I need to change your sheets." Mom leans over the bed and tries to help me up. I feel weak, as if all my muscles have evaporated to nothing. "The doctor's coming to see you today."

"Why? There's nothing wrong with me."

"Because you were addicted to drugs, and we need to make sure everything is moving along in the right direction."

"I wasn't addicted," I say to Mom. But in my heart, I know I was. Mom nods her head, though she purses her lips tightly. She rips the fitted sheet off the bed, and I see her cry. I'm breaking her, destroying the hope she has of me recovering. "I'm sorry, Mom," I say as I sit on the floor while she keeps making my bed.

"For you, I'd walk to the end of the earth, and still have the strength to kill anyone who'd hurt you. But when you're hurting yourself, that breaks not only my heart, but my soul."

"I'm trying," I say in a small voice, more to myself than to Mom.

Mom nods again. "I'll make you something light to eat. You need to put some weight back on. You're lucky if you're ninety pounds, you've lost so much. But your skin is already looking better."

"When do you think I can get out of here?"

Mom's shoulders stiffen, but she gathers the dirty bedding, lifts it, and shakes her head. "For now, this is your sanctuary."

"You mean my prison? I'm better, I don't need to be locked in here."

"Hannah," she stretches my name in a sigh. "We can't let you go anywhere until we know you're clean."

I push myself off the floor, and my legs nearly collapse beneath me. "I'm fine!" I shout. "I just need to get out of here, it's driving me crazy looking at this place. I go from here to the bathroom, and back here again. I can't see any of my friends. You've got me locked in here. I'm a damned prisoner."

"You don't have any friends. You ruined your relationship with Kristen, and until she knows you're clean, she doesn't want to see you."

"I have other friends. Like Sky. She'll be worried about me."

"Tell me about Sky."

I want to pace back and forth, but I've run out of energy. I quite literally can't. My eyes become heavy, and I want to collapse on the bed, and go to sleep. "She's a girl I met. She's really nice."

"What does she look like?"

Lying on the bed, I try to concentrate so I can remember her features. But, my memory is hazy. As if all my memories of her are under a veil of darkness. "She's really nice, Mom. She helped me."

"How did she help you?"

Again, I can't answer, because I can't remember anything specific she actually did. "Oh," I say surprising both Mom and myself. "She got me a job." Instantly I feel my face burn with embarrassment. "Never mind," I just as quickly retract the statement. How do you tell your mother she got you a job in a nasty brothel doing things with men for drugs? Even though I know that happened, it's still hazy and unclear. Wait, maybe it didn't happen. I don't know anymore. I'm not sure Sky's even real, because I can't remember her face, or her voice, or what we ever did together.

"Hannah, crystal meth really messes with everything about you. Look at your arms, see those scratch marks?" I look down to my arms, and notice the sores all over them. "They're because you thought there were things under your skin and you tried to scratch them out."

"No, I never thought anything like that." Did I? I really can't remember. Maybe I've been asleep all this time, and nothing actually happened. Maybe, I'm in a dream right now, and I'll wake soon. If I pinch myself, maybe, I'll wake from this horror-filled nightmare.

"Then how do you think you got these scars?"

I'm not even sure any more. My mind can't make sense of anything. "I'm tired," I say.

"I'll be back soon when the doctor arrives."

I barely acknowledge Mom. I just need to close my eyes for a minute. A familiar smell invades my nose, an aroma I miss. My eyes spring open, as if by some magic remedy, I'm fine. I push myself up, so I'm sitting in bed and search the room for where that delicious scent is coming from. I just need a little bit. A taste, then I'll be over it. I won't want more.

I can't find where it's coming from. I search everywhere, but there's nothing in the room. The smell is getting stronger, and sending me rampaging like a hungry wild animal. I need it. I have to have it.

No, keep it together, Hannah.

A small taste. My hands tremble, and my lips quiver with the anticipation of having the pipe for just one more time.

A sad realization happens. I'm imagining the smell. Maybe even hoping for it. Falling to the floor, I grasp at my hair pulling at the strands. Tears fall from my eyes, and I rock back and forth on the spot. I rip at my hair, it gives me something else to mourn. I want my pipe, but instead, I'm tearing at my hair, literally pulling out clumps of it. The pain is a welcome distraction from my reality.

I'm a fucking junkie, and I'm climbing the walls, desperate for more. Willing to do anything for a little rock of ice.

I can't believe this is happening. What have I done to myself?

Will this feeling of impending doom actually end? God, will I ever feel normal again?

The hair I'm pulling out hurts, but at the same time, I'm feeling something. I need this pain. I need something to help me.

Please… let this end.

Chapter 26

Day Six.

THE SHAKES HAVE EASED. I'M NOT VOMITING. IT'S HARD, SO HARD. But Mom and Dad have been here around the clock. They're helping me the best way they can. I'm determined not to let them down. I need to do this, for them.

The door unlocks, and I look over to see who's coming in. "How are you feeling, sweetheart?" It's how Dad always greets me when he enters the room.

"Still tired, but not as bad. I'm going through all kinds of emotions though, I'm not sure how to cope with things."

"Remember what the doctor said. She said you'll need counselling, and tools to cope. You are an addict, but you're cleaning yourself up."

I look at Dad and shake my head.

"Oh, honey, you're doing so well."

I swing my legs over the bed and sit on the edge. "I'm not

sure I could've stopped if you and Mom didn't... " I pause and smile, "... kidnap me."

"We did what we had to do."

"I've been terrible." Shame overtakes me. "There's nothing I've done that can make you proud of me."

"We've always been proud of you. But the drugs, they altered you."

This is a conversation we're constantly having. I try to make sense of things, but I'm still too screwed up to even attempt and clarify it in my head. "It's the only thing I can think about." A tear falls from my eyes. "All I want is to get more of it. It's got such a strong hold over me." I turn to Dad, and I'm crying full-force now. "I'm not sure I can do it."

"We'll be here with you. Every step of the way. We'll drive you to your appointments; we'll be in there with you, we'll do everything we can." Dad's strong arms hug me tightly to his body. Although the shakes and vomiting have passed, my skin still feels like I've been doused in gasoline and set on fire.

It takes a few moments to finally cry all my tears. "I'm okay." I lay back on the bed, cover myself with the blanket, and hold in a sob. I've put them through enough, I can't keep doing this to them. It's not fair.

"Do you need anything?" he asks. I shake my head, and go back to wallowing in self-pity. Dad closes the door, and locks it.

The sound of the lock reminds me I'm not free. And I doubt I ever will be. Depression beckons to me. And no wonder. I'm being kept a prisoner in here, so I can't escape and go back to the life I was living. A life of self-hatred, self-delusion, and self-destruction. There's a stabbing pain in my chest, like my heart has been ripped out and lies shattered on the floor. Maybe that's how my parents felt when I left home and turned to drugs.

Although I'm sad, I also can't help but think of Edgar. I wonder where he is, and what he's doing. Does he think of me? Does he think of what we had? Does he want it back again?

He's my one true love. A man who loved me and wanted nothing but the best for me.

"Hannah?" I didn't even hear the door unlock. Mom opens it and comes in. "Martin's here to see you." I crinkle my brows. Martin? The cop? "Would you like to come out and see him?"

Edgar's pushed to the back of my mind. The pipe is too. As is the sadness of my life.

"Sure," I say and try to piece together as much sanity as I can muster. I drape a cardigan over my shoulders, and try to fix my hair. I hate to think how I look, but at the same time, he's seen me at my worst.

I follow Mom out to the family room, where Martin's pacing back and forth. He's not in his uniform. He's wearing a t-shirt and jeans, and looks quite handsome. "Hi," I say as I approach him, but still keep my distance. I can't quite remember much about him. I know he called my parents. He and Dad forced me into Dad's car, where Martin sat in the back with me, and made sure I didn't jump out and run.

I think I'm thankful for that. I'm not sure.

The pipe still compels me, but I'm trying to fight through the control it has over me.

"You look so much better than when I saw you last." He smiles and steps back to sit on the sofa. He looks behind me to the arm chair, hoping I sit too.

This is the first time since I've been home that I've been out of my room other than to go to the bathroom. "Thank you," I gingerly say as I lower my head in shame. Martin starts saying something, but I hold my hand up to him to stop talking. Lifting my head, I say, "I'm sorry. I'm not sure what I said and did to you, but I'm sorry."

"I've heard and seen worse," he says. The atmosphere in here is tight. Mom's standing in the kitchen, and Martin and I are struggling to talk. Not that I know what we're supposed to say to each other. "How are you feeling?"

"Like my body isn't mine, and I was invaded by someone who looks like me, but isn't me. I feel like shit. I can't stop thinking about the pipe, everything about it draws me in. Truthfully, I'm struggling."

"That's the most honest thing I've heard you say." I smile, not knowing how to respond. "That's what happens when you detox. You begin to regain yourself, and your brain. With drugs, you're under their control. They rule, and you're nothing more than a vessel."

I rub my hand against the tension in my temple, trying to relax. "I'm sorry, but so much is hazy. Did you tell me about someone who died from drugs?" I ask.

Martin's smile tightens, and I notice his demeanor. There's something about him that says he's young, but he's seen a lot. Almost like he's wise beyond his young years. Is that why he called my parents? Because he actually wanted to help, rather than follow protocol?

"You knew I was underage, but you chose to call my parents instead of taking me to the police station. Why did you do that?" I only now notice he's halfway through a sentence, and I cut him off. I'm not even sure what he was saying. But I need to know. It doesn't make sense.

"My brother died." I nod my head, vaguely remembering him telling me about it. "I found him." Oh... crap. "He had a pipe, and a needle. He'd taken both crystal meth and heroin. One sent him high, the other was a large enough dose to kill him."

"I'm... "

"Don't say you're sorry unless you're committed to changing your life. Because if you say you're sorry and relapse, it's an insult to me, my brother, and my family." I gasp, unsure on how to respond. "That's the hard reality, Hannah. There's no sugar coating it."

Suddenly, a blanket of silence falls over us. It's an awkward situation. I *am* sorry, but his brother isn't me either. I'm not sure how to respond considering Martin just shot down what I was going to say. "I'm tired," I say and offer him a weak smile. It's the best I can do.

I don't want a lecture about how I screwed up. I don't want to hear it.

Standing, I give Martin a small nod and turn to head down the hallway toward my room. I can hear footsteps behind me and know Mom's only a few feet away. "Hannah," she says. But I close the door, and for the first time wish the lock was on the inside, so I could lock the world out.

I don't need to feel any worse than I already do.

Lying on the bed, I hear my door creak open, then close a moment later. I listen for anything. But I can't really hear any noise coming from outside my room. My head pounds with a heavy pain, and my body responds to what I once thought of as safe. I want the pipe again. I need it. It helps me cope. It's the only real thing I've ever had that's helped me through life.

Crying, I curl myself into a ball and try to get past all this shit going through me. I can't keep thinking that the pipe is the answer, if I'm going to stay clean. But it's still got a hold on me.

The hold is incredibly strong, but I'm fighting it.

Chapter 27

Day Eight.

MY MIND IS CLEARER. IT'S STILL INCREDIBLY DIFFICULT TO THINK, but at least it's clearer than it has been. I'm not filled with haziness and fog. Actually, no, that's not right. I am, but it's lifting a little bit more every day.

I think about the pipe every second, of every minute, of every hour. I can also recognize how I'm still a slave to it. And I'm not so delusional as to think I could've stopped whenever I wanted. The fact is, I wouldn't have stopped. I probably would've died with a pipe lying beside me, just like Martin's brother.

My parents took me, kidnapped me, and if they didn't, I have no doubt I would've died. I do think about Sky, though, and wonder how she is. I hope she's got someone searching for her and that they find her. She never talked about her family, or at least, I can't remember if she did. Every moment we spent together was about us getting high. Me with the pipe, her with a needle and sometimes the pipe.

I shake my head to try and dislodge those memories. Not because I'm ashamed of them, but because the bitter, yet slightly sweet taste of it still coats the inside of my mouth. The smell makes me close my eyes as I imagine the aroma. It had a slight hospital smell to it, with a touch of sweetness. It's hard to describe, but I knew when someone was smoking it close to me. It's like a marker of stability and strength that locks onto you and doesn't let you go.

I catch myself drooling, salivating with a desire to be near a pipe again.

The yearning is broken the moment my door opens. "Hannah, Kristen's here and wants to see you."

"What?" I ask as I turn on my bed. "I'm not sure I... " I want to say no, but I also want to see her. I need to apologize to her, and grovel for forgiveness for my behavior, even though I'm not entirely sure what I've said to her. I just know it wasn't good.

"She's come to see you."

My heart hurts and my stomach cramps with worry. "Okay," I sigh. I try to delay getting out of bed, but I know she's not going 'til she sees me. I have to face her, regardless of how I feel.

I stand to my feet, and with wobbly knees and clammy hands, I head out to the family room. When I reach it. Kristen is looking like the beautiful blonde bombshell she always was.

"Hannah," she says and moves forward to hug me.

I step back, not wanting her to touch me. "Don't," I say as tears form in my eyes. "Don't let my dirty rub off on you."

"You're not dirty," she says, her eyes taking me in.

"I mean my dirty past."

She hangs her head slightly, then nods. I'm so ashamed. "Will you sit, and talk with me?" She sits where Martin was, and I sit in the single arm chair again. "You're looking so good. Your skin is clearing up beautifully." She smiles.

"These past few days have been hell. And I've had time to think about everything I've said and done. But it's all so foggy for me. If I've done anything to you, I'm sorry."

She lifts her brows, and I see the sparkle of tears in her eyes. "You've not been a good person."

An arrow is shot straight through my heart. "I'm sorry," I say again. But what else can I say?

"I got into college." She changes the subject, that for me is the kindest thing she can do. I don't want to relive my dark days. I just want to move on from them.

"Yeah? So, you'll be studying interior design?" I ask. "Living the dream." She smiles and I smile, but inside I'm dead. I'm not living the dream I wanted for myself, I'm detoxing and thinking about nothing but the smell and taste of the pipe.

"I am." It's quiet and tense. "A lot of people heard about what happened to you at school."

My throat constricts. "Yeah?" I ask, my voice squeaky and high.

"Some not very nice things were said, but mostly, everyone was hoping you'd get clean."

"Yeah?" My stomach knots and I feel like I'm going to hurl.

"Some people weren't so nice though."

I look around, and hope Mom can save me, but she's not in the kitchen. I'm not sure where she is. I lift my shoulders and wipe at the tears that are falling. "I bet," I respond. It's not meant to be malicious, but I can just imagine what I'd say if someone I knew got hooked on drugs, back when I was clean.

"So many videos made the rounds, and that was brutal to watch."

"Videos?" I ask. "What videos?"

"The porn movies you made."

"Porn movies?" My heart's beating like crazy inside my chest. "What are you talking about?" Shit, did I make porn movies? Did I consent to having sex in front of the camera? Oh shit... oh shit.

My heart is beating like crazy, and my pulse is rushing so high, I can feel tightness across my chest. "You don't know?" Kristen stares me, her mouth open and the color draining from her face.

"There are porn movies out there I'm in?" I ask slowly, making sure I have all the information.

"A few of them, on PornHub."

I gag from the vomit, trying to hold it in. My breathing is short and shallow but rapid. "I didn't make any movies like that," I barely manage to say through my shortness of breath.

"Hannah, you did. I saw one and nearly threw up. I couldn't believe that was you. I didn't want to believe it, but it was."

Standing, I run. I run straight out the front door, and I'm surprised it wasn't locked. I keep running down the street and away from here. I made those videos, and I don't remember making them. What is wrong with me?

My lungs are burning as I keep running, I'm not physically fit, I'm still recovering from all the drugs in my system. But I have to push and get away from here.

Do my parents know?

Do my neighbors know?

Oh my God. This is something else.

This is much worse than I thought it was. Tears keep falling, making my vision blurry. But I don't care, I need to get somewhere away from everyone so I can think. I don't know where to go.

I don't care either. I just need to be gone.

I keep running, taking back streets instead of the main streets. I know my parents will come looking for me. I also know Kristen and Martin will be searching for me too.

I keep running until I can't run anymore.

My feet are sore from running on the rough, coarse pavement in my slippers, and my heart feels like it's going to explode out of my chest. I have no idea how far I've run. Maybe a mile, maybe two or three. I don't know. I don't even know where I am. Everything from before drugs is fuzzy. I don't even feel like I own my body. I'm merely a host for whatever's taken over.

I keep walking, looking behind me in case they've caught up with me. I can't let them see me like this. They'll think I'm lost.

Maybe I am.

I don't know anything anymore.

I head down a side street, and keep going, jogging until I finally hit another street. This seems familiar, but I don't know where I am.

A familiar bridge comes into view and I run toward it, still unsure of where I am, but I know it's somewhere I've been before. I cross the bridge, looking around me. I've definitely been here before.

My feet know where they're going, but I don't. I keep jogging, I'm not even sure how long I've been gone for.

Finally, I stop and bend at the waist. I brace my hands on my knees and take several deep breaths, trying to get air into my lungs. Straightening, I keep walking, trying to think where I am, rubbing at a stitch in my side.

I hate this constant state of confusion I'm in. I keep going, opting not to stand still for too long because I don't know where I am. But the problem is, I don't know where I'm going either.

I stick to back streets, making sure I'm not seen by anyone. I have no idea where I am.

"Hannah?"

I turn to see a girl standing in front of me. She's a mess. She's smiling, and I see her teeth are black and rotting. She'd be pretty, if it wasn't for the marks all over her. She steps toward me, and opens her arms for a hug. "Sky?" I ask, unsure of if Sky was my imagination, or a real person.

"Where have you been? I thought you were dead." She hugs me tightly. Her odor hits me right in the nose. I don't breathe in while she's hugging me. She looks terrible. "Look at you. Have you gotten clean? I always said you're too good for a place like this." She throws her hands out, indicating the streets.

"Wait, do you still have the apartment?" I ask.

"Yeah, had to suck the landlord off for last week's rent. But I got him money this week. He won't be throwing our asses out for at least another week. But rent is on you this time."

"I don't have any money," I say feeling sorry for her.

"Oh shit. Well, Justin's been asking about you. He got so mad you didn't show up to work. Said if I saw you to tell him. It's okay, I worked it off for ya. You owe me." She smiles again, showing me her rotten teeth. "You coming back home?" She starts walking quickly in the direction of the room.

I shouldn't, but I need to get my head clear before I go home. I'm so ashamed of those movies, that I don't know what to say to my parents. "Just for a bit. Hey, have you got a phone?" I ask.

"Yeah, I do. Swiped it from a client today. He won't have an idea I took it 'til he wakes up. He took a pretty big hit of the needle before I left. Doubt he'll wake soon." She giggles.

We walk together, but she's leading me back to our apartment. I can't remember where it is, or anything about it. She's talking, and I'm not really listening. Instead, Kristen's words keep playing on repeat in my head. "Hey," I say as we head into a building resembling something out of a dystopian movie. It's crumbling and falling apart, but I suppose if this is where Sky lives, I really shouldn't judge.

Hell, I was living here with her.

We walk up two flights of stairs, and I can't help but notice the condition of the interior. It's dirty and dingy. And any minute, I feel like there's going to be gunfire from the hall.

She goes to a door, and unlocks it. I walk in behind her, and I remember everything about this apartment. It's small, and incredibly dark. There's not much furniture, just an old sofa, a small kitchen, and a bathroom with a spread of needles, a spoon, and a lighter on the counter. I was hazy, and couldn't remember a lot about my drug-fueled days. But I remembered this place.

I see the pipe.

My old pipe. My stomach churns, and suddenly I feel excitement. "Have you got any?" Sky asks as she throws her handbag on the small kitchen table.

"Nah, I'm quitting."

"Yeah? Good for you. I always knew this wasn't a life for you." She picks up a rubber tourniquet and ties it around her upper arm. "Want some?" she offers as she catches me watching her.

"Nope." I swallow back the desire. Everything in here is slowly breaking down the barriers I've worked so hard to build. The beautiful, toxic smell, the bubbling of the heroin on the spoon.

"Sure?" She draws the dirty-colored liquid back in a syringe that's been used many times before.

"Yeah."

"Okay. Give me a minute." She smacks at her arm and tries to find a vein. "Bastards have collapsed," she says. "Here." She finds a vein, sticks the needle in and starts pushing the contents of the syringe through her veins.

Her face softens, then goes slack as she closes her eyes. She's chasing a high. And by looks of things, she's well on her way to finding it. She's quiet for some time, and I'm left in this room, reminiscing about my own highs and lows.

The pipe taunts me. But I'm using every ounce of strength not to look at it. I can't help it though. It's calling me. Beckoning me to pay it attention.

This innocent little piece of glass has single-handedly captured all of my attention.

"So... " she says as my focus stays on the pipe.

"Um, the phone? Can I borrow it?"

"Sure thing." Sky's high as anything. She's barely able to stand. "Who are you calling?"

"I have to know if it's true."

"If what is true?" She's struggling to focus as she rifles around her bag.

"I made some porn videos."

"Shit, yeah? Did you get paid a lot for them? I've made some before. They pay well. How much did you get?"

"I don't remember making them."

She grabs the phone and tosses it over to me. Giggling, she collapses back against the sofa, and nods her head. I'm not sure what she's giggling at. Her eyes are drooping, and she's breathing very slowly.

"What's the password, Sky?" I ask as I slide my finger across the screen.

"Um. He put in... " She closes her eyes again, half way through the sentence.

"Sky!" I nearly yell.

She startles but opens her eyes. "Yeah?" she asks already forgetting what I've asked.

"What's the password?"

"Oh yeah. Real original. One, two, three, four."

I type in the numbers, and I shake my head. Are people really that dumb? Apparently so.

The phone unlocks, and I get the numerical keypad up on the screen. I dial Edgar's number. The phone rings only twice before he picks it up. "What?" he barks into the phone.

His voice is like hot molten chocolate. It's smooth and delicious. His voice alone sends goosebumps over my skin. For a second, I'm speechless. "Edgar," I say with a shaky voice.

"Who's this?"

"It's me, Hannah."

The silence is deafening. I'm not sure what he's going to say, or even if he's going to say anything at all. "Hannah."

The sensual whisper draws me back in. I nearly can't speak. I'm barely able to manage any words. My heart is beating loudly, my skin is burning for him, and my body reacts just by the sound of his voice.

"I need to know if I made any pornographic movies?"

Silence, again.

The quiet is making me think he's not there, but I can hear the whirl of the tires on the road. I know he's there.

"Are you clean?" he asks.

I'm nodding my head, but of course, he can't see me. I'm not sure I'm strong enough to say the words. I respond by crying. He's affecting every part of me. I'm craving him, but I need to stay strong. "I am," I say with an even smaller voice. But I can't hide how I'm feeling. My voice betrays me, even though I don't want it to.

"Where are you?"

"No. I can't do this with you. I just need to know if you made pornographic movies of me and uploaded them. Or worse still, sold them." Don't see him, you're not strong enough for that yet. "Please," I finally beg. "Just tell me."

"Only if you have a coffee with me."

I close my eyes and hold the phone to my forehead. He's breaking my walls down. He has ultimate control over me. He says *jump,* and I ask *how high?* "No." My resolution is crumbling. Please, don't ask again. I can't. I just can't.

"Meet me outside."

I swallow hard. "I don't know where I am."

"Are you with Sky?"

He knows Sky? How? My mouth opens and I answer before I have a chance to stop my response. "Yes."

"I'll be there in a minute. Wait for me outside."

"No," I weakly say, fighting the monumental pull he has over me.

"I'm driving up now, be downstairs."

I nod my head. I don't bother speaking, he knows and I know I'll be there waiting for him.

"Hey, Sky. Thank you for the phone, but I have to go."

"Oh, okay," her voice is soft and sedate. I've seen her go ballistic when she's had a hit, and I've seen her be calm and sweet. Mostly, she's always been sweet, well at least to me.

"I'm going to do my best to come back for you."

Sky lifts her hand and waves to me. "Bye."

Leaving the phone on the kitchen table, I go to the door and leave. Walking down the ill-lit stairs, I'm careful not to step on anything, like a discarded syringe. When I get outside, I walk to the end of the street and notice how the sky's turning darker. The sun is sinking, and soon night will be upon us. I need to get back home. I can't stay out here. I have to get back to my parents. They'll be worried about me. I just got up and ran out after what Kristen told me. Now, I'm about to get the answer I need. After which, I'll have to overcome yet another hurdle, and move on with my life.

I have to.

The black car rolls around the corner toward me. I don't even have to look to know it's Edgar.

He slows to a stop only a few feet from me.

My heart's hammering inside my chest, and I'm shaking like a leaf. The back door opens.

Out steps one of the most beautiful men I've ever laid eyes on. He's dressed impeccably in a suit, his hair is neat and slicked back, and his dark eyes lock onto mine. "Hannah." His voice is pure opium. It hooks me in. But I have to fight it.

Straightening my shoulders, I hold my head high. I can't let him do this to me. Stepping closer, I'm careful not to get too close. If I do, he'll overcome me and I won't be able to stop myself.

"Just… tell me. Did you sell a video of me having sex?"

"Get in, I'm taking you for coffee."

"No, Edgar, I won't. I just need to know if you sold or uploaded a video of me having sex!" I'm more forceful, but inside, I'm barely holding on.

"Get in." This demand is final. If I don't get in, I'll never find out if it was him, or someone else. I have no idea what to think. I'm so confused. But I need answers.

I fight with myself. If I get in, he'll have his talons in me in a matter of minutes. If I don't, I'll never know if it was him, or Justin from the brothel. God, I hope it's not Edgar. That would snap my heart. Break me completely.

"I… " I stop what I want to say, because I don't actually know what it is.

"This is your last chance." He gets back into the car and closes the door.

My body is screaming, I want to get in. But I don't. The slim level of control I have over my brain is slipping.

I walk to the other side of the car, and get in.

He's sitting back, smiling. He's relaxed and confident. The way he's always been. I feel like I'm a mouse in the lion's den; trying to escape his power before I'm consumed like I'm nothing more than a meal.

"Did you sell or upload?" I ask again. My resolute is completely gone.

"Is that all you're worried about? If I uploaded or sold a little video here and there?" He casts his gaze over me, travelling all the way down my body. The car's in motion, and for a split second I'm contemplating jumping out. I can't be in here with him. My control is nearly gone.

"Did you?" I ask. Tears are threatening, but I'm holding strong. I'm not sure how many more seconds I'll be able to hold onto my strength.

His lips begin to smile. That sexy smile he'd give me. "Oh, kitty," he says with that dangerous dark tone.

His voice. God, his voice. It holds onto me. Comforts me, caresses me.

"Please?" my pitch breaks. I can hear the desperation.

"Kitty," he says again. This time I respond with a shiver. Goosebumps cover my body. "You're looking good. Just like I remember you." He reaches over and places his warm hand over mine. With his thumb, he gently strokes the soft skin on the back of my hand.

Closing my eyes, I fight the pull he has on me. He owns me, and he knows it. I can't help it. I lift my hand slightly, and try to link fingers with his.

What are you doing, Hannah?

I can't let him back into my life. I can't.

My head is hazy, but not like it used to be after the pipe. It's more a blanket of want *for him.*

I remove my hand, finally controlling myself. Opening my eyes, I look over to him. "Did you do it?" I ask, not letting this subject go.

Edgar pulls his hand back, and reaches into his jacket pocket. He brings out my old friend. My foe. My best friend. *My enemy.*

"What are you doing?" I ask, afraid, yet strangely excited about what he's showing me.

"This?" He holds the pipe up, and shows it to me.

I'm desperate. I want it. Just like he used to give it to me. He'd hold it, and I'd climb on his lap, straddling him then I'd wrap my lips around the pipe and suck in deeply. "Please." I scrunch my eyes tight, and turn my head away from him. But this is futile. I know what he has, and I know in a matter of minutes, I'm going to want what he's offering.

I hear him tapping in a couple of crystals. I hear the flick of a lighter. *No, no! I can't.*

"Would you like to try this?"

"No," my voice is weak at best. Exactly like I am.

"Are you sure?"

I peel my eyes open, and turn to him. The pipe is in his hand, the crystals in the bottom. The lighter in his other hand.

I shake my head, too scared to speak, because I know if I open my mouth, it won't be to speak, but to suck in the smoke.

"For old time's sake."

I shake my head again. The taste is in my mouth. It's right there, teasing me. He holds his hand out a bit further. Something overtakes me, something so strong, I've never felt anything like it before. It's more than a want, more than a need, more than hunger, more than the need for air.

I move closer to him, and before I even realize, I'm straddling his hips. "That's it," he says.

He lights the pipe. Instantly, relief floods me.

Yes, that's it. This is what I've been missing. I need this. I can't escape it. I won't escape it. Just one more time. I've stopped before, I can stop again.

I lean forward. The pipe is only a hair's breadth from my mouth. I could pull back and refuse it, but I want it. One more time. Just once.

"I…"

"Shhh, kitty. I've missed you."

"You've missed me?" I ask.

"I love you."

That's all I need. "Please, don't let me go as far as I did last time," I beg.

He guides the pipe closer to my mouth. "I promise, I won't."

Happiness overtakes me. I'm no longer fighting this. Edgar loves me, and he'll look after me. This is right.

One more time, and I'll stop.

Chapter 28

Two weeks later

"Sky, I need some money."

"Justin said you can go back to work any time you want."

"Edgar won't let me. He says I'm not allowed to whore myself out anymore." I giggle as I light up my pipe.

"What do you need money for? He gives you what you need." She wraps the rubber tourniquet around her arm, draws the liquid heroin back and smacks her arm to find a vein. The moment the needle is in her arm, she slumps back, and lets out a sigh. "This is good shit," she says in a slow and calm voice.

"Yeah?"

"Yeah."

"I need money," I say again.

"Ask your parents, they'll help you out."

I burst out laughing, finding what she's saying funny. "Yeah, after they beat the crap out of me. You know how they kidnapped me? They didn't feed me once, and they didn't let me go the bathroom. I had to shit myself. They don't give a crap about me. They're too invested in themselves. I hate them so much."

"Then come back to Justin's."

I shrug. "I might go back home, and see what I can get. I gotta make sure they're not there though." I stare at the wall. I feel like I've got so much energy. I don't want to sit any longer. "I'm going," I say as I jump up off the sofa.

"Yeah? See ya," Sky responds.

I open the front door, and run down the stairs. I have so much energy, I don't know what to do with it. I'm walking so fast, I'm almost running. I don't even know where I'm going. I'm just going.

"Hey, you're hot," some guy yells out of the window of his car as he drives by.

I stick my middle finger up to him.

He slows, then yells, "Whore!" before he throws his soda can out the window toward me. It narrowly misses me. I flip him the bird again.

My feet are walking on their own. The high from the pipe is strong in me. It lasts longer than it's ever lasted before. I try not to have it all the time, but it's so good. I can't help it. It makes me super horny, and gives me so much energy.

I love how I feel. It's the best thing ever. Edgar's coming over tonight, so I have to make sure I'm home then. He's taking me somewhere special. I can't wait.

Before I know it, I'm standing in front of my parents' house.

How did I get here? Did I walk all this way? Crap, I hope they're not home. I walk up to the front door and knock. I can't hear anything. Phew, they're not home.

I walk around the back, and see the kitchen window is ajar. I giggle to myself. Idiots. They left the window open.

I remove the screen, and slide the window open, then I haul

myself up and squeeze through the opening. "Hello?" I yell, in case someone's here. I'm never getting stuck in this hellhole again.

My parents are vicious and brutal. They chained me to the fucking bed, and kept me there.

Who'd do something like that?

I hear nothing.

Yes, I've got some time before they get home. I go straight to my parents' room. I take out their drawers, one by one, and tip them upside down. I need to find money. They better have some. I need some. Edgar told me I'm gonna have to start paying for the rocks, but he won't let me work at Justin's.

I go through all their drawers, I haven't been able to find anything.

I go into the kitchen, and look through everything there too. "Jesus," I say to myself as I look for things.

"Hannah?" Dad's voice booms from behind me.

Before I look at him, I roll my eyes. God, these people are such monsters. I turn and display a fake smile on my face. Dad's in a towel, his hair glistening from the shower. I don't recall hearing the water. "Daddy?" I say as I step toward him. He's staring at me. His mouth is gaping open, and I can't help but feel like he's judging me. "What?" I yell at him.

"You're using again." He clasps at his heart as if he's shocked.

"I'm clean," I say. "But I need money."

"No. No money."

"This is bullshit. You owe me after the way you treated me."

"What?" he asks, looking confused. "I can't talk to you when you're using. Because I'm not talking to my daughter, I'm talking to the drugs. Crystal meth?" he asks.

"I'm clean," I say again.

"Really, and that's why your skin is filled with those terrible spots. Your arms have got scratch marks again."

"There was something crawling under my skin, but I got it out now." I start scratching again, feeling something crawling.

"Let me help you." He steps closer and lifts his hands in surrender.

"I don't need help, old man. I need money. Are you gonna give me some, or not?"

"Hannah, I can't. All you'll do with it is spend it on drugs."

I roll my eyes and huff in frustration. "Here we go again. What are you gonna do? Keep me here chained to my bed again? Sorry, old man, but those days are gone. I have someone who loves me and takes care of me. Unlike you and that bitch of a mother."

He shakes his head, and a few tears roll down his cheeks. "We're devastated," he says in a small voice. "This isn't what we want for you."

"No? Prefer to beat me instead?" I ask as I step back from him.

"I can't argue with you. Because in your head, you believe the words you're saying. We've never beaten you. We've always given you everything you've wanted. We've never denied you."

"You haven't? With what, *Dad?*" I spit his name as if it's something dirty. "You've gambled everything away. And Mom… she's a whore," I smugly say. Dad looks confused. As if he has no idea what I'm talking about. "Don't pretend. You're a gambler, Mom's a whore and you're worried about me occasionally having the pipe? You're a loser."

"Hannah, you've said those words before, and I know you believe them. But it's not true."

I look away, not believing a thing he's saying. "Whatever," I say. "Give me money."

"No, but I can get you help."

"I don't have a problem."

"Yeah? Prove it to me. Let me get you into rehab."

"You think you know everything, don't you? I don't need

rehab, I just need Edgar." I straighten my shoulders and smile. "He takes care of me now."

"Obviously. Look at you. When was the last time you had a shower? Or ate? Or even looked in the mirror? You're a shadow of the girl you used to be. You've fallen under the spell of drugs again, and if I'm guessing right, I'd say this Edgar is the guy who's feeding them to you."

"Edgar does feed me!"

"Drugs. Drugs that are made with chemicals that could kill you."

"Whatever!" I shout and throw my arms up. "Give me money." I hold my hand out to Dad.

"No." He's standing his ground, but I'm not leaving without money.

"I tell you what. How about I give you something in return?" This I can do, because let's face it, men love sex.

"Hannah." Dad's voice becomes more strained. "Don't do this." His face twists in agony.

"Come on, it's only sex. For fifty." Dad cries while he shakes his head. He rakes his hands through his hair, then buries his face into his palms. "Don't act like you don't want to have sex with me."

"Hannah Rose Mendes!" I hear my Mom's voice from behind me.

"Shit," I mumble. "Hey. I need money."

Mom storms over to me, and grabs me by my upper arm. "Get out!" she screams as she drags me through the house toward the front door.

Something takes over, and I turn. With my hand in a fist, I punch Mom as hard as I can in the nose. Bloody spurts out all over the place. "Hannah!" she screams as she cups her nose.

"You think you can tell me what to do?" I smack her again. This time punching her in the eye.

"Stop!" she pleads.

"You're a stupid bitch!" I smack her again, this time to the side of the head. She stumbles back and falls to the ground, hitting her head against the leg of the table in the family room.

Dad grabs me by the shoulders, turns me so I'm facing him, and slaps me across the face. "Get out now before I call the police. When you're ready to get clean, call us and we'll be there for you. But for now, you're nothing more than a junkie." He shoves me, and before I know what's happening, he's pushed me out the front door and slammed it in my face.

"FUCK YOU!" I scream at the top of my lungs and beat on the door. "FUCK YOU!" I turn and walk down the driveway, leaving this house of hell behind, once and for all.

Neighbors are coming out of their houses, looking to see what's going on. "Screw you all and your peaceful neighborhood. Watch yourselves, because I'll come for each and every one of you bastards."

Most of them slink away back in their houses, closing the doors behind them. Gutless pricks. "Hannah," one of the neighbors' yells toward me. "Please."

I storm up to her, standing on her front lawn. "You want a piece of this? I should kick your fucking head in. You rapist pedophile! You'd come into my room at night, and touch me."

The woman looks at me, shakes her head. "You need help," she says. "I've known you for years, and I've never touched you."

I lift my sweater, and show her my breasts. I start to fondle them in front of her. "This is what you used to do to me."

She looks horrified. "Child, I hope you get the help you need." She turns her back on me.

I lower my sweater, and leave. Everyone's gone back in their houses. *Gutless.*

With anger pumping through my veins, I walk back to my apartment.

Chapter 29

WALKING HOME FROM MY PARENTS' HOUSE, MY ADRENALIN IS pumping hard through me. I can't believe my mother. How dare she call me a whore. Who does *she* think she is? She's the one who's sleeping around with everyone. Not me. Edgar takes care of me, he looks after me.

My hands tremble as I angrily walk back toward the apartment. I know where I left the pipe, it's on the small table in the kitchen. I need it. It has to calm me down. It's the only thing I can have that'll settle my nerves.

And my father. The nerve of him offering me fifty dollars to have sex with him. He's my God damned father. My own father. I laugh out loud. I bet Mom's no good in bed, and that's why he offered me the money to sleep with him. He's desperate for a good lay, and considering Mom wasn't home, he thought it would be a good opportunity to get him some.

Sick bastard.

Who does shit like that?

But then again, my parents are highly dysfunctional. The

most screwed up anyone can be.

Dad dropped his towel and started stroking himself in front of me. Mom tried to kiss me. Ugh, they make me sick.

The anger fuels my walk. I need to get back to the apartment quickly. I need the pipe. Just a small drag should be enough to calm my wild mind down.

I see the building in the distance, and run the rest of the way. It's not particularly well-lit, but I can tell by the shape and the graffiti on the walls that it's where I live. Night has started to fall, and soon, it'll be pretty black out.

I look up to the sky, trying to find the moon. But it's not out tonight, nowhere to be seen. There are a few clouds in the sky. They look dark and looming, as if they're warning me that something shadowy is on the horizon and that I need to beware of it.

But what could possibly go wrong?

I have the best guy in the world in love with me.

The best roommate I could ever ask for.

I just wish I could go back to Justin's to work. Edgar keeps telling me I need to pay for my crystals, and they cost him money. I owe him a little bit, and he knows I'm good for it. I just have to get a job.

Maybe, I can beg Justin for my job back, and keep it a secret from Edgar. That could work.

I reach the building, open the front door, and run up the stairs. One of the dirty junkies from the floor above us is on the stairs, shooting up. "Go to your room and do that," I angrily spit toward him.

"Yeah," he responds in a wistful voice.

He's high and has no idea what I've even said. Sad really, to be that dependent on drugs. I'll never get like that. No way. Never again. Now I do it more for fun than anything else.

I open the front door, and search for my pipe.

Sky's in the kitchen getting a hot drink. "Hey," she says as she stares at me. "Where have you been?"

"Went to my parents."

"Yeah, that's right. How'd it go? Got any money? I could do with something to eat."

"Nah, they wouldn't give me any. But Dad wanted me to suck him off for Jackson."

"Did you do it? 'Cause we got no food, and we gotta pay rent."

"Eeew. That's sick. No, of course I didn't do it." I search for some crystals, and realize, I'm out. Shit. Shit. *Shit.*

"It's just a blowjob," Sky says. "You used to blow heaps of people at Justin's."

I'm frantically ripping through here, trying to find anything I can so I can smoke it. I'd settle for a shard, a small taste. I'm tearing the cushions off the old sofa, overturning everything in here. "Shit!" I groan as I keep searching.

"What? Just go back to your parents."

I need my damn pipe, and I need it now. But something inside snaps. The molten lava spills over, and I turn to Sky who's now moved directly behind me. She's got a mug in her hands. I grab it from her, and throw the contents over her face, burning her. My anger keeps building; I can't stop. She's screaming, but I don't care. I need a fucking crystal, and I need it now. "Shut up about my fucking parents."

She's on the floor, with her hands covering her face. I've got a fistful of her hair, and I'm pounding her head into the floor. She's screaming. I'm smashing her.

"Hannah," she sobs as she's cowering away from me.

I stop for a split second. Reality comes over me. "What have I done?" I whisper. Standing, I back away from Sky. She's on the floor, crying and writhing around in pain. My heart breaks.

Shit, I did this to her.

"I'm sorry," I say.

She sits up, her face is red from where I threw the tea at her. Her hair is a bloody mess. "Get out!" she screams.

"Sky… " I move forward.

She backs away from me, wedging herself in a corner of our small kitchen. She gropes blindly on the counter, and lifts a fork to me. "Get out!" she screams in a pitch I've never heard before. It's a cross between anger, and pain. "Don't come back."

I stand staring at her and know she means every word she's spoken. I turn and grab my pipe, shoving it in my pocket. "You tried to steal from me, and I'm the one being thrown out. Great friend you turned out to be," I say.

"You're delusional," she cries at me as I leave the apartment.

Anger is the main emotion pumping through me. Great. I walked in on her going through my stuff to steal from me, and I'm the one being punished. What a bitch. I hope she dies. I hope she dies a slow and painful death. I hate her so much.

I make my way down the stairs, the junkie from above is still on the steps, passed out with a needle in his arm. "Fucking junkie," I spit toward him as I leap over and keep making my way out.

Dark is now here. There's a bite to the air, a definite chill factor. I stick my hands in my pockets and try to warm up. That bitch threw me out of my own house, into the cold. I should go back there and kill her for doing that.

But I need a crystal. One damn crystal.

My body's trembling, but I can't tell if it's because I need the pipe, or because it's cold. My head is fuzzy; I can barely think straight. All I know is I have to stay off the main streets, because I bet you anything my parents are looking for me. If they find me, I know they're going to kill me. My Dad yelled it at me as he pushed me out of the house. He told me he's going to kill me if he finds me, and started counting to give me a head start.

I have to stay in the shadows, until I can find somewhere to stay. I hit the main street. It's quiet this time of night. The odd car drives by. Most of the stores are closed. There's the all-night café, and I walk past it trying to keep my head down.

Inside the café, a group of guys are sitting, talking, and laughing. I recognize them from Justin's. They're low-level dealers, friends of Sky's. I keep walking. An older man walks toward me. He lowers his chin and avoids eye contact with me. But I need a crystal, just to get me through.

"Wanna party?" I ask him as he approaches me.

He scrunches his mouth, shakes his head, and continues walking.

"You probably couldn't get up if you tried," I tease as I walk backward yelling.

I stick to the darkness. I can't be seen. I'm in fear of my life. My parents will kill me. There's no doubt in my mind.

I wish I could use the phone to call Edgar. He always looks after me, he'll protect me. He'd come and get me. He loves me.

I hide in a small alleyway, looking around.

The hurt my body is going through is grueling. My heart itself feels like it's going to explode. My lungs yearn for a smoke. A small inhale, God, it's all I need. Just one small inhale.

I hear a commotion from down the street. I peep out to see who's making all the noise.

It's the dealers from the café. They're walking toward me. They may be my only chance to score. I hear them get closer, and I shove my hands into my pockets so they can't see my desperation for the pipe.

They approach, and I step out from the darkness. Leaning against the wall, I make myself as sexy as possible.

"What do we have here?" one of the guys asks as he steps in front of the others.

"Hmm, I foresee a little bit of fun," another says.

There's four of them in total. I can handle four. I can do this, but they better be willing to pay. "I like to party," I say in a cute voice. *Just think of the crystals, Hannah. You can get iced, and feel as good as you ever have. Think of the crystals.*

"Yeah, what's your choice?" another asks.

The four of them look real friendly. All five of us are now walking together. Two of the guys have hung back a bit and are whispering.

My shakes are getting worse. God, I hope they have the goods. I need the pipe. "Meth," I answer. "I'm not a junkie though," I add in case they think they're getting me for nothing.

"How about you blow all of us, and we'll spot you an eight-ball?"

Holy shit. These guys are idiots. An eight-ball and all I need to do is blow them? An eight-ball is worth two-hundred dollars. Yes! These guys really have no idea.

"Yeah, alright," I say as calmly as I can. But, damn it, an eight-ball. *Yes.*

"How about down there?" One of the guys points down an alleyway. It's dark, with an overhead street lamp nearly half a block away. It gives little illumination, just enough so I can see what I'm doing.

"Fine, but first, I want to see it." I wasn't born yesterday. They can pretend to have it, get a blow-job from me, then leave.

We walk further down the alleyway.

I turn to look at them.

I get punched in the head, knocking me to the ground. The pain vibrates through my temple. Panic spikes.

"Grab her," one says.

"Rip her pants down."

I try to yell, but someone stuffs something in my mouth and holds their hand over it. My screams are muffled. I can't yell. I can't make a sound.

I feel my clothes being torn off me. I'm completely exposed.

"Wear a condom. You have no idea where this dirty slut has been."

One by one, they take turns.

Each face looks down at me. I'm crying, bawling hot tears, but I'm helpless. I can't move. They all take turns, some pinning me down, others raping me. They take turns spitting on me.

Help... please... help.

Once they've finished taking turns, they take turns again. They keep going. They're not stopping.

My body is being used over and over again.

My tears have dried. There's nothing left of me.

Help.

But help doesn't arrive.

Why would it? This is the worst part of town, in the middle of the night. An alleyway that sees no foot traffic. I'm going to die here; I know it.

I'm not even shaking anymore. My mind is clear, and I know exactly what they're doing to me. I can hear their laughs, and their jokes about how easy I am. They're commenting on my body, how I'm a whore and a junkie.

My heart doesn't stop beating rapidly. It can't calm.

I'm broken.

I'm dead.

It feels like hours have passed, and I think they've finished. My limp body is so broken and exhausted, I can barely lift my head. "Dress the slut," someone gives instructions. He's the same voice who said to pin me down.

The others laugh. One kicks me in the ribs. He kicks me again.

My torture is no longer just being raped, now I'm a punching bag too.

After they roughly pull my clothes back on, one takes my arm and pulls up my sleeve. I can hear a lighter igniting, and a faint hope it's being used to light a pipe rushes through me. Now I hear the sizzle of liquid boiling in a spool. I look over in time to see them suck the spoon's contents through a cotton ball and into a syringe. I know this routine. I've seen Sky do it a hundred times.

Another man wraps a tourniquet around my arm, just above the elbow, and ties it off tight. My brain tells my body to struggle, but it can't. I feel someone slap my arm, then a needle slides into my vein. There's pressure, then an overwhelming numbness travels all through my body.

"Are you sure that's enough to kill her? No one can know what we did," the same voice tells the others.

It's getting lighter in the alley. The sun must be rising. I flick my gaze to each of them; etching their faces into my memory. Their smell is so deeply embedded, I'll never forget them. They all smell like cigarette smoke. Stale smoke and beer.

I stare up at the sky, watching as the sun is rising. My body shakes.

This is where I die. In an alleyway. I have no one. I am nothing. And this is where my life will end.

Chapter 30

"IS SHE DEAD?"

Groaning, I try to roll over so I can see where the voice is coming from.

"She's moving. We have to help her," someone else says. Their voice is breathy, sounding panicked.

My limbs are heavy, my head is fuzzy, and I swear I can hear my mother's voice.

"Hannah, are you high?" She aggressively holds my chin and stares into my eyes.

"No, Mom," I respond, and giggle.

"Your eyes are bloodshot, and you're barely looking at me."

"I'm just tired," I say and giggle again.

"What's so funny?" she asks as she lets go of my chin and steps backward.

Shrugging, I look around the room.

"We need to call an ambulance," someone says, reminding me that my mother isn't here with me.

My vision is blurry. I can't focus on anything at all. Turning my head, I look straight into the eyes of a girl. She's probably around my age, but I bet she hasn't seen half the stuff I have. She kneels beside me, and behind her are another two girls and three guys. One of them looks bored; he's scrolling on his phone.

"What do you want?" I bark toward her, but my voice comes out broken, and slurry.

"Jasmine, she's a junkie. Look at her. Just leave her. She's not our problem," the bored guy says.

"We can't just leave her," she snarls back at him.

Suddenly, my stomach starts contracting, and my breathing becomes challenged. Gasping for air, my body tightens with spasms, trying to get oxygen into my lungs.

"Shit, she must be overdosing. We gotta get out of here before anyone finds us," bored guy says.

"I'm not leaving her. She's just a kid."

"She ain't my problem. I'm outta here," the bored guy says and takes off, the others going with him.

The girl stays with me, and as I try to focus on her, all I can see is the pretty chain around her neck. It looks like it's worth a lot, I'm sure I could give it to Edgar for some crystals. Man, maybe a few days' worth. I need money big time.

"I'm going to call an ambulance," the girl says as she takes her phone out of her pocket and dials it. "What have you taken?" she asks.

Everything is fuzzy. Her voice sounds disjointed and almost robotic.

Reaching for my pipe, I scream in pain. But she doesn't seem alarmed by my screams, maybe I'm actually not moving. Everything hurts.

"I need an ambulance..." her voice is frantic as she tells the operator where she is.

My eyes keep drifting shut, and she screams at me to open them again.

"She's frothing at the mouth, and she's barely moving."

I try to turn over, but whatever those fuckers gave me was strong. It's weighing me down. I can barely move.

"Her breathing is shallow…"

If I can just get up, I'll find my way back to Edgar's. He'll look after me. He always does. Sometimes he asks me to do stuff for him. "I'm alright," I mumble.

"She's trying to say something," the girl says into the phone. "Okay, I won't touch her." Her eyes are filled with pity and sadness. I stare up at her, and can see how concerned she is. I can see her. Can she see me?

"There's a syringe beside her. I think she might have injected something. There's a pipe, too. Maybe she smoked crack or meth?"

Yeah, baby. Crystal meth. Meth. Crystal. Ice. Tina. Glass. I love it. I love getting iced. It's the best feeling in the world. Being invincible, even when there are a million people in the room. Being free. Floating. That floating is what I love best. Anything can be happening around you, and when you smoke a bit of ice, you're floating above everyone. Free and happy and high.

"I'm here!" The girl jumps up and waves her arms frantically.

"Thank you for calling, we'll take it from here," another woman says to the girl.

The girl steps back and continues to stare at me. I'm being rolled over, and talked at by someone in a uniform. "What's your name?"

"Hannah," I respond.

"She's unresponsive," the woman says as she looks up to someone. She presses into my chest plate with her knuckle, and a shooting pain rips through me. "She's barely coherent. Heart rate is down, pulse is weak. She's overdosing."

"Get me back to Edgar's," I say.

"She's crashing. Administering Narcan."

There's a tightness in my chest. Pain soars through me, every part of me is like someone is stabbing multiple sharp knives into my body.

A darkness overtakes me.

A blanket of warmth is thrown over my entire body. My last breath escapes past my chapped lips.

Suddenly, I feel weightless. This must be what heaven feels like. It's so peaceful.

"We're losing her!" I hear someone yell.

Who's losing who? What's happening?

"ETA sixty seconds," someone else says in a calm voice.

I'm not sure what's happening, all I know is I like the quiet.

"Breathe, damn it, breathe!"

"Great, another dead junkie," someone snickers.

"I haven't lost her yet."

"She's just a junkie, Sally. Who cares if she dies? It's another one off the streets."

"Hey, she's someone's daughter. You want to be the one to knock on her parent's door?"

I hear a grumble from behind me. More like a pained sigh.

Who's talking?

What the hell is happening?

As it turns out, this is far from the end of my story.

Chapter 31

One month later.

"GIRL, I THINK YOU'RE GOING TO BE OKAY." ANNA HUGS ME. HER dark brown hair has a slight red tinge and a sweet smell to it.

I pull out of the hug, and look down at my feet. "I'm so nervous," I say. My voice shakes with anguish. "I've been such a terrible person, I'm not sure I can face them."

"It's part of the steps. You know that. Humility is a major part of sobriety." Anna's shorter than me, maybe by half a head, but she's a straight shooter. She's been with me every step of the way. Detoxing was hard. The drugs coming out of my system was… I can't even think of the word to say just how awful it was. "You're going to be okay." She runs her hands up and down my arms. Warmth is instant where she's touching me. Anna's my biggest supporter, next to my parents, of course. They've been with me every step of the way. From when I cried and told them I hated them, to today. My last day in rehab.

They've been there through it all. My biggest support system.

"What if I relapse again?"

"You've got your meetings set up, you know where they are. You know what to do. I've never seen anyone as determined to succeed as you. You won't relapse, and you know how I know?" I shake my head in response. "Because I'll kick your ass if I see you in here again."

I smile. That's Anna for you. Tough, supportive, but also, she has a sense of humor. I hug her again, but this time, I cry. "Thank you, for everything."

"Right. I have work to do, and I don't like talking to the riff-raff." She winks at me, and I smile again.

"You made my time here… " I pause for a second, thinking of the right word to say. It's not been comfortable, or easy by any stretch. "… safe," I finally find the right word. Safe, yep, perfect. "It wasn't easy. And I know I'm a drug addict for life, regardless how many years of sobriety I have. But I never felt like I was in fear of my life while being here. And that's because of your kindness. It must be hard for you. Seeing people like me coming through, and trying to show us kindness only to have us spit, yell and try to hurt you."

Anna smiles. Her face lights up as she's nodding. "But these moments right here make it all worth it. Because I know you're going to walk out of here, and not only are you going to survive, but you're going to thrive. Hannah, you have a story to tell. You've lived through becoming another number, and have come out the other end. Keep that fire burning. Never let it go out, and I know you'll be stronger than you ever have been."

"I don't feel strong. I feel vulnerable."

"Good, so you should. And you should feel humble too. You've put a lot of people through shit. And now's the time to make it right. Remember, don't get frustrated when they don't trust you straight away. Because, that's gone, for now. But it doesn't mean you can't earn that trust back."

"I know." I shake my head and look down to my shoes again. "I'll spend a life time trying to make it right to everyone I've done wrong to."

She hugs me again. I like Anna's hugs. They're genuine, like she is. "Now, go and say goodbye to everyone else. Remember, this isn't somewhere I want to see you again. I'm not going to say I'll miss you, because I won't. Instead, I'm going to believe you'll leave here and spread those wings. Soar, Hannah, soar." She turns and walks away, leaving me in my room.

I sit on my bed, the bed I've had for the past month, and look around at the off-white walls. It's somewhat sterile, but this has been my safe room. Where I've cried. Where I've begged them to let me leave. Where I've come to terms with what I've become and what I've done.

"Knock-knock," Mom says as she comes into my room.

"Mom," I hug her tight and don't let go. "I don't know if I can do this." I cry into her hair.

"You can," Dad says from behind Mom. I extend my arm to include him in the hug. The three of us are huddled together.

"I still struggle with reality, and delusions. But, I think I'm getting better. I know what my reality is now, but I'm still not sure what did and didn't happen while I was using."

"We'll help you, sweetheart," Dad whispers. "We'll always be here." I step out of the hug, and turn to get my bag. "I'll take it." Dad places his hand over mine which is over the handle. I smile at him.

Walking out of here is bittersweet and surreal.

Growing up I never imagined I'd be in a place like this. I never thought I'd become addicted to drugs, and I never thought I'd do and say the most horrible things to the people who love me most.

But here I am, a drug addict, leaving rehab.

The bars on my windows are gone, and my room is bright. This is my happy place. Mom's changed the bedding. It's bright and yellow and it gives me hope that I'm going to be okay.

"Are you okay?" Dad asks as he wheels my bag behind him.

I nod, then slowly my nod turns to a shake. Tears fall as I try to really grasp the reality of this all. "I've screwed so many things up."

Dad doesn't give me a chance to sit, he hugs me. His hands rubbing my back gently. "Yes, you have. But you know this. And now you've got the tools to cope with making everything right."

"I feel so bad." He doesn't say anything, but I can feel him nodding. "I have to make it right."

"You do, but everything has to be done slowly, Hannah. You've only been clean for a month. What's happened to you, what you've been through, it's going to take more than a month to understand the full effect. Be kind to yourself. And be forgiving."

"I'm sorry, Dad." I cry into his chest.

This has to be the hardest day of my life. I'm facing all my demons. Every one of them.

"I know." He kisses me on the forehead, then leaves.

Sitting on my bed, I gather the courage to do what I have to.

First and foremost, I need to make peace with my neighbors. Especially Mrs. Drew who I accused of being a pedophile. I stand from my bed, and make my way out to the family room. Mom and Dad are talking in a low voice, and I'd be a fool to think they're not talking about me. "Everything okay?" Mom asks.

I nod and smile. "I'm going to knock on every house, and apologize to them."

"You don't have to do that," Mom says as she steps toward me.

"I do," I reply. "I have to be accountable for my actions. And this is the first thing I need to do."

"It can wait 'til tomorrow. Just stay here, settle into home life before you do that. We'll get pizza."

"Mom." I take a deep breath. "I need to do this now before I lose my nerve. Starting with Mrs. Drew. If I don't, I won't be able to sleep tonight. I need to do this, for them and for me."

Mom looks me over and nods. She decides I'm right. I do need to be accountable for my actions. "Do you want me to come with you?"

I want to say yes, but I did this alone. I caused this terrible rift between the neighbors, not them. "Can you stand at the door please?"

"Of course."

We walk together. My hands are sweating, and my heart is beating like a hummingbird's. But I need to start regaining control over my life. I have to. There's no other way.

I open the door, and walk across the lawn to Mrs. Drew's home. It seems like it takes me a long time to get up the nerve to actually knock. When I do, she opens immediately. I wasn't expecting her to be here so fast. "Hannah," she says with a warm smile.

I look down at my feet. I don't deserve her warmth. I deserve her to be angry at me. "Mrs. Drew," my voice cracks, but I hold onto the little bit of strength I have.

"Yes, dear."

Mrs. Drew is old. Maybe in her late sixties. Her thinning gray hair, and wrinkled face tells me she could even be older than her sixties. I take several deep breaths. I want to run and hide, but I have to do this. I have to confront the monster I once was, and own it. I breathe out a shaky breath.

Lifting my head, I look her straight in the eyes. "I'm a drug addict," I say owning my worst. "I said horrible things to you. I called you a pedophile, and I accused you of doing horrible things to me." She nods her head. Her eyes don't change, her expression remains the same. "I'm… " I begin to break. I'm trying hard to hold in the tears, but I can't. I need to do this. For me and for her. "I'm sorry for everything I said and did." I break. Spectacularly.

Mrs. Drew doesn't move to touch me. She takes a breath herself. "I know you are," she finally says. "And I accept your apology, Hannah."

"Thank you."

I don't know what else to say and do. If I could tell her I'm sorry for a lifetime, I would, but I can't. I have to move on. I turn to leave. "Hannah," she calls me back.

"Yes, ma'am," I reply and turn around to face her again.

"Become a warrior and make a difference," she says and offers me another smile.

"Yes, ma'am." Although I don't exactly know what she means. I'm barely hanging on to my sanity, how am I supposed to be a warrior and make a difference? "Thank you," I say again.

She closes the door.

And I slowly walk to the next neighbor.

As I walk from house to house, the humiliation doesn't get easier. I'm eternally humbled by the fact they all accept my apology. They don't have to, but they do.

Walking back home, I hug my parents before collapsing on the sofa in a mentally exhausted state.

Tonight, it's the neighbors, but tomorrow it's Kristen and Martin.

Chapter 32

"MARTIN'S HERE," DAD SAYS AS HE STANDS AT MY DOOR.

I'm dreading this. Really terrified, but I need to do it. It's part of my recovery. Last night I slept like shit. I tossed and turned all night. I'd sleep for what felt like hours, but it was only a few moments, then I'd wake, anxious about today.

"Thanks, Dad." Standing, I head out to the family room. Mom and Martin are talking.

"Here she is," he says as he approaches me and gives me a hug. "You're looking really good.

"Thank you."

"Would you like coffee, Martin?" Mom asks.

"Yeah, I would, thanks."

"Can I have one too please, Mom?"

"Sure thing."

Martin and I sit over on the sofa, next to each other. "First, I have to say I'm sorry."

"You've been saying sorry every time I'd come to see you in

rehab. You can stop apologizing now."

"I really can't. The crap I put you through, I'm so ashamed."

"I know." He smiles.

Mom brings over a coffee for Martin and a mocha for me. I pick mine up and blow on it. "Why did you try to save me?" I ask.

"I told you why, because of my brother."

"But you have to see so many drug addicts, you can't save us all."

He frowns, and looks away from me. "I don't know why, but I've always felt protective of you. There's something that makes me want to wrap you in a blanket, and keep you warm at night. There's just something there. When you left your parents' home, after you'd detoxed, I tried to find you, so I could bring you back."

"Why?"

"Because you're different. And you're special. You weren't meant for a life of drugs, you were meant for something more."

I chuckle, then take another sip of my mocha. "Funny, because Anna in the hospital said something similar. And so did Mrs. Drew."

"Mrs. Drew?" he asks.

"Neighbor, down the street." I point toward her direction. "I said some horrible things to her, and I wanted to apologize for them. So, I went there yesterday, looked her in the eyes and told her I was sorry. Kristen's next. She's coming over later." Mom is in the background, in the kitchen. She's hanging around, in case I need her.

"It takes a lot of courage to admit when you've done something wrong. You have to take it easy, be kind to yourself." I laugh, though it's more like a snort. Yeah, be kind to myself after everything I've done to everyone. "Don't do that." He points to my head, knowing what I'm thinking.

"I'm not doing anything."

He tilts his head to the side, as if he can read my thoughts. "You're beating yourself up for every bad word, every wrong action, everything you've done." I hug my coffee cup closer, trying to set a barrier between us. But I'm a fool to think he can't see through it. Martin's always been able to see through every one of my actions. Every one.

"I'm… " A huge lump rests in the pit of my throat. I want to say more, but I'm unsure what to say.

"You've been through something life-altering, Hannah. You don't come out the other side of severe drug abuse without it changing you." I nod my head and look down at the cushion on the sofa. "And when you look at the big picture, it's not just the drugs you've survived." I nod again, too ashamed of myself to say anything. "Abuse in any form is difficult. Confronting it, and dealing with it is freeing, and courageous. Don't feel shame, Hannah. Feel powerful because you've made the decision to actually do something about it."

"I shouldn't have people tell me they're proud of me for coming clean. I shouldn't have gone down that road to begin with."

"No, you shouldn't have. But, you did. And then you made another choice, to get clean."

I chuckle ruefully. "I didn't make the decision, it was thrust on me. I was raped, left to overdose, and found beaten in a dirty, dark alleyway."

"You had a choice. You always have a choice. Because instead of being here with your parents, and with me, you could be out there, being a prostitute and smoking crystal meth. This is your choice. Am I proud of you?" I look at him and wait for his answer. "You better believe it. Not because of what you did, but because of what you're *choosing* to do right now."

My gaze falls to my now empty mug. "Thank you," I whisper. I feel better knowing Martin's here. I feel safer. I know I can be strong with him. Not because he builds my confidence up, but because he honestly cares about me. "One day, when I'm more okay here." I point to my head. "I'd like to take you out on a date."

His brows shoot up, and I can see him trying to hold in the smile. There's joy in his eyes, and his cheeks are turning pink.

"I'd like that," he finally says.

I lean in and give him a hug. I like Martin. He's proven to me that no matter what I go through, he's here for me and for my family.

I pace inside my room. Kristen is due to come over, and although I can't wait, I'm also nervous. She visited me once while I was in rehab, and we talked about everything. She said she forgave me, but I'm still not sure where we are on the friends scale. Are we passing acquaintances, or are we 'hey let's go to the movies' friends? After today, I'll see, I guess.

I go out to the family room and look through the front window to see if she's here.

She's not.

God, what if she's changed her mind and she doesn't want to come anymore? My stomach churns with fear and worry. I don't know what I'd do if the roles were reversed. I'd like to think I'd give her another chance, but I don't know.

I hear a car, and look out the window again. It's not her.

My shoulders drop and sadness forms in the pit of my soul.

I've been horrible. Maybe I don't deserve a second chance. I don't know. Maybe I do. But, why do I? I haven't been a great friend to her. I kept her in the dark about everything. Asked her to lie for me, and treated her horribly.

I go to the kitchen to try to occupy my mind. I need to move my thoughts away from the (very real) possibility she won't come. I open the dishwasher, and begin to offload all the dishes. I'm humming around the kitchen, trying to keep myself busy. As the moments tick by, I get a twisting pain in my gut, just knowing she's not going to come. A bitter feeling of defeat keeps churning in my head. She's not coming; I know it.

My eyes begin to well with tears, and I desperately try to think of something else. But the yearning, the need for the pipe is right here, about to break through. I want it, only a taste to make me feel better.

"Mom!" I call. My hands shake and I've gone into full flight mode. I need to get out of here, go and find a pipe. "MOM!" She's going to help me through; I know she will. I brace myself on the kitchen counter, close my eyes and repeat in my head: Drugs are not the answer, they're the cause. Drugs are not the answer, they're the cause.

"Sweetheart, what's wrong?" Dad's deep voice booms from across the family room.

"I need you," I say and run to him. I throw myself in his arms, and hold him tightly.

"It's okay." He gently pets my hair, holding me.

My breathing is crazy, the craving and need for the pipe slowly retreats. I knew this would happen. It was always bound to happen. Challenges will send me into a spin, but it's how I handle them that distinguishes the person I am from the person I was.

Suddenly, as I regain my control, there's a knock at the front door.

I pull back from Dad. "You okay?" he asks, knowing I was at the start of a meltdown. I nod. "Go." He looks to the door.

My hands sweat as I slowly walk toward it. It takes me a few seconds to get the confidence to actually open the door. My hand rests on the handle, reluctant. But I need to know if we are okay, or are we strangers now?

I open the door.

Kristen stands, looking as beautiful as always. Her thick blonde hair cascades down over her shoulders. Her big, blue eyes are glued to me. Staring? Judging? Her body is tense, too.

I deserve her wrath. I deserve it all.

I don't speak. Neither does she.

I don't know what to do.

A tear falls from her eye, and she lifts her hand to wipe it away. I feel something wet on my cheeks, and realize I'm crying too.

This is raw, for both of us.

She can turn and walk out of my life, or she can come in and be part of it. I won't blame her for leaving. I won't allow myself to hate her if she does. She's never been anything but kind to me.

We stare at each other. We're both crying.

She drops her shoulders, and throws herself into my arms.

We both sob uncontrollably.

"I'm so sorry," I say through thick, fast tears.

She kisses my cheek, and holds me like I'm her own life raft.

"I'm so happy you're back," she whispers.

So am I.

Epilogue

A TEAR FALLS FROM MY EYES AS I STARE AT THE PAPER ON THE podium. I can't bring myself to look up at the hundred-plus pairs of eyes, all of whom are sitting quietly, watching, and listening to me.

Today is especially emotional, because it marks my five years of sobriety.

My parents sitting here, supporting me. They don't often travel with me, but I knew today was going to be difficult, and I knew I was going to need them and their support. Martin travels with me and comes to all my events. He's become the protective partner, but he's always been that way when it comes to me.

The hall is quiet. Only the whirl of the air conditioners can be heard. In my ears, I can hear the pounding of my heartbeat. It takes me a long few moments to compose myself before I have the courage to lift my head and look at them. It's not always this hard, but sometimes I can't deal with the shame of what I did. Nor can I deal with everyone knowing about my past. But I've become the warrior Mrs. Drew encouraged me to be, because my story needs to be heard.

I wipe at my cheek, clearing the wetness from my face. I know this is hard. But it's also worth it.

It's not about humiliating myself, it's about educating these kids. If one person is thinking about picking up the glass pipe for the first time and they hear my story, maybe they'll decide to take a different path.

Breathing a few deep sighs, I finally look up.

In the front row, I can see two girls sitting next to each other. Both have been crying. Both are wiping at their faces with tissues. There's always someone who responds the same way when I read passages from my book. I get it. It's raw and confrontational. You'd have to be made of stone to feel nothing after reading *Addiction*.

A student's hand flies up from the center of the auditorium.

This is the most painful part. Sometimes I get asked questions that I don't want to answer, but I have to because I made the commitment to educate teenagers on the risks and dangers of addiction.

"Yes," I say and point to the girl whose hand is raised.

She stands and straightens her shirt. "How hard was it for you to write *Addiction*? I mean, there's some deeply personal things in here." She holds up my book, showing me the cover of the girl walking down a lonely road. What an apt cover, because that's exactly what my addiction did to me. It isolated me from everyone who loved me.

"Writing *Addiction* was the hardest thing I've ever done. I thought when I went through rehab, that nothing could be harder than that. But once I started writing, I found I had to be real and tell the truth. No matter how much it hurt me, I needed to write everything down. It serves as a constant reminder of how easy it is to fall prey to and become a victim of something you were never looking for."

She sits down with a satisfied smile that I've answered her question.

Another student from the high school where I've been asked to speak stands. It's a male student, which I find interesting because usually the males don't ask a lot of questions. The males usually sit and listen. "Was there anything you left out of the book that you wish you could've added?" he asks before sitting and waiting for my answer.

A sick feeling twists in my stomach. I hate being asked this. It doesn't happen often, but when it is asked, I tell the truth. They need to see how bad this can be. And I was a lucky one, because I made it out of that world alive. "I did something I'm extremely ashamed of doing," I say as my voice cracks and another tear falls.

"Worse than stealing your grandmother's jewelry?" the same boy asks.

Turning to my Dad, I see the tears glistening his cheeks. He knows what I have to say, and I'm not proud of it at all. "I wrote it, but decided to take it out. I'm still so ashamed of it." I wipe my hands over my eyes, trying to hold onto whatever dignity I have left. But I know I *do* have dignity, worth, and self-respect. Because I fought tooth and nail to get myself out of the heavy addiction I once was victim to. "At my lowest, I went back home and tried to steal whatever I could carry. I thought my parents would be at work, but Dad was home." I swallow back the tears and shame I have in myself. These kids need to hear it, they need to understand what lengths a drug addict will go to. "I was in a bad state, coming down off a high, needing money for drugs." I shake my head, ashamed by my low. "I asked my Dad for money, told him I needed to eat. He said no." I look at Dad, almost seeking his permission. He nods his head. Mom is crying, Dad is crying, and I'm in tears.

"What happened?" the boy asks.

"All I could think about was where I was going to get the money for my next hit. It's all I wanted. I yearned for it. It burned through my veins. It was pounding through me, like a tsunami of desperation." I take another deep breath. "Dad and I were arguing. I wanted crystal meth. I craved it, more than a drowning man at sea would crave air for his lungs. More than a mother would crave the touch of her newborn baby. I needed it, like nothing I've ever felt or known. I *had* to have it."

"And what happened?" he asks again, pushing.

"I asked my Dad for money again. He told me no. I begged him, promised I'd pay it back. He said no."

"Is that the worst of it?" another boy asks whose sitting in the front row.

Shaking my head, I grimace at the remembered, painful memory. "I told my father I'd have sex with him if he'd give me fifty dollars." Everyone gasps. I look up, and see so many mouths are gaping in horror. "My Mother walked in when I made my offer. He backed away from me and told me I needed help, and my Mother grabbed me and dragged me outside. In a fit of anger, I hit her a few times. She fell back and hit her head. My violence sent her to the hospital for stitches." I hear more gasps. "That was the day I tried to kill my junkie roommate. And that was the day I was raped by four men who then tried to overdose and kill me so I wouldn't identify them for raping me. They've never been caught," I add in a small voice.

"Oh my God," I hear someone whisper.

The hall is quiet, but it doesn't take long for another hand to fly up. I point to the girl in the back. She stands and says in a loud, confident voice, "What happened to Mr. X?" I changed the names in my book for legal reasons. Mr. X is Edgar.

"Wow, I knew this question was coming." I half chuckle, knowing my answer will horrify these teenagers. But I've vowed to keep it real. I refuse to lie. "I wasn't able to mention anything about Mr. X in the book, but now I can. Mr. X is serving five life sentences in prison."

"Because of the drug dealing?" the same girl asks.

"Strangely enough, no. The drugs weren't the reason for his prison sentence. He decided movies would be his thing. And went from the pornographic material he was filming with me to what's called 'snuff films.'"

"What's a 'snuff film'?" this girl is really curious.

"Snuff films are real-life torture and murder that occurs on film, and they sell it to the highest bidder."

"Oh, my God," she says with a gasp.

"He killed two girls." Ginger, whose name I changed to Jade, and Sky who I called Cat in the book. "He killed them by slashing their throats on camera. The blood sprayed all over his face. What he didn't know was that one of the girls he murdered had AIDS. Some of the sprayed blood got into his eye, and mixed with his blood. Mr. X will die in prison, because he didn't know he had HIV and didn't get treated for it. It developed into AIDS."

"Yes!" I hear a lot of people collectively mumble and scattered applause erupts.

"I don't wish death upon anyone," I say, although, Edgar deserves whatever fate wants to hand him. I take a moment and hold my hand up, where I'm wearing my grandmother's ring. "The one good thing that happened was when the police raided his home, they seized all his property. My parents filed a police report for this, of which he'd kept, and I got it back."

"You never said what happened to Hunter in the book," another eager male asks. Hunter being Zac.

"I see him around from time to time. He told me how sorry he was for not standing up to Mr. X. As it turns out, Hunter was terrified of Mr. X. I can see why, and I don't hold any bad feelings toward him." A long silence falls over the students.

"How do you feel about Mr. X now?" a different student asks.

I smile. "I used to think I loved him. That he was what I wanted and needed. But the reality is I just wanted what he got me hooked on. I thought there was a pull toward him, but that's what predators do. He created a wedge between my parents, my friends and me. He even went so far as to falsify those documents he gave me. He conditioned me. Made me need him, made me think he took care of me. He took me on our first 'date,' and I use that term loosely, because after he was arrested his method of operation came out. The restaurant meeting wasn't a date, but an audition. The men who were having dinner there offered Mr. X money for pornographic movies with me in them. He knew what he was doing, from the moment he met me. Everything was a lie. He was a seasoned predator. How do I feel about him?" I shrug my shoulders. "He's getting what he deserves."

Another hand flies up to ask a question. "You seem to be so…" They pause thinking about the word they want to use before adding, "… normal. How are you finding life now?"

"It's a struggle. Every day I think about my old life. But I'm lucky, because *Addiction* is now going to be made into a major motion picture. I know this book and the movie will be able to reach so many people at the same time. I love traveling from school to school to talk about my experiences. Because one of you, or a few of you will at some point be offered drugs. And when you are, think about what I went through. Think about the pornographic movies of me that are out there on the Internet, and will probably be out there for eternity and ask yourself if that's the road you want to travel." I see a lot of them nodding their heads. "They say the truth will set you free." I take a deep breath and try to look at as many faces as I can. "My truth is this… " I pause for a further second, looking at more eager faces staring up at me.

The students are watching me, waiting to hear what I'm going to say. Their eager faces are glued to me.

Relief floods me. The words I'm about to say were something I once completely refused to acknowledge. I wasn't an addict, a junkie. I wasn't like them. I wasn't dirty, and I wasn't a hooker.

But my reality is here in print for everyone to see. *I was.* My strength increases every time I say the sentence aloud.

I turn to my parents and see the pride in their eyes. I'm proud of myself too. I survived.

"My name is Hannah Rose Mendes, and I'm a drug addict."

The End

Phone Numbers

Drug Abuse Hotline US: 1877 978 1523/1877 659 9350

Life line Australia: 13 11 44

SupportLine Telephone Helpline UK: 01708 765200

Action on Addiction UK: 0300 330 0659

From the Author

I first saw the cover to Addiction, and noticed the simplistic beauty of it. The girl, walking down an isolated road with small bruises on her arms. It immediately took me to a dark place and made me question *why* she was there. And *why* she had those bruises. What was she escaping from? Who was she running from?

Hannah came to me like a bullet. She began telling me what a wonderful family she had, and how her parents loved her more than life itself.

She showed me snippets of the man she was seeing, the man we know as Edgar, and how in love she is.

Of course, Edgar isn't a nice a man. We know that now, and so does Hannah.

As Hannah told me more and more about her life story, I became increasingly frustrated with her, and her choices. There were many times I wanted to slap her face, shake her and tell her how much of an idiot she was. Being in the mind of a drug addict was one of the most difficult things I've ever had to do.

The fact I could see Edgar's deceit and she couldn't, was frustrating to me. I hated him from the moment he interjected himself in her life. Many a time, I would have to get up and walk away, especially when he was in a scene. He angered me, and sent my blood pressure sky rocketing. His manipulative ways were obvious to me, but not to Hannah. Hannah isn't stupid, she's simply naive. Something a lot of people are, not through choice, but because of lack of experience.

While writing Hannah's story, I often asked myself, what I would do if my child became dependant on drugs. I never want to be in that position to find out. And I hope you never have to either.

Addiction is by far the most challenging book I've ever written. Because I've never been dependant on drugs, so I didn't know how it felt to be hooked. But while writing, I got a very clear image, because essentially, although I'm not drug dependant, I had an insight into the mind of a drug addict through Hannah.

I never write a book with sensitive subjects without doing my research. Yes, this *is* fiction, but to many it's reality. The research alone had my mind jumbled with so many statistics. I can only imagine what clouding it with actual drugs would do to someone.

Addiction has taught me something. And that is, to have compassion. The war on drugs is epic, the casualty numbers are climbing. Anybody can become a statistic.

Acknowledgements

Addiction wouldn't have been written if it wasn't for the encouragement from certain people.

First and foremost. We are not friends (LOL), but your sprinting helped me when I was stuck and couldn't write. Dzintra Sullivan.

To my dear editor. We finally get to meet! YAY! You always make my words shine. Whenever I send you my books, I'm worried about how crappy they are. It's the critical writer in me. And you read them and tell me exactly what you think. I love how you're honest, and I love the magic you spin to make my words pretty. Thank you.

My beautiful cover is designed by Kellie from Book Cover by Design. She's been making my covers for years, and with every cover they are more beautiful. She's truly talented.

Tami from Integrity Formatting has always found time to take my pages, and make them perfect. Tami, I love how attentive you are, and I love how you work so closely with me to make the pages sing. Thank you.

And my friend, Kylie from Give Me Books. I'm eternally thankful how you always make the effort for me, and spend time putting together the packets and sending them out to bloggers.

To my proofreaders, Terry, Sam and Mandy. You ladies take time to read my books, and to find anything I may have missed. Thank you for being on call.

To my beautiful friends who always encourage me. Bek, Lyndal, Anna, Kimmy, Jodi, Britt and Halle. You ladies are awesome. You're so inspirational to me. Whenever I need a swift kick in the butt, you give it to me.

And of course, to my readers. You motivate me to keep bringing you books that push the boundaries. I can't do sweet and pretty. All I can do is me. And I hope I've bought you the best version of me possible.

Thank you for reading.

Margaret X

Keep reading for Previews of:
Drowning
Ugly
Mistrust
Dying Wish
The Gift

Also by MARGARET MCHEYZER

Drowning

I'm a cutter.

I cut because I find solace in it.

I cut because it helps calm my frantic mind.

I cut because the voice inside my head tells me to.

I cut because this is the only way I know how to handle life.

The Gift

I have something people want. I have something they cannot take or steal. I have something they'd kill for.

The something I have, isn't a possession, it's more.

Much, much more.

It's a gift.

It's part of me.

The Curse

It's been the butterfly effect.

I changed the course of my life because I warned a man.

I thought what I had was a gift, but it's quickly turning into my curse.

Now I realize I'm much more than a girl with an ability.

Because now... I'm becoming a weapon.

Dying Wish

I have three major loves in my life: my family, my best friend Becky, and ballet. Elijah Turner is quickly becoming the fourth.

He's been around as long as I can remember. But now he's much more than just the annoying guy at school.

My life was working out perfectly...until it got turned upside down.

Mistrust

I'm the popular girl at school.

The one everyone wants to be friends with.

I have the best boyfriend in the world, who's on the basketball team.

My parents adore me, and I absolutely love them. My sister and I have a great relationship too.

I'm a cheerleader, I have a high GPA and I'm liked even by the teachers.

It was a night which promised to be filled with love and fun until...something happened which changed everything.

Ugly

This is a dark YA/NA standalone, full-length novel. Contains violence and some explicit language

If I were dead, I wouldn't be able to see.

If I were dead, I wouldn't be able to feel.

If I were dead, he'd never raise his hand to me again.

If I were dead, his words wouldn't cut as deep as they do.

If I were dead, I'd be beautiful and I wouldn't be so...ugly.

I'm not dead...but I wish I was.

Chef Pierre

Holly Walker had everything she'd ever dreamed about – a happy marriage and being mum to beautiful brown-eyed Emma - until an accident nineteen months ago tore her world apart. Now she's a widow and single mother to a boisterous little 7-year-old girl, looking for a new start. Ready to take the next step, Holly has found herself a job as a maître d' at Table One, a once-acclaimed restaurant in the heart of Sydney. But one extremely arrogant Frenchman isn't going to be easy to work with...

Twenty years ago, Pierre LeRoux came to Australia, following the stunning Aussie girl he'd fallen in love with and married. He and his wife put their personal lives on hold, determined for Pierre to take Sydney's culinary society by storm. Just as his bright star was on the upswing, tragedy claimed the woman he was hopelessly in love with. He had been known as a Master Chef, but since his wife's death he has become known as a monster chef.

Can two broken people rebuild their lives and find happiness once more?

Grit

*** Recommended for 18 years and over ***

Alpha MC Prez Jaeger Dalton wants the land that was promised to him.

Sassy Phoenix Ward isn't about to let anyone take Freedom Run away from her.

He'll protect what's his.

She'll protect what's hers.

Jaeger is an arrogant ass, but he wants nothing more than Phoenix.

Phoenix is stubborn and headstrong, and she wants Jaeger out of her life.

Her father lost the family farm to gambling debts, but Jaeger isn't the only one who has a claim to the property.

Sometimes it's best to let things go.

But sometimes it's better to fight until the very end.

Smoke and Mirrors

Words can trick us.

Smoke obscures objects on the edge of our vision.

A mirror may reflect, but the eye sees what it wants.

A delicate scent can evoke another time and place, a memory from the past.

And a sentence can deceive you, even as you read it.

Yes, Master

** THIS PROLOGUE CONTAINS DISTRESSING CONTENT. IT IS ONLY SUITED FOR READERS OVER 18. **
ALSO CONTAINS M/M, M/M/F, M/F AND F/FSCENES.

My uncle abused me.

I was 10 years old when it started.

At 13 he told me I was no longer wanted because I had started to develop.

At 16 I was ready to kill him.

Today, I'm broken.

Today, I only breathe to survive.

My name's Sergeant Major Ryan Jenkins and today, I'm ready to tell you my story.

A Life Less Broken

CONTAINS DISTRESSING CONTENT. 18+

On a day like any other, Allyn Sommers went off to work, not knowing that her life was about to be irrevocably and horrifically altered.

Three years later, Allyn is still a prisoner in her own home, held captive by harrowing fear. Broken and damaged, Allyn seeks help from someone that fate put in her path.

Dr. Dominic Shriver is a psychiatrist who's drawn to difficult cases. He must push past his own personal battles to help Allyn fight her monsters and nightmares.

Is Dr. Shriver the answer to her healing?

Can Allyn overcome being broken?

My Life for Yours

He's lived a life of high society and privilege; he chose to follow in his father's footsteps and become a Senator.

She's lived a life surrounded with underworld activity; she had no choice but to follow in her father's footsteps and take on the role of Mob Boss.

He wants to stamp out organized crime and can't be bought off.

She's the ruthless and tough Mob Boss where in her world all lines are blurred.

Their lives are completely different, two walks of life on the opposite ends of the law.

Being together doesn't make sense.

But being apart isn't an option

HiT Series Box Set

HiT 149

Anna Brookes is not your typical teenager. Her walls are not adorned with posters of boy bands or movie stars. Instead posters from Glock, Ruger, and Smith & Wesson grace her bedroom. Anna's mother abandoned her at birth, and her father, St. Cloud Police Chief Henry Brookes, taught her how to shoot and coached her to excellence. On Anna's fifteenth birthday, unwelcome guests join the celebration, and Anna's world is never the same. You'll meet the world's top assassin, 15, and follow her as she discovers the one hit she's not sure she can complete – Ben Pearson, the current St. Cloud Police Chief and a man with whom Anna has explosive sexual chemistry. Enter a world of intrigue, power, and treachery as Anna takes on old and new enemies, while falling in love with the one man with whom she can't have a relationship.

Anna Brookes in Training

Find out what happened to transform the fifteen-year-old Anna Brookes, the Girl with the Golden Aim, into the deadly assassin 15. After her father is killed and her home destroyed, orphan Anna Brookes finds herself homeless in Gulf Breeze, Florida. After she saves Lukas from a deadly attack, he takes her in and begins to train her in the assassin's craft. Learn how Lukas's unconventional training hones Anna's innate skills until she is as deadly as her mentor.

HiT for Freedom

Anna has decided to break off her steamy affair with Ben Pearson and leave St. Cloud, when she suspects a new threat to him. Katsu Vang is rich, powerful, and very interested in Anna. He's also evil to his core. Join Anna as she plays a dangerous game, getting closer to Katsu to discover his real purpose, while trying to keep Ben safe. Secrets are exposed and the future Anna hoped for is snatched from her grasp. Will Ben be able to save her?

HiT to Live

In the conclusion to the Anna Brookes saga, Ben and his sister Emily, with the help of Agent rescue Anna. For Anna and Ben, it's time to settle scores...and a time for the truth between them. From Sydney to the Philippines and back to the States, they take care of business. But a helpful stranger enters Anna's life, revealing more secrets...and a plan that Anna wants no part of. Can Anna and Ben shed their old lives and start a new one together, or will Anna's new-found family ruin their chances at a happily-ever-after?

Binary Law (co-authored)

Ellie Andrews has been receiving tutoring from Blake McCarthy for three years to help her improve her grades so she can get into one of the top universities to study law. And she's had a huge crush on him since she can remember.

Blake McCarthy is the geek at school that's had a crush on Ellie since the day he met her.

In their final tutoring session, Blake and Ellie finally become brave enough to take the leap of faith.

But, life has other plans and rips them apart. Six years later Blake and his best friends Ben and Billy have built a successful internet platform company 3BCubed, while Ellie is a successful and hardworking lawyer specializing in Corporate Law.

3BCubed is being threatened with a devastatingly large plagiarism case and when it lands on their lawyers desk, it's handed to the new Corporate Lawyer to handle and win.

Coincidence or perhaps fate will see Blake and Ellie pushed back together.

Binary Law will have Blake and Ellie propelled into a life that's a whirl wind of catastrophic events and situations where every emotion will be touched. Hurt will be experienced, happiness will be presented and love will be evident. But is that enough for Blake and Ellie be able to live out their own happily ever after?

.

Made in United States
North Haven, CT
04 January 2024

46984769R00173